PRAISE FOR THIS BOOK

'All the charming and not-so-charming characters are back. Another great read by Nicola May – five stars'
Devilishly Delicious Book Reviews

'Warning: this sequel is so GOOD you might find daily life a struggle while reading it. If you were crazy about *The Corner Shop in Cockleberry Bay*, then expect your book craziness to soar to new heights with the sequel'
BlondeWriteMore

'Filled with lots of love, laughter and emotion, this is a great addition to this series. Hopefully we shall have many more visits to Cockleberry Bay'
Stardust Book Reviews

'A story of emotion, drama, romance and life in general. Such a great read'
Me and My Books

'Nicola May expertly weaves together threads of drama, emotion, and romance in this delightful story'
Audio Killed the Bookmark

'A soap opera in story form – a whirlwind of a read'
Just 4 My Books

'I loved *Meet me in Cockleberry Bay*, I was hooked from the start. I'm excited to find out what else this wonderful place had to offer'
Baby Dolls and Razorblades

'Coming back to Cockleberry Bay was like coming back to a place I know and love. Great characters, perfectly descriptive location and a plot that has humour, romance, friendship and unexpected escapades. I predict that, like Book 1, this too will become a bestseller'
Chocolate Pages

'A fun, tense, absolutely enjoyable ride'
27 Book Street

'There are some fabulous characters in this book [who] ended up seeming like old friends by the end. I hope this isn't the last we'll hear from Cockleberry Bay'
Over the Rainbow

'An endearing and compelling romcom that's warm and light-hearted yet deals with some serious subjects. Once you pick it up, you won't want to put it down'
Dash Fan

MEET ME IN COCKLEBERRY BAY

NICOLA MAY

Lightning Books

Published by
Lightning Books Ltd
Imprint of EyeStorm Media
312 Uxbridge Road
Rickmansworth
Hertfordshire
WD3 8YL

www.lightning-books.com

First published in the UK in 2019 by Nowell Publishing
This edition 2019
Copyright © Nicola May 2019
Cover design by Ifan Bates
Cover illustration by John Meech

Nicola May has asserted her right under the Copyright, Designs and Patents Act 1988 to be identified as author of this work.

British Library Cataloguing in Publication Data
A catalogue record for this book is available from the British Library

Printed and bound in Great Britain by Clays Ltd, Elcograf S.p.A.

ISBN 9781785631559

This edition published in collaboration with Canelo Digital Publishing Limited

To Joan B, Joan D and Brenda M
– for your continued support,
guidance and sage advice

In the end, it only really matters
what you think of yourself
Elizabeth Taylor

PROLOGUE

'Oh Titch, why didn't you just ring for an ambulance?'

'I did, but they're always so slow getting down to the Bay and I knew you'd know what to do. I'm sorry, Rose. *Oooh…*'

Hot Dog, Rosa Smith's excitable mini-dachshund, was now running around the Corner Shop making whining noises similar to the ones coming from the young girl in labour.

Flustered, Rosa snapped at him, 'Hot, will you just stop it?' She reached for her friend's hand and said more gently, 'Come on, we need to get you upstairs.'

'No! No, I can't move.' Titch was bent over, clutching at the counter. 'Oh no – I think I'm ready to push!'

'Shit! OK, OK, don't panic.' Rosa hurriedly turned the Corner Shop sign to Closed, dragged the biggest, comfiest dog bed off a shelf and carefully eased her friend to the floor. She then darted into the downstairs kitchen and grabbed a whole handful of clean tea-towels from the drawer.

As she tried to remove Titch's lower clothing without hurting her, Rosa said as calmly as she could manage: 'OK, start doing the breathing you learnt at your anti-natal classes.'

'Problem is, I didn't go to any. *Aaarrrggghhh!*' Titch writhed on the floor, tears streaming down her bright red face.

'Look mate, hold on. The ambulance will be here soon and I've watched enough Sir David Attenborough to get us through this.'

'Ow! So not…funny…at this minute,' Titch panted, sweat standing out on her forehead. And as another earth-shattering contraction took hold of her skinny little body, she let loose with a string of words that would have made one of the local fishermen blush.

In what seemed like minutes, with the air now bluer than the autumn sky and with an almighty cry that even the circling seagulls couldn't drown out, Theodore Ronnie Whittaker entered No. 1, The World, Cockleberry Bay.

CHAPTER ONE

Rosa took in a deep breath of fresh sea air as she shut the Corner Shop door behind her. Hot, knowing that his morning walk was imminent, ran in and out of her legs emitting excited yaps and nearly tripping her up with the lead.

It had seemed just days ago, not months, that she and her four-legged companion had arrived on the train here in Devon, with a battered leather briefcase and a bin bag full of clothes. In fact, a lot of what had happened still felt like a dream. The words of the London solicitor informing her of her mystery inheritance remained etched on her brain.

'You, Miss Larkin, are now the official owner of the Corner Shop in Cockleberry Bay.'

The Corner Shop and flat above, both closed and empty for five years, had needed some love and care, but using the cash that had also come with the legacy Rosa had somehow got everything cleaned and upcycled, and had ordered enough stock in to be able to re-open the shop. She had decided to sell pet supplies as she didn't know much about anything, apart from dogs.

Having lived in foster-care all her life, Rosa had not a single clue who might have left her this amazing opportunity. She had been beside herself to find out, but the hidden letters she had discovered by chance, explaining everything, became uncomfortable reading. In fact, finding out where she belonged on her family tree was connected to one of the saddest love stories she had ever read. But in Cockleberry Bay, Rosa Larkin knew that she had, at last, come home.

As she and her beloved sausage dog made their jaunty way down the steep hill to the beach, they passed rows of picturesque old cottages with their bright front doors and polished steps. Shops and eateries in the narrow streets offered well-thought-out window displays and mouth-watering baking smells. Taking in all the new window activity, Rosa made a mental note that she too must get ready for the pending half-term holiday surge. Amid the pet supplies sold at the Corner Shop, she had cleverly added lots of trinkets that the visiting kids loved, and stocks were running low.

If somebody had told her last Christmas that by the following autumn the whole spirit and energy of this place would already be ingrained in her, she would have called them ridiculous.

Titch clumsily negotiated her second-hand pram into the corner shop, and on seeing Rosa put her hand to her face.

'What have I done, Rose, having a baby? It's a nightmare. He hardly ever sleeps, then sucks the life out of my nipples when he wakes up. It bloody hurts.'

'That's what babies do, isn't it?' Rosa smiled. 'Here, sit behind the counter, do you want a hot drink?'

'I want an *alcoholic* drink.'

'Titch, it's only ten o'clock. I'm making us a cup of tea, all right? Hot and I are missing you, if that makes you feel any better.'

On hearing his name, the little dachshund appeared and

barked his approval at Titch's presence. He sniffed lengthily at the pram, nearly cocked his leg to do a wee on one of the sandy wheels – but then on seeing his mistress's expression he trotted over to his sheepskin bed in the corner and flopped down, one ear up.

'I'll be back here soon, don't you worry, Mr Sausage,' Titch said fondly.

'He's knackered, thank goodness; been chasing seagulls on the beach.'

'I wish I'd just got a dog now, instead of a baby.'

'Oh Titch, you don't mean that. And surely now is the time to stay home and enjoy the little darling for a bit. I mean, he's only four weeks old, isn't he?'

'Hmm. The thing is, I've actually come down to ask if I could start back – like next week maybe?' Titch added hurriedly, 'That's if you didn't mind Theo being here too. I can detach the top of the pram like a carrycot and he could sleep upstairs. It's OK living with Mum, but you know the plan has always been for me and the little man to have our own place. We didn't start the Titchy Titch fund for nothing, you know.'

'I could do with the help, but only if you're sure?'

'I'm sure – and if I just do part-time, I can express some milk and Mum can look after him sometimes too.'

'OK, well, let's see how it goes. But I think you might be underestimating how tired you will feel.'

'When did a twenty-six-year-old, childless shop-owner become the guru on nursing mothers anyway?'

'Well, I did help deliver him on this very floor, so I'm allowed to class myself as an expert of some sort.' Rosa blew out a breath. 'How crazy was *that* day?'

'I know.' Titch seized her hand. 'And I will be forever grateful. If I was religious, you would be his godmother.'

'I'll take that.' Rosa smiled. 'I shall be his spirit mother instead. You know I'll always be here for him and you.'

'Don't, you'll make me cry. I was proper hard-faced before this pregnancy. Now even the news headlines send me into a blubbering mess.'

Just then, little Theo murmured, causing Rosa to peer in his pram. 'He really is the cutest baby.' She stroked his tight black curls and caramel skin. 'Not quite the fair-skinned redhead we dreaded, eh?'

'Yes, and what a relief. I am so pleased he has nothing to do with Seb Watkins.' Titch gulped. 'Throughout the pregnancy I was secretly worried that I wouldn't be able to love my baby properly after what that wanker did to me.'

'I was slightly concerned about that too.'

Titch gently readjusted her baby's blanket. 'However, sleep deprivation, leaky nipples and a sore fanny aside, Theodore Ronnie Whittaker really is the best thing that has ever happened to me. If true love could be put into words, this is it.'

'Ronnie is an unusual name, but I like it.'

'My brother.'

'Aw, sorry, of course.' Rosa knew that Ronnie had died far too young. 'That's sweet and he is *so* adorable,' she cooed. 'So, if he's not Seb's, who is the father then?'

'A stag party came into the Ship – I think they were Welsh.' Titch let out a little groan. 'The bloke in question sang the whole of "All I Want For Christmas Is You", whilst trying to tie a bauble around his huge chocolate log before we did the deed.'

'Titch! You can't say that.'

'I just did. It gets on my nerves that you can't say anything these days without offending someone. It really is quite ridiculous.'

'Well, at least Theo's dad could be passing on a sense of

12

humour.' Rosa grinned. Then something struck her. 'Please don't tell me it was *the* Stag himself who impregnated you.'

'I'm bad, but not that bad. Actually, I retract that. I am, or should I say *was* that bad. Anyway, things are changing from now on. I need to do everything right by this little one and men are just not in the equation.'

'You say that now whilst your bits are out of action.'

'No, Rose. I mean it.'

Rosa still found it so endearing that her friend called her Rose. 'And the father, are you going to tell him?'

'Even if I wanted to, which I don't – all I have to go on is his name: Ben. I know that he has family in the Caribbean and probably sings in a choir in the valleys.'

'Big Ben by the sound of it,' Rosa joked, and disappeared to the back kitchen to make tea. She could hear Titch serving a couple of regulars with dog food and bird seed, and smiled. The teenager had always had an easy way with the customers.

Rosa brought through two steaming mugs of tea and a big plate of biscuits to keep her mate's strength up. The new mum began to dunk and scoff digestive biscuits one after the other.

'Grabbing the energy whilst I can,' she mumbled, spraying crumbs. 'He'll be awake soon. Anyway, Rose, enough about me. How are Mr and Mrs Smith doing?'

'We are wonderful, thanks. Still can't believe we are married, to be honest. It all happened so fast.'

'So romantic though. I aspire to find a love like you two.'

'Yes, my Josh is rather gorgeous, I'm not going to lie. Although I am getting sick of him working away in the week and we still haven't had any sort of honeymoon to mention.'

'Like I said, I'm happy to come back to work in the shop as soon as possible. Mum has even knitted me a special breastfeeding cape with dolphins on, so as not to be flashing my tits at the locals.'

'That'll be a change then,' Rosa grinned.

'Oi.'

'You know I love you, Titch Whittaker.'

'And me thee.' Titch jumped down off the stool just as Theo started to scream his little lungs off. 'Here we go again!'

'He could become the next Tom Jones and then you won't be moaning.'

Titch took the baby upstairs for a feed and to change his nappy, while Rosa got on with tidying up the shop and checking the stock. When Titch reappeared, with a now-sleepy Theo, Rosa helped her to manoeuvre the pram out of the door.

'Call me!' Rosa shouted after Titch, who faux-flicked her blonde crop then stuck her tiny bottom out in a farewell twerk.

CHAPTER TWO

'All right, duck?' Mary Cobb was just coming out of Seaspray Cottage as Rosa and Hot approached.

'Morning.' Rosa pointed to her mother's windowsill. 'New crystal? That's nice.'

Before meeting her birth mother, Rosa had spent long lonely nights in the children's homes dreaming that she had been born to a famous actress who'd given her up due to a sordid affair with an Arabian prince. On finding out the truth – that she had been born to a reformed alcoholic who lived in a two-up-two-down terraced cottage and worked in the Co-op in Cockleberry Bay – it wasn't quite the fairy tale she had hoped for.

Mary's array of stones and crystals outside was a tradition started by Rosa's great-grandmother Queenie, who had also lived at Seaspray Cottage but who had sadly passed away earlier in the year. In fact, with their unconventional spiritual ways, and before Rosa knew that Mary was her mother, she had named the pair the Cockleberry Coven.

Despite knowing her for such a short time, Rosa missed the old lady. At ninety-three, Queenie's whole being was steeped in wisdom and secrets. Her long hair was as white as the driven snow and her face furrowed with experience. Rosa had memorably been there inside the cottage on the day her great-grandmother had decided it was the right time to die.

Rosa had never forgotten her first visit to the cottage, when Queenie had insisted on reading her tea leaves and proceeded to predict many things that had come true. Abiding by the old lady's 'save nothing for best' motto Rosa still often wore the gold necklace she had inherited from Queenie, and had worn it for her recent wedding to Josh. Looking at it for the first time, Rosa had marvelled at the huge sapphire pendant, set in gold and with the words *Meet me where the sky touches the sea* engraved on the back.

Mary reached over to the window sill and picked up the stone, saying, 'Yes, it's Rock Crystal, one of your birth stones, Rosa.' Hot started barking at her feet. She bent down to fuss him, her jet-black hair almost touching the pavement as she did so. 'Where are you two off to anyway?'

'It's poo time for the hound. You?'

'Just going for my own daily constitutional too, but you'll be pleased to know that *I've* just been.'

They both laughed. Rosa commented, 'I'm so proud of your new fitness regime.'

'Well, you and I know it helps my COPD' [Chronic Obstructive Pulmonary Disease] 'and I need to be fit for those pending grandchildren when they come, don't I?'

'Mother! What have I told you! Josh and I need a bit of time to ourselves first.' Rosa linked arms with Mary. 'Come on, let's walk down the hill together. Hot is dying to chase seagulls on the beach.' At the 'seagulls' word Hot started running around in circles yapping. 'We can have a cuppa in Coffee, Tea or Sea and watch him from the window.'

'We won't be able to do that for much longer. Not with the same owner anyway. She wants to sell up.'

16

'Oh?'

'Yes, I found out this morning.'

Rosa laughed. 'You find out everything, before anyone else.'

'Sara – without an H – wants to retire. She's evidently selling the cafe as a going concern. Buying a big old place down in St Ives.'

'Retiring? But she can't be much older than fifty, can she?'

'True. What's more, it's a little goldmine in *and* out of season. I remember old Harry Trevan having the place before her. It was just called simply Harry's then. He retired with a tidy penny too.'

'I've always quite fancied running a café. Ever since I worked at the one near to Josh's house in London.'

'Didn't you tell me you walked out of there?'

'I walked out, or I was fired from every job I did. It's different now I am my own boss.'

'Oh Rosa, I think you should be very grateful you've got the shop. You've only had it five bloody minutes and your great-grandfather worked his socks off to ensure you were well looked after.'

'I am grateful, you know that, but it is quite small.'

'"The most pitiful among men is he who turns his dreams into silver and gold".'

'Is that what Kahlil thinks?' Rosa smiled. Mary nodded. She was forever quoting her favourite prophet, Kahlil Gibran. 'I know money doesn't necessarily bring happiness, but it does bring freedom. And as the shop is so small, the earning capacity is capped really.'

'You have Josh now, too.' Mary was feeling a bit wheezy so she stopped and took a blast on her inhaler, holding her breath for as long as she could manage before releasing it in a long whistling sigh.

Rosa waited until she'd done before saying, 'Yes, I do have Josh, Mum, but I don't want to rely on him or anyone. You never know what's going to happen in life.'

'When did you get so wise, little lady?'

'It's called being a survivor and having you as a mum and Queenie as a great-gran. I so wish I could have met your mum too.'

'So do I.' Mary looked up to the sky. Maria, her mother, had died giving birth to her. 'Come on, no more doom and gloom. It is such a glorious morning and we are spending this time together.'

'I know. Lovely that it's such a mild October, too. Can't be doing with winter yet, especially as my dear husband will be away for a lot of it.'

'Remind me what it is that your Josh does again? He tells me – and *whoosh*. I forget immediately.' Mary flung her arm in the air to demonstrate.

'I don't know the ins and outs either, to be honest. He's still at the same trading firm in the City. And he gets a mega-bonus each year, so is going to stick it out, for now anyway.'

'And remember, before getting too maudlin about him being away, you managed well enough without him before you married.'

Had she? Had she really? Thinking back to her countless one-night stands in London, then her affair down here with Joe Fox, the Editor of the *South Cliffs Gazette*, Rosa sighed. Joe had fooled her into believing that he was unhappily married, about to divorce his cheating wife, and it wasn't until Mary cleverly set her up to meet the wife that Rosa had realised what was going on. The couple had a teenager, five-year-old twins and a baby on the way. Rosa felt so disillusioned. Apart from Joe, she'd had a sex-only relationship with Luke the plumber, whose mother was the devious landlady at the Ship Inn. So no, it wasn't true. She hadn't managed at all; she had muddled through relationships in the only way she knew – until Josh, that was.

'Keep your sense of identity, Rosa.' Mary took her daughter's hand as they walked down the steep street to the beach. '"Give your hearts but not into each other's keeping. For the pillars of the temple stand apart and the oak tree and the cypress grow not in each other's shadow".'

'Mary! Enough of Kahlil now, thanks.'

'All he means is that space is good in a relationship.'

'Says the woman who's never had one,' Rosa tutted.

Hurt, Mary released her hand. 'You don't know that.'

Rosa felt a sudden anger rising. 'And anyway, I don't need your advice,' she said bitterly. 'Thanks to you, I've been on my own in many ways and for many years.'

Mary squeezed her daughter's shoulder. 'And for that I am truly sorry.'

Rosa softened. 'Oh, I'm sorry…I didn't mean…I think what I'm trying to say is that I've found love now, with Josh – and with you, of course. And I want to spend as much time as possible living and breathing it. It's all so bloody confusing.'

'There is no rush. Let it all happen naturally. Although Josh is thirty-one now, isn't he?'

'What's that supposed to mean?' Rosa reared up again.

'I know you had a miscarriage, love.' Rosa flinched as Mary promised, 'If you ever want to talk about it, you know you can.'

Rosa thought back to the painful and ongoing period she had suffered not long after the wedding.

'In sickness and in health, my dear,' Mary said gently.

'I was just late, that's all,' Rosa lied, 'and I tell Josh everything normally. I was just so happy about the wedding. Didn't want to make a fuss and spoil things.'

They reached the beach and Rosa bent down to let Hot off his lead. The excitable dachshund immediately tore down the beach towards a group of unsuspecting seagulls.

Mary stuttered, 'I d-do love you, Rosa.'

Giving her mother a watery half-smile, Rosa turned and started to run over the sand towards the sea's edge and away from the mutual affection they both struggled to accept and convey.

CHAPTER THREE

'Rosalar!'

Josh flew through the Corner Shop front door and scooped his petite, curly-haired wife up into his arms. The happy couple had known each other for two years now. Their paths had crossed after Josh became her landlord 'with benefits' in the East End of London before Rosa had – out of the blue – inherited the shop. It wasn't until they had spent time apart that they realised how much they missed each other, and that was when their up-and-down relationship began.

Rosa felt warmth flow through her and said through Hot's rapturous barking: 'You're a day early, you bugger.'

'That's a nice welcome! Imagine, we are more than a month married now and already you won't even acknowledge me.' Hot was jumping up and down by now. 'Aw, my best boy.' Josh put his wife down and swept the little doggie up in his arms.

With Hot licking his face, Josh strode over to flick the Open sign on the door to Closed, and pointed upwards.

'Get your beautiful little being up those stairs, Mrs Smith. I need you and I need you right now.'

'But…'

'No buts, the pet population of the South Hams are not going to starve. I'll only be about ten minutes, and that's if you're lucky.'

Rosa laughed out loud. 'Husband, I bloody love you.'

Rosa lay back in post-coital ecstasy. 'I needed that – and you, of course,' she sighed.

'You're only human.' Josh stroked her thigh lovingly.

'I can't bear it that you're away in the week.'

'I know, I know. But listen up, I have a compromise. Like today, I will come back on a Thursday, so every other week it's just four nights I will be away.'

'Hmm, that's a little better, I suppose. But don't think you're getting any extra-curricular bedroom activity for being such a good boy.'

Josh laughed and wrapped his big muscly arms around her. 'I'm doing this for us, Mrs Smith. For our future. You know the bonuses at the bank are too good to turn down. It just makes sense.'

'And I guess it's October now, there's only a few more working weeks until Christmas and you'll be done.'

'Er...'

'Oh Josh, what? No more!'

'If I do one more year then we will have such a good pot of money. I can rent out my place in London and we'll be able to afford to buy somewhere on the cliffs at Polhampton Sands. Just like you've always wanted.'

Rosa screwed up her face and objected, 'Money isn't everything.'

'I know, Rosa, but security is. I've worked bloody hard to get where I am, and this will be the making of us. I don't want to burn out. So, I do mean it when I say one more year.'

'A whole year?' She stuck out her bottom lip.

'Imagine when I'm back. I can help you with the shop and do some consulting work and with us keeping the place in London, we can have the best of both worlds. Now, how does that sound?'

'It's all so organised, it sounds a bit boring.'

'Boring? Rosa, really? It is just one year.'

'I'm joking. You know what I'm like.' She snuggled back into Josh's arms, secretly unsure whether, in fact, she was joking or not.

CHAPTER FOUR

Monday morning, bright and early, with Josh having gone back on the train to London, Rosa was heading into the Co-op to get some milk when she heard the familiar voice of Jacob shouting her name from the door of the Lobster Pot.

'Hello, stranger.' Jacob kissed her on each cheek. His smooth skin, trendy haircut and designer jeans defied his early forties age tag. He flatly denied her Botox inquiries and said his youthful looks were all down to being married to the equally handsome Raffaele, who was many years his junior. The couple had instantly befriended Rosa on her arrival last Christmas, and she had welcomed a part-time bar job with them to give herself some extra set-up cash.

The men had sold up in London to make a life down in the South-west and were able to buy not only the Lobster Pot and turn it into a desired gastro pub, but also a beautiful cliff-top home in Polhampton Sands. Jacob ran the show, while husband Raffaele did the cooking.

'What do you mean, stranger? I only saw you last week. And I've been busy *entertaining* my new husband, don't you know.' She emphasised the word *entertaining*.

'Well, I've missed you, darling, and I'd be entertaining him too, given half the chance.'

Rosa laughed. 'He's mine, all mine.'

'Have you got time to come in for a coffee? I'm just waiting for a delivery, then heading back home.'

'Go on then.' Rosa followed him inside the familiar surroundings of his pub.

'I'm excited actually. My sister and Brad are working both today and tomorrow, so I get to put my feet up at home at the Sands and spend a bit of quality time with my Italian stallion. Guess what else we are doing?'

'Going surfing?'

'In October? Are you mad, darling? No, we are looking at expanding the Sharp-Marino canine contingent.'

'You dark horse. You didn't mention you wanted another dog.'

'We didn't, but we saw an ad on the internet with the most adorable photos and fell in love.'

'I'm jealous. Maybe Ugly and Pongo will be as well. They will surely have to give their Pug paws-up approval though?'

'Now, don't tell me off, Rosa, but…it's not a Pug this time.'

'Oh Jacob, it's not a sausage, is it?' Rosa's voice rose an octave with excitement.

'Yes!' Her camp friend clapped his hands together in seal-like fashion.

Rosa started speaking at a hundred words a minute. 'I want to come, but I can't come, or I would just have to have one. Mind you, Hot would hate it if he wasn't numero uno.'

'You're not cross with me, are you?

'Cross? Of course not. I can't wait, they are so cute when they are puppies. But Jacob, I have to warn you, if you think Hot barks a lot…'

'You can share the little bundle with us anyway. And think of all the new collars and coats you're going to sell to us, kidder.'

'Are you getting a girl or boy?'

'Raff informs me that he wants to stay the only bitch in the family.' Jacob laughed. 'But we are going to pick the most pretty or most handsome puppy, of course.'

'Of course.'

'Where's your furry little fella anyway?'

'I was just running up the road for milk and he was asleep under his favourite smelly blanket, so I just left him there.'

'He's such a character, that one. How long is Josh away for this time, sweetie?'

'Back Friday.' Rosa groaned. 'I hate saying goodbye to him.'

'I know it's hard – but look what Raff and I achieved by working our nuts off in London before moving down here. It does make sense. And you are both so young.'

'I guess so.'

Jacob lifted his cup. 'Top-up?'

'Yes, just a little one, please.'

Jacob reached for the coffee jug and as he refilled their cups, he said, 'I heard some bad news for us both today.'

'Go on.'

'Sheila Hannafore is going to be back in the Ship Inn really soon. The refurb is complete. Rumour has it her son is coming down to help her attract a younger crowd.'

'Which son, Lucas?'

'I guess so, since the other one lives down here anyway, doesn't he?'

'How do you know all this?'

'Your mother told me.'

'Ah, of course she did.' Rosa nodded. 'I've missed this one.'

'She literally caught me when I went to get my paper, so you'll get the lowdown later, I'm sure.' Jacob took a slurp of coffee. 'I still can't believe how that canny old bag Sheila wriggled out of that hit-and-run business.'

'I know. Last heard of, she was staying with her sister in Exeter whilst the work was being done on the pub. I was hoping she would be away a lot longer.'

'Me too. We've been enjoying the extra business, to be honest,' Jacob said, then added wickedly, 'although I'm sure some of the locals who go in there have got six toes.'

'You can't say that!' Rosa laughed. 'But you're right, it's not quite your normal clientele down that end of town.'

'I still can't get over why Sheila would be party to running her son's girlfriend over. And I can't believe you were nearly framed too.'

'Nobody is ever good enough for her boy, maybe? I don't know.' Rosa stirred some sugar into her coffee.

'Bit extreme though, running someone over. Although saying that, I'm sure it was Sheila who arranged for our stockroom to be torched when we first arrived and threatened her business.' Jacob's expression had turned grim.

'True, that is a bit scary.' Rosa made a face. 'Sheila Hannafore also paid for Seb Watkins's lawyer, and he got off. Yet he was bang to rights in that hit-and-run. We know that a hundred per cent. Sold his van straight after it happened. I mean, if that didn't show his guilt… He so should have done some prison time.'

'I wonder where he ended up?'

'I don't know, but just hope it's a long way from here.'

Despite her closeness to Jacob, Rosa said no more. Titch had sworn Rosa to secrecy over what had happened with Seb. The young girl had decided for her own reasons that she didn't want to drag the dreadful affair through the courts and Rosa had respected her decision. So, it had been a complete relief that

Seb Watkins hadn't shown his face in Cockleberry Bay since.

Rosa drained her coffee cup. 'Right, much as I would like to stay and gossip all day, I had best go and open that shop. Another day, another dog collar and all that.'

Jacob yawned. 'I want to go back to bed…oh, and I can later today if I want to. So there.'

Rosa mock-swiped him. 'It's all right for some. Enjoy your time off. Love to Raff – oh, and I want a photo of *all* those furry chipolatas as soon as you can, please.'

CHAPTER FIVE

Squatting down to fill the bottom shelf with tins of dog food, Rosa heard the shop door ring, but didn't turn around. 'Won't be a minute!' she cried.

'I'd recognise that pert little arse anywhere,' said a familiar voice.

Jumping up in shock, she knocked over the box of tins, causing the contents to roll around the floor. Hot came running over from his bed in the corner to see what the fracas was about.

Lucas Hannafore knelt to pick them up. 'Ah, Mr Sausage, have you missed me?' He stroked the dachshund, who disloyally licked the handsome one's hand.

'I can manage this, thanks.' Rosa knelt beside him. 'And do you always have to be so coarse?'

'Hark at you! What's all this then – has marriage turned you into a lady suddenly?'

Rosa took in his brooding dark looks, and remembering how they'd had abandoned and particularly good sex on her sofa last New Year's Day, conceded to herself that he did have a point.

She got up and dusted down her knees. 'What are you doing here anyway?' She wanted to confirm Jacob's findings.

Lucas stood up too, and remained a little bit too close for

comfort. 'Here as in right here? Or here as in down in the boring Bay?'

'Only boring people get bored.' Rosa was irked that despite her happily married status she still found him attractive. She wasn't usually keen on men shorter than five-ten either.

'You didn't find me boring before posh boy staked his claim on you.'

'Answer my question, Luke.' Rosa squirmed slightly inside. Even his eyelashes were longer than hers.

'Mother dear is back in the pub, that's why I'm here. It's looking great actually. I said I'd take a couple of months out of London and help her with marketing the place. Get some live music booked, et cetera. It's what this dump needs.'

'Not exactly the season for it, is it.'

'Cockleberry Bay is not all tourists, you know. There are a lot of locals who like live music too and it will be Christmas again before we know it.'

'And you're a plumber, Luke. Or did I miss "music mogul" on your cv?'

'Still sharp as a tack, I see. I'm a plumber, yes, and I intend to do some local jobs, but that doesn't stop me from having the gift of the gab to market the place and it's not exactly hard to deliver a flyer or two.'

'You're *so* flexible,' Rosa replied nonchalantly.

'Well, you would know.' Rosa was annoyed to feel her cheeks reddening. 'And I love it that you can't let the Luke bit go. I find it kind of sexy.'

'It reminds me of how you duped me when we first met, that's all.'

Luke aka Lucas Hannafore had been set up by his mother Sheila Hannafore aka landlady of the Ship Inn to pretend to be a local plumber just so that he could find out everything that was going on at the Corner Shop when Rosa had first arrived to take over. Put out that the shop had been inherited by a mystery benefactor, a few of the locals had been far from welcoming to Rosa. She was bitterly resented (a) for being an outsider and (b) for having the Corner Shop and upstairs flat literally land in her lap without apparently having done anything to deserve it.

'Anyway, Mrs Smith, how is married life treating you and where is your hunk of a husband?'

'He works away in the week.'

'Oh, does he now? That's handy.'

Rosa shook her head. 'You're unbelievable.'

'Thanks.' Lucas grinned. 'And talking of boring, what about your new name, Mrs Smith? Rosa Hannafore sounds *so* much better.'

'I wouldn't marry you if you were the last plumber on earth.'

'I'm not asking you to marry me, Rosa.' Lucas stared right into her eyes, winked and picked out a cat keyring from the basket on the counter. 'Purrfect.'

Pressing three pound-coins into her hand, he stroked his fingers against Rosa's palm. 'See you around, sexy.'

Relieved to hear the door click shut, Rosa took a deep breath. Yes, she was a married woman now, yes, she was very much in love with Josh and yes, her promiscuous past was behind her.

But that still hadn't stopped her from feeling the charge that had just sparked between her and bad boy Lucas Hannafore.

CHAPTER SIX

'Bliss.' Rosa turned over, wrapped her arms around Josh and gently kissed his broad back. It was the first Saturday in ages that she hadn't had to get up and open the shop.

Josh took her hands in his, kissed them and snuggled into her. Just as they had both dozed off into a lazy lie-in, the doorbell rang, causing Hot to jump up from his bed on the landing and start barking loudly.

'I'll go.' Rosa sleepily pulled on her dressing gown and went down to open the shop door. She was greeted by a grinning Titch and a gurgling Theo in his pram.

'Sorry, Rose, I thought you'd be up. I forgot the key.' Rosa didn't speak, just lifted her hand in acknowledgement. 'Go back to bed,' Titch said. 'I will text you if I need anything. I take it everything has got a price against it?'

Squinty-eyed, Rosa nodded, then waved and turned to go back up to bed. She assumed the former position with Josh, then, on feeling a little horny, began to push her tiny frame and full breasts into his back.

'Little minx.' Josh turned over and began to kiss his new wife passionately, rising to the occasion in seconds. Rosa gasped as he entered her and their love-making commenced.

It had taken a while for Rosa to accept love in its highest degree. So devoid of proper emotion throughout her childhood and adolescence, she had seen sex as purely a short-term answer to love; she felt undeserving of anything other than that. How lucky was she that Josh had seen through that to find the loving, albeit slightly wild character that lay below all the bravado.

Josh held her tightly into his chest. 'God, I love you, Mrs Smith. And I was thinking the other day just how beautiful our babies are going to be.'

'As long as the girls come out petite and green-eyed like me and don't grow into six-foot rugby-playing Tight Head Props like you.'

Josh laughed. 'Yes, and they have to have your dark brown mops of curly hair.'

'And really hairy legs.' Rosa kissed his nose.

At that moment Hot tried to jump up on the bed and failed miserably. Rosa wriggled free from her husband and scooped the little hound up on top of the covers. 'Don't be jumping up, you'll hurt your little back.' Her hair tickled Hot's ears and he shook his head frantically, his ears whipping back and forth. 'But for now, this is our little family and I don't think I could be running a shop and looking after a baby all on my own. It would just be so hard.'

'I hear you, but we don't want to leave it too long.'

'Josh, I'm only twenty-six."

'I know, but I'm thirty-one and I don't want to be an old dad in the playground. Maybe we should start trying. Why don't you come off the pill? I mean, it might take us ages.'

Rosa knew that it wouldn't, since she had only missed two contraceptive pills in all the flurry of getting married and had fallen pregnant before the wedding. But she wasn't ready to give up her freedom yet, and seeing how shattered Titch was had made her doubly certain. And what if Josh changed his mind about her, stopped fancying her?

Josh read her face. 'I'm not going to leave you in the shit ever, Rosa, you know that. I love you so much.'

'But you're away so often and I do still wonder why you chose me over one of the glamorous City girls.'

'Rosa, not again. I want *you*. My pretty, funny, adorable, slightly crazy, warm and loving *you*. Work is just work. I literally count the days until the weekend to be back with you.' And when Hot started to lick his chin: 'And yes, I want you too, of course, my boy.' He buried his face in Hot's coat and breathed him in. 'Where's all this come from today anyway?' he asked in a muffled voice. 'I thought needy Rosa had gone away.'

'I'm fine. I think it's because I know I've got another year of a part-time you.'

Josh turned and wrapped her up in his arms again. 'OK. I will be here as much as I can, I promise. So, how about we plan a baby to arrive when I'm back? You won't have time to miss me then.'

'More plans?' Rosa asked with a sarcastic smile. She had always hated the word. 'Life doesn't work like that, husband, and I've made more plans this year than I have in my whole life.'

'Good, isn't it?' Josh teased and kissed her forehead. 'Talking of plans, how about we go for a long walk up West Cliffs and then have a lazy lunch at the Lobster Pot? It will be nice to catch up with each other and the boys.'

'Now that, gorgeous man, is the kind of plan I do like!'

CHAPTER SEVEN

On reaching the top of West Cliffs, Rosa lifted her arms out either side and ran into the oncoming wind. Hot charged after her, his soft brown ears flailing behind him. Rosa then pelted back to where Josh was standing taking in the amazing views.

'You are both mad.' He ran his hand lovingly through his wife's curly mop, saying, 'It's such a relief, being out of London. They've got Christmas stuff in the shops already. I can't believe it.'

'I can't say I miss it that much. Aside from sometimes wishing there was a cinema and some bigger shops near to us, there isn't really anything I would change. Well, apart from you being here all the time, that is.'

'I know, but time will fly. I mean, look how quickly the months have gone by already since you arrived.'

'I guess so.' Rosa glanced down at Hot, who then charged off to join a family flying kites on the cliff along from them. 'Look at this.' She pointed to the endless sea. 'We are so lucky to live here.'

'Yes, we are. And let's hope we have the same long love story as Queenie and your great-grandfather. Despite what happened, they were deeply in love.'

Rosa said quietly, 'This is the exact spot where Ned's wife

Dotty took her own life, heartbroken about his affair with Queenie, my great-grandmother.'

'Remind me about it all again on the way down the hill. I still have trouble getting my head around it.'

Arm-in-arm with her husband, Rosa relayed the story of how Ned, her great-grandfather, had been married to Dotty for years and how both ran the Corner Shop. Unable to have children with Dotty, Ned started to have feelings for his wife's best friend Queenie. They did all they could to stay apart but the pull of true love was too strong. 'I do believe he loved Dotty too though,' Rosa insisted. 'Anyway, Queenie got pregnant by Ned and went away to London to live and to have her baby in secret. She always vehemently denied to Ned that it was his child. That baby was Maria, my grandmother, Mary's mother. With Maria dying in childbirth, Ned and Queenie had to take Mary on as a daughter and so the rest you remember, right?'

'Yes. Mary went off the rails and became an alcoholic, hence you being taken into foster care after she got drunk and dropped you, causing this scar.' Josh stopped and caressed the tiny lightning-shaped scar on his wife's left cheek. 'Sorry, that sounded a bit hard. I'm just so glad I am here for you and that Mary did come good in the end.'

'We are still working on our relationship though. No doubt it will take time. I still find it hard calling her Mum.'

'Of course, it will be hard, gorgeous girl. Being told a stranger is your mother – I can't even comprehend it. And living practically on her doorstep and having to make it work. You've been amazing with what you've dealt with. You've taken it all in your stride and for that I admire you so much.'

Rosa felt tears welling. 'I keep thinking of Queenie and Ned. For the rest of their long lives, they never had any other lovers, they just had their own special relationship.'

'It is a film-worthy love story,' Josh said.

'Yes, it is. When Queenie went off to London, they sent each other so many letters, which they would always close with "Meet me where the sky touches the sea".' Rosa looked out again at the vast stretch of water in front of them. 'I love that it was about this very horizon, and that those actual words are engraved on the necklace Queenie gave to me – the one I wore on our wedding day.'

'Never seen you so soppy, Mrs Smith.' Josh squeezed her hand. 'Their relationship was probably better than most conventional ones. In fact, maybe separate beds are the answer for us?'

Rosa poked her husband in the ribs. 'Oi, we would never come to that. I just wish that Queenie had allowed herself to love Ned openly, but due to her guilt, even after the Cockleberry rumours died down, she carried on pretending that they were just friends. Mary wasn't even told that Ned was her grandad, but deep down she always knew.'

'His final hurrah, and what I think is even more romantic and special, is that Ned felt compelled to leave the shop to you, Rosa. He obviously knew what had happened and it must have taken ages for Queenie and Mary to find you: Ned and Queenie's one and only great-granddaughter.'

Hot was craving attention and began weaving in and out of their legs. They were nearing the dangerous edge of the cliff path, so Josh clipped on his lead.

'It will be tough moving out of the flat with so much history steeped in it,' Rosa murmured.

'But you do want to get a house, don't you?'

They reached the beach and released a now restless Hot, who started pouncing on an unsuspecting seagull that was absorbed in pecking at a dead crab.

'Yes, it'll be so much better for Hot if we have a garden, and

I'd love a constant sea view too. We do have to remember that we can't sell the shop though.'

'Ned will never know,' Josh joked.

'I do hope you're not serious. His words are etched on my mind.' She began to recite: '*One proviso of my gift to you is that you must NEVER sell the Corner Shop in Cockleberry Bay. When you feel the time is right, it can only be passed on to someone you feel really deserves it, and only then.*'

'That's the shop, not the flat.'

'Oh Josh, stop it. They are one and the same in my view. I must honour Ned. Without him I would still be roving from one rubbish job to another, and the same with men. He has changed my life. Without his legacy, you would still be believing that I was useless, and so we would never have got married.'

'I have to stop you there, missus. I loved you even when you worked at Poundworld.'

'Really?'

'Oh Rosa, stop this.'

'OK. But I do think the shop has been a complete and utter catalyst to our happiness.'

'I hear you, darling wife.' Josh grabbed her hand. 'And there is no rush for anything else, so don't worry. We have all the time in the world.'

'Oh yes there *is* a rush for something. Last one to the pub does next weekend's early poo walk.' Rosa screeched and began to sprint up the hill, leaving a bemused Josh to put on Hot's lead and follow at her heels.

An out-of-breath Rosa squealed in delight as Jacob appeared behind the bar carrying the cutest, miniature version of Hot she had ever seen. The new puppy was small enough to fit into his hand.

'I can't believe you didn't tell me you were getting him today!' she cried. 'I wanted to help you choose.'

'And I wanted to surprise you. We decided on a *her* in the end, despite Raff's initial objections. So, Lady Dolce Vita Petunia Duchess Barkley, please meet my dear friends Rosa and Joshua Smith.' Hot was now careering in circles around their bar stools, barking his head off.

Picking Hot up so he could sniff the new little lady, Josh joked, 'Blimey, mate, what do you call out if she runs off?'

Just then, Raffaele appeared in his chef's whites and came over to tickle the little dog under her chin. 'She's our little Duchess, *piccolo amore*.'

'Duchess – that's what we will call her.' Jacob smiled as the handsome Italian greeted the pair with air kisses either side.

You could see the hearts in Rosa's eyes. 'I so want another fur baby. Can we, Josh, please?'

'I see. It's easier to get one of those out of you than a real one.' Josh grinned. 'Come on – are you really ready for a puppy running around the shop and all that training involved too?'

'Hmm. You may be right. I just missed out on Hot being a puppy, that's all.'

Jacob put a pint of bitter and a red wine down in front of them. 'That's because you stole him when he was a grown-up, Rosa.'

'He was being beaten, it was terrible. I *had* to dognap him.' Remembering the day she had saved her beloved pooch from the cruel woman outside Poundworld, she put Hot on her lap for comfort. 'The poor little fella had welts all down his back.' She looked lovingly at the new arrival. 'How old is the Duchess, Jacob?'

'She's sixteen weeks already. She was the runt of the litter, so they kept hold of her a bit longer. Little angel. That just makes her extra-special. Right, enough excitement.' Jacob took the puppy back upstairs to join the pugs in their big bed. When he reappeared, he shook Josh's hand firmly. 'Anyway, it's good to see you, mate.'

'You too. We've just been up on the cliffs. The Ship's re-opening next weekend by the looks of things.'

'Hate to say it,' Rosa chipped in, 'but it does look quite smart. They've repainted it so it's bright white, and put a new sign up.'

'We're not too worried. Our menu is excellent, and we now have as much reliable trade in the winter with locals, without the holiday barrage. We are a very different pub from the Ship, and that's how I want it to stay.'

Josh put his hand on top of Rosa's. 'Promise me, wifey, you won't be going in there anytime soon?' he said in a low voice. Whilst Rosa had been running off earlier Josh thought he noticed Lucas's plumbing van pulling into the pub car park.

'Err, no. Why would I?' Rosa screwed up her face.

'I know how much you love your live music, especially if you've had a drink.'

'I rarely go out without you, if you want to know the truth, and after the hit-and-run debacle I doubt if Madam Hannafore would serve me anyway.'

'Have you seen or heard from that awful son of hers lately?'

Without thought or expression Rosa replied with a quiet no.

'Good.' There was bad blood between the two men, since Josh had discovered Lucas getting angry with Rosa for not covering his alibi to the police after the hit-and-run incident. Josh had subsequently launched the cocky plumber down the stairs of the flat and out on to the street. This was without him ever knowing that his wife had slept with the bloke.

'So, Rosa, you promise?'

'Josh! OK. I promise. Now, what are we eating? I'm starving.'

CHAPTER EIGHT

Titch turned the volume up on her phone and began dancing around the lounge of Rosa and Josh's flat.

'I love this tune.' She threw open the French doors to the balcony area. The uninterrupted views of the bay it offered were stunning whatever time of day, whichever season. The seagulls were already screeching their goodnights in the dark sky. Hot followed the young mum out and cocked his leg on a plant pot.

'It's cold, Titch, shut it up,' Rosa called from the kitchen. 'Do you want another drink?'

'Is the pope catholic?' Titch came inside and shut the double doors behind her. 'Where do you think seagulls sleep, Rose?'

'Er, I've never really given it much thought.' Rosa appeared in the lounge carrying two glasses.

'Happy Halloween!' Titch jumped out from behind the sofa.

Shocked out of her skin, but luckily not enough to spill the drinks on the carpet, Rosa screamed loudly. 'You little cow! That is possibly the freakiest mask I've ever seen.'

'Good, isn't it?' Titch jigged around with it on. 'Here.' She handed Rosa a replica mask of *The Scream*. 'Got one for you too.'

'I see no point in bloody Halloween,' Rosa grumped. 'It's got so big over here now.'

'So why is the shop fully decorated with cobwebs and pumpkins? And you've been selling Halloween pet costumes and giving treats to the kids all week, haven't you?'

'It's called keeping up with the Boneseys.'

Titch laughed out loud.

'Shocked myself with how funny that was actually.' Rosa had a good look at the mask and tutted. 'Anyway, my question to you is: are you allowed alcohol when you are breastfeeding?'

'I've expressed some milk, it's fine for tonight. I'm thinking of just doing bottles soon anyway. I do love the bonding bit, but the leaky, sore tit business isn't for me really. Especially now I'm back working already.'

'I wondered about your implants too?'

'Seem to be fine. I did double-check with the midwife. Evidently as they are saline, there is no risk to my little man. He does scoff a lot though! Eat, sleep, poop repeat, eat, sleep, poop, repeat. That's my life now.'

''I know, I don't envy that bit, but he is SO gorgeous.' Rosa handed her friend a glass of Prosecco. 'OK, as long as you are sure re this.'

'I'm sure.'

They chinked glasses.

'Cheers. I can't tell you how nice it is to be out. Don't get me wrong, Theo is my world, but after being pregnant for nine months, this tastes like nectar.' Titch plonked herself down on the comfy cream-and-blue striped sofa and reminisced, 'Remember when you first moved in and you had that shitty old sofa.'

'Yes, I did make do and mend. But it was still homely then and I loved it. I was even rather fond of the avocado green bathroom suite.'

Titch laughed. 'It's all clean and new now.'

'Yes, it is, but we would like to get a house now that we are married. More space would be nice, especially as Josh keeps going on about us starting a family too.'

'Well, if you ever need a tenant, look no further.' Titch drained her glass. 'This flat would be perfect. Theo could have the smaller bedroom. And what more do I need than a great-size lounge, kitchen and bathroom? Outside space too.'

'You do realise the rent is going up each time you open your mouth,' Rosa teased. 'Fancy a tequila?'

'Blimey Rose, what's happened to you?'

'Nothing. We haven't had a blast for ages.'

'It's good to have you back, girl. I was getting a bit bored of sensible married Mrs Smith.'

The music stopped and they both heard a frantic scratching noise. Rosa rushed to the balcony doors, where Hot shivered outside, barking his indignation. 'Sorry, my boy, that nasty girl locked you out.'

The music coming from the Ship was so loud it had even frightened the seagulls off to wherever they might be sleeping.

'Titch! I should have known you didn't just want to go for a walk at this time of night,' Rosa hiccuped.

'Come on, it's their opening night. I've always wanted to see that group Shore Thing play live.'

'But I promised Josh.'

'Here.' Titch pulled the masks from her bag.

'You scheming little…' Rosa shook her head.

The poster on the door stated it was a Halloween Party and WEAR TO SCARE! Leading her friend past the smoking area contingent of ghost and ghouls, straight into the heaving and very noisy pub, Rosa suddenly felt a pang of both apprehension and excitement. Josh was right, she did love live music and with this mask on and her mind in drunk mode, she told herself that surely no one would ever know it was her.

However, on first sight of Sheila Hannafore appropriately donning a witch's hat behind the bar, Rosa had a slight wobble. This was the woman capable of organising and pinning a hit-and-run on to someone else. This was also the woman who had paid for Titch to have an abortion as she thought the girl was pregnant with her precious son's baby and didn't want his life ruined. Most importantly of all though, Rosa had also promised her new husband she would not come in here.

Titch found Rosa on a bench overlooking the bay. Near enough the pub to hear the music, far enough away to be keeping her promise.

'Here.' The girl handed Rosa a glass of fizz. 'Get that down you. And what are you doing out here, being a party pooper?'

'Titch, have you got no sense whatsoever? Have you forgotten about Sheila's pay-off?'

'Of course I haven't. The money's in my ISA and hasn't been touched, ready for when Theo and I get our own place.'

'Did Sheila speak to you?'

'She didn't recognise me with the mask on, and I managed to get Ritchie from the chip shop to buy our drinks. I'm not that stupid, Rose.'

'But there is going to come a time when she knows Theo is not Lucas's.'

'She will have to prove it. They've got the same colour hair, even if Theo's skin is slightly darker. Nah,' she took a sip of her bubbles, 'I reckon the old bag won't bother to fight it anyway.'

Rosa had to applaud the gall of her young friend, if nothing else.

The band struck up with 'Mustang Sally' and both girls adorned the masks and started to dance around on the beach, laughing their heads off as they did so.

'I need a wee so badly. Wait here.' Titch ran back to the pub as Rosa carried on dancing and singing along to the music. An autumn moon lit up the relatively calm October sea, while the lights from the pub created a rainbow of colours on the wet sand. For a moment, Rosa felt a sense of pure happiness.

Then she screamed as a hand touched her shoulder and span her around.

'Mustang Sally...' The smoke-and-beer-tinged breath of a Werewolf hit her right in the face. 'Apt mask you've got there, lady.' Recognising Lucas's voice, she hit him on the arm and threw her mask to the ground.

'That's a bit of an overreaction, isn't it?' Lucas began to dance seductively close in front of her. 'Ride, Rosa, Ride.'

'You bastard, you scared the life out of me.' Rosa steadied herself on the bench. Damn, she was drunker than she'd have liked.

'This is a bit of déjà vu, innit?' Lucas said. 'If you believe in all that baloney. Ha, but with a witch for a mother like yours, of course you do.'

Rosa's mind flashed back to the night that Lucas had embarrassed her in front of everyone here when she had first arrived, and yes – this song *had* been playing.

'I knew you wouldn't be able to resist coming down here.' Lucas discarded his cigarette on the sand. 'And the mask may have covered the face, but like your arse, those pretty little tits of yours remain etched in my proverbial wank bank too.'

'You're disgusting.'

'You love it.'

'And I thought you were bringing the pub into the twenty-first century, not playing the same old crap.'

'Touché. Even your wit still makes me hard.' He pushed his mask back over his head.

Taking in the brooding hazel eyes, long lashes and full lips in front of her, Rosa resisted the urge to admit that, regrettably, his intentions still made her wanton.

The music stopped. 'You'd better get back in and serve, hadn't you?' she said icily.

'I know you still fancy me, Rosa.'

'I'm a married woman now.'

'That didn't answer my question. And I bet big bold hubby doesn't know you are here, either.' Removing his mask completely, Luke leaned forward to kiss her. Quickly moving her head to the side, she avoided the kiss on her mouth; instead, he planted one right in the middle of her cheek.

'Mmm, cheeky.' Luke smiled and put his index finger on her nose. 'I'll be seeing you…Mrs Smith,' he murmured before swaggering his way back into the pub.

As Rosa was thinking that maybe it was time she set up a 'Wanker Bank' of her own, a drunk Titch appeared with an even drunker Ritchie. A gangly six foot two to her titchy five foot, they made for a comical couple.

'Ritchie says we can go back to his dad's chip shop, Rose,' Titch piped up. 'There are some battered sausages to be had.'

Rosa's 'I bet there are,' fell on deaf ears. Times like this reminded her that her dear young friend was still only a teenager and not the worldly grown-up she so ably pretended to be.

CHAPTER NINE

Rosa looked around to see that every table in Coffee, Tea or Sea was full. She loved this little café. She had come here a lot when she first moved in, mainly to use the free wi-fi and because the excellent coffee was only £2 a cup and worth every penny. The place was completely dog-friendly, which made it perfect. The quirkiness here suited Rosa's style, for the shelves were adorned with seaside-themed knick-knacks, plus a variety of books were dotted around everywhere, accompanied by an old battered sign announcing *Read me, Replace me, Replenish me*. Despite it being early November, on the counter there was already a lit-up reindeer sporting a Christmas hat, being kept company by a ceramic burlesque dancer money box, holding a sign that said *Nice Tips*. Rosa had seen them on her very first visit to the café last year. Titch had worked here back then too. There was also the added advantage of a view over the beach. Hence why it was usually packed to the rafters, even out of season.

Rosa hoped Mary hadn't taken real offence when she'd said that she had always dreamt of running a little café. Rosa hadn't wanted to seem ungrateful about inheriting the Corner Shop; it was just she did like the idea of the buzz and excitement that running a place like this would bring.

'Penny for them?'

'Sorry?' Rosa looked up to see a broad, auburn-haired man, with thick-framed brown glasses and a short pointy beard looking down at her. He was taller than Josh and with Josh being six-feet two, that was tall!

'Do you mind if I sit here?'

'Of course not,' she lied, and put her bag down beside her, causing Hot to make a funny snuffling noise, before going straight back to sleep on her feet.

'I reckon everyone must have been in the Ship last night for the grand re-opening,' the stranger remarked.

'Er…yes.' Rosa, whose head was banging, was in no mood for polite chit-chat. She had only come in here to use the toilet after walking Hot on the beach, but then realised that a bacon sandwich and a cup of strong coffee would see her fit to open the shop. Titch had had the foresight to book the day off today, and Rosa really had to get herself together, as Josh would be back this evening too.

The big man put his coffee and Danish pastry down on the table, then held out his hand. 'I'm Alec, by the way,' he said, introducing himself. 'Alec Burton.'

'I'm Rosa.'

The big man had noticed her London accent straight away.

'I'm not from down here either,' he confided. 'I've lived all over the place, but most recently Windsor in Berkshire. Do you know it?'

'Only because of the Queen and her castle there. And because of Harry, Meghan and Archie.' Rosa felt a bit queasy.

'Anyway, I'll leave you to your thoughts.' The newcomer opened his leather man bag, pulled out a newspaper and began to read.

Rosa reckoned he must be forty-odd years old, and despite

his size he had a very calming demeanour and presence. Remembering how hard it had been to fit in when she had first arrived, she didn't want to come across as unfriendly. It was time to make a bit of an effort.

'My thoughts are probably the same as everyone else's who was there at the Ship last night,' she replied. 'In other words: *how exactly am I going to get through the day with a hangover like this?*'

Auburn Alec's open face lit up, even his teeth were big. Rosa didn't dare check out his feet.

'I didn't see you there last night,' he let on.

'No, no. I was celebrating Halloween at home with a friend. Well, mainly at home. I did pop into the Ship and then straight out again.' She had no idea why she was telling him this. He was just the sort of person you meet and feel you can reveal your soul to them before you even notice what colour eyes they've got.

'So, hungover Rosa, originally from London by the sound of you, what brings you to these parts?'

'I run the Corner Shop in Main Street.'

'Excellent. I literally only arrived yesterday and noticed it on my way down. I've got a Labrador; Brown. I didn't bring him this morning as I wasn't sure if dogs were allowed in here.'

'Brown Burton, eh? That's a very grand name for a dog.' Rosa laughed.

'Ha! I hadn't thought of that.' Alec revealed his big teeth again.

Beginning to feel a bit better, Rosa told him, 'That's one of the joys of being down here; Cockleberry Bay is really dog-friendly. That's what encouraged me to sell pet stuff. I knew there would be a market.'

'So you own it, not just run it? Forgive me for saying this but

49

you seem really young for that type of venture.'

'I was really lucky to inherit it…but that's a long and sensational story and I'm sorry, but just making small-talk is my limit this morning.'

Auburn Alec laughed heartily. He liked Rosa already. He was all for small-talk; so often it led to big-talk.

The waitress put Rosa's coffee and sandwich down in front of her and Hot stirred before continuing to snore gently at her feet.

'How about you? Why have you left the realms of Royal Berkshire?' she asked, before taking a large bite of her food.

'I got divorced.'

'Oops, I'm sorry,' she mumbled, her mouth full of delicious crispy bacon and Devon bread and butter.

'It is what it is. In a nutshell, half the money from the sale of our marital house in Windsor could only allow me to buy a cupboard if I stayed in the area, but down here I could afford a proper home. We always came to Devon for holidays and I love it here. My son's studying medicine in Cardiff, so it's just me and Brown, and I thought, Why not?'

'So, did you buy in the Bay?'

'I haven't done anything yet. I wanted to suss out the area first so I'm renting a place in Fore Street.'

'Good plan. I didn't have that luxury. Threw myself in feet first.' Rosa swigged some coffee and sighed happily. It tasted so good.

'Any regrets?'

'Not yet, although my husband still works in London and it's tough sometimes, as he's just home weekends.'

'Enjoy a bit of freedom, I say.'

Rosa sighed and rubbing her hand down her face, she groaned slightly before taking several more sips of the piping hot drink.

'That bad?' the big man said sympathetically.

She longed to confide in him, but thankfully, before she had time to blurt out her sorry tale of allowing Lucas close enough to kiss her, Hot let out a resounding string of barks.

'Oh no, I'm so sorry, little fella,' the big man said, stricken. 'I didn't even know he was under there; I think I must have caught him with my foot. Oh dear.'

'Shush, Hot.' Rosa tried to appease the startled hound, but to no avail. She wrapped her half-eaten sandwich in a napkin and handed Auburn Alec a ten-pound note. 'Would you mind sorting the bill? I'd better get him out of here before there's a hangover revolt.'

A slightly flustered Alec stood up and pressed the note into her free hand. 'Please take your money back. The least I can do is pay. Once again, I'm so sorry.'

'Well, thank you so much, but it's fine, honestly. Hot Dog is a complete drama queen.' She looked back as she headed to the door. 'Pop into the shop, we'd all love to meet Brown.'

'Will do.' The newcomer watched the curly-haired bundle of energy walk out of the café and smiled to himself, thinking that if this was the sort of reception he was going to get from the locals, then he had definitely made the right decision in moving down here.

CHAPTER TEN

Rosa couldn't quite believe how busy the shop was that morning. It was as if the whole of the Bay knew she had a hangover and were coming in to punish her for getting drunk on a school night. Mind you, she couldn't complain; she had a large pet-food supplier bill to pay so a sharp intake of cash was just what was needed.

The half-term visitors were very much out in force. The regulars with their weekend and holiday cottages often popped by to see if Rosa had any new leads or coats in for their precious pooches. And thanks to Jacob's insistence that she should also stock designer gear for the better-heeled visitors, with the sniff of winter in the air, she suspected she would be making a tidy profit this week. The Corner Shop also stocked very reasonably priced dog and cat food, which was a steady earner, bringing in a regular stream of punters, who then often went on to treat themselves to other products.

She brightened as she saw the familiar face of Jacob coming through the door.

'Hiya, darling. That cute little weather presenter on *South Cliffs Today* tells us it's going to be minus two this week, so I simply must get the pack kitted out with some new winter warmers. Saying that, I need to get some gloves and a hat myself. It's Bonfire Night this weekend.'

'Oh yes, I love fireworks, although I know the poor animals absolutely hate it.' Rosa started checking through her rail of canine coats. 'Is it usually a good show down here?'

'I forget you haven't been before. Yes, it really is something. The Cockleberry Bay Residents Association put one on every year. I always throw in a fifty when they come around for donations.'

'Titch did mention that someone had come in. I said to give them a tenner out of the till, then forgot all about it.'

'On Saturday night the beach will be packed, as they set the fireworks off near the lifeboat station. And now that old Ma Hannafore is back, she will no doubt be doing a barbecue and music as usual.'

'Brilliant. Josh will be around too. You having a night off then?'

'Not really. My sister and Brad are holding the fort whilst we pop down and then we will hurry back after the fireworks, as the whole town will be busy.'

'How are you getting on with the Duchess?'

'She's a complete little bitch, with her constant barking and tantrums, but we all adore her. Even Ugly and Pongo are treating her like a princess. It's very amusing to watch.'

Rosa grinned. 'I bet. How about this for her?' She pulled out a dainty little pink woolly coat with a big red heart on. 'A present from the Smiths.'

'Love, love, *love* it, darling. Thank you so much. The Duchess will look a picture. Put that in the bag and I think it could be Burberry season for the boys.'

'Delivery for those coming later, I'll pop a couple up.'

'That would be fab, thank you.'

'OK, see you soon. Josh and I are going to come in for a drink and probably food later anyway.'

Thirsty and desperate for a drink of lemonade, Rosa put on Hot's lead, stuck her *Back in* 20 *minutes* sign up on the door and trudged up the hill to the Co-op. On the way, she phoned Titch. When the girl finally answered, Rosa could hear baby Theo screaming in the background.

'Remind me never to drink again, unless I have a babysitter for the whole day after too,' the girl said in a harassed voice.

'And there was me feeling sorry for myself,' Rosa joked.

'Get over yourself, love, this is like torture. Thankfully Mum has just taken him off to settle him down and then he will have a nap, as will I. He woke me practically every hour last night.' Titch gave an enormous yawn. 'I'm sure he knew I'd been out and was punishing me.'

'He was probably being kept awake by the tequila fumes,' Rosa giggled. 'Anyway, how was the hot sausage?'

'I'll have you know that Ritchie Rogers and I are just good friends.'

'Heh. That hasn't stopped you before.'

'That was when my insides weren't like a pound of liver.'

'Ew, Titch! You are so gross. Anyway, I just phoned to see how you are and to let you know we are probably going to the fireworks Saturday night.'

'Oh yes, I forgot about the fireworks. It depends what Mum says. Mind you, if I wrap my boy up well, I could pop down with him for an hour. I always said he wouldn't stop me doing what I wanted. Hmm. I don't know if it would be too loud. He might get scared, and it is really cold at the moment. I need to ask Mum what she thinks.'

'Also, I would like to discuss set days you can work if

that's OK.'

'Oh Rose, can we do this Monday when I'm back at the shop, please? I feel so rough; in fact, I think I'm going to be s...' The line went dead.

Rosa tied Hot up outside the mini-supermarket and waved when she saw Mary at the till.

'Hello. I thought you were off on a Friday.'

'I am usually, duck. Bloody Doreen Lacey rang in sick,' Mary complained in her rich Devonian twang. 'She has the flu jab, then only goes and immediately gets the ruddy flu. Every year she does it, but that lovely doctor on *Good Morning Devon* was only saying earlier that it's not possible.'

Rosa went to the drinks fridge and grabbed herself a can of lemonade.

'Put that back, love, and pop into the cottage for a sec if you have the time. There's plenty of lemonade there. I'm done now. Colette is just putting her uniform on out back.'

A few minutes later, Rosa and Mary arrived together back at Seaspray Cottage. When Mary opened the front door, Merlin, the huge black cat, hissed on seeing Hot, then shot out of the door at a million miles an hour.

Despite Mary saying she was going to have a good old clear-out after her grandmother Queenie's death, she had never got around to it, and the little cottage looked more or less the same as when Rosa had first seen it. The front door led straight from the pavement into a cluttered lounge. A small TV sat in the corner with a huge amethyst perched on top – to protect the telly from going wrong, as Mary had explained once – and a comfy green settee looked inviting. The armchair in the other corner had been Queenie's special place, with a threadbare footstool drawn up in front of it where she used to rest her legs. Rosa noticed that the chair was now covered in a knitted blanket with a catnip mouse sitting on top. There were a few black cat hairs to be seen.

Aware of Rosa's gaze, Mary said, 'Well, I couldn't sit there, could I? No, I could never take *her* place, duck. Merlin guards it, keeps it warm.' As she spoke, the room lit up with a shaft of sunshine, and the low fire sparked behind the fireguard.

Rosa followed Mary into the kitchen, which was immaculately clean as usual. There was a small open fire in the corner in here too, and the cottage felt cosy.

'I'm sure that cat is the devil reincarnated,' Mary grumbled. 'Honestly, he's worse than he ever was when we both lived here.'

'Maybe it's because he misses Queenie but still feels her presence. Animals are all-seeing, we know that.'

'You're right. I know I still miss her,' Mary replied quietly.

'I bet you do. She was such an incredible life force. She was not only your gran, but your mum too really. A massive part of you.' Rosa paused. 'A massive part of *us*.'

Mary went to the fridge. 'Lemonade, or I've got a Diet Coke if you'd rather?'

'No, it's got to be lemonade.'

'So are you hungover? Oh Rosa, don't tell me you've got drunk again.'

'I haven't been drunk for ages.' Rosa's voice rose an octave in annoyance, despite being inwardly pleased that her mother was beginning to know her so well – even for the wrong reasons. 'And I'm not like I used to be, you know that.'

For years, just like Mary, alcohol had been Rosa's crutch, her escape from reality.

'And I'm happier. I don't feel depressed or have the need to send random unsuitable texts to random unsuitable men.' She laughed. 'I've got Josh now. He just gets them instead, but he knows what I'm like.'

'I just worry about you, that's all.'

'I don't have an alcohol problem, if that's what you mean,' Rosa snapped guiltily.

'I didn't say that, now did I, young 'un? I just want you to be at peace with yourself now; that's all.' Mary handed Rosa a tumbler of ice-cold lemonade, which she downed in one. Hot whined and Mary placed half a carrot on the floor, which he began to crunch noisily.

Rosa sat at the kitchen table. 'I can't be too long, I only put a 20-minute sign on the door.' She fingered the crystals on the table and sniffed at a pack of unopened candles through their plastic. 'I thought you were having a clear-out.'

'You know me. I have to think about it a lot before I do anything.' Mary poured herself a glass of water. 'Trouble is, I like my own clutter.' She took a sip of her drink. 'I do think we need to get that young Titch in for a reading though. Just casually – tea leaves will be enough.'

'Why? Have you seen something?'

'Just get her in, Rosa.' Mary put a hand on her daughter's shoulder. 'And here, take this.' She placed a small green crystal down on the table in front of her. 'Pop this in your bedroom.'

'What is it?'

'Peridot.' Mary took an apron from the back of Rosa's chair and tied it around her waist. 'Right, back to work you go.' Rosa stood up slowly and clipped Hot's lead on while he sniffed around the floor for leftover morsels of carrot. Her mother ushered her towards the front door, saying, 'You are going to have an even busier afternoon.'

Rosa and Hot scurried the short distance down the hill to the Corner Shop, where two customers were waiting patiently outside. She apologised for keeping them waiting, let them in to browse and while they were having a good look round, she quickly turned to Mr Google on her phone.

Peridot can help with issues of self-worth, bringing relief to unhealthy emotions such as anger, resentment and jealousy.

CHAPTER ELEVEN

Rosa was dozing on the sofa when a text brought her back into reality.

Hi wifey. Bloody signal problems outside Exeter. Going to be late. Sorry. Love you XX

She checked her watch and tutted. That meant that even if they sorted it right away, Josh wouldn't be home until at least eight-thirty. She was hungry and hungover-tired. Hot nuzzled her free hand.

'Come on, boy, let's feed you. Daddy's late home again. It's hardly worth him coming at all on a Friday sometimes.'

She put Hot's bowl down and despite her hungover state poured herself a large glass of white wine.

'Hair of the dog, eh?' She raised her glass to Hot, then started flicking from channel to channel on the TV.

This part-time marriage business was getting on her nerves. On previous Friday nights, she would have been in the pub and having fun by now. And with another whole year to go she wasn't sure if she could stand it. It wasn't as if she could go out and have fun with anyone else. Especially now that Titch was a mum. And Jacob always went home to his house in Polhampton when he was off duty.

Hi wifey. Getting ridiculous now. Going to be at least 10 until I get home. Will eat from the buffet car. Love you XX

Rosa reached for her phone to call Josh, but it went straight to his answerphone. She dialled another number. 'Hi Ritchie, it's Rosa. Can I be cheeky and order a cod and chips ready to pick up in fifteen? Yes, salt and vinegar, that's great, thank you.'

Two large glasses of pinot grigio and a fish supper down, Rosa felt relaxed and sleepy. So sleepy that two hours later she didn't even feel the big arms of her husband sweep her up gently and place her in their comfy king-size bed.

On Saturday morning Rosa awoke to the relaxing sound of rain pouring against the bedroom window. There was a warm patch beside her, but no hunk of husband. No Hot in evidence either. She then reached for her phone, usually on the bedside table – but couldn't find it. She'd only had two glasses of wine, she knew that much, but had been so tired she didn't even remember getting into bed. She was shocked to realise she hadn't even taken her clothes off.

Sleepily she got up and went through to the kitchen to make some tea. It had been such a wonderful summer and autumn that it seemed almost alien to have bad weather. She checked her phone, which was lying on the work surface in there, to find messages from Josh, one saying that he was on his way from the station. It was timed at 11 pm, so no wonder she'd fallen asleep. And the other informed her he was taking Hot for a walk on the beach. *After all, you did win the bet!* the message ended. She smiled, remembering her mad dash to the Lobster Pot and him owing her a lie-in. If and when they did have kids, there would be a lot more bargaining for that slot, she thought.

She got back into bed and drank her cup of tea. Mary had kindly said she would manage the shop today so Rosa could spend some much-needed time with Josh. It upset her that she had already missed a whole evening with him. It would be a relief to talk to Titch on Monday about getting into some sort of routine. For as much as she loved running the shop, six days a week had become all-consuming without any help, and ideally, she wanted most weekends free for Josh now. Thinking about this also aggrieved her slightly, since if he were home in the week, cramming time with him at weekends wouldn't be necessary. But on the other hand, she did understand his motives and they were in an enviable financial position compared to a lot of couples their age. Her current life seemed beyond her wildest dreams all those months ago when she had been fired from Poundworld for timekeeping issues.

Checking her watch, it seemed like Josh had been gone for ages, especially in this foul weather. She got up again and pushed open the French doors to go out onto the balcony, craning to see if she could spot her two best boys walking back up the hill. It was cold, but at least the rain had stopped.

She rang Josh, and on hearing his phone ringing, realised he had left it in the kitchen. Pulling a jumper on over the T-shirt she was still wearing from the night before, she grabbed her trainers and put them on. She could do with the fresh air and was excited to see her husband after his week away. Sleeping through his homecoming wasn't exactly romantic, was it, and it wouldn't be fair for her to moan to him, when she couldn't even make the effort to stay awake for him after his long journey. She would surprise him, Rosa decided; they could have breakfast together on the front. Quickly, she cleaned her teeth and ran a comb through her hair.

Taking her waterproof coat off the rack and pulling on a hat, Rosa walked through the shop and headed down to the sea.

Greeting various shop-owners and locals as she marched

down the steep street, Rosa realised just how far she had come in the past twelve months. It was nice to have gained the respect of so many, but on the flipside, there was none of the anonymity she had enjoyed in London (Josh's nosy neighbour Ethel Beanacre aside). Now, if she was to so much as fart the wrong side of midnight, someone here would know about it and the word would spread.

Lucas's van was still in the Ship car park, and Rosa could make out the silhouette of Ritchie's mum Edie in the public bar, doing the weekend cleaning. She reached the beach and pulled her coat around her more tightly. There was a strong wind coming off the sea and even the gulls were quieter than usual as they soared around trying to fly against it.

The beach was peaceful, aside a young family screeching as they ran in and out of the bubbling edge of the surf in their wellies, and a lone blonde lady walking her Great Dane. Hmm, where *were* Josh and Hot? Rosa decided she wasn't going to hang around here to find out, as the only person she knew with a dog that huge was Joe Fox, editor of the *South Cliffs Gazette* and Rosa's former lover. It was strange to see his wife out on her own; on the rare occasions Rosa had seen her in the town, the woman had always had her new baby daughter with her.

'Rosa? Hi.' It was Alec Burton towering above her. 'Looking thoughtful again?' They both laughed as he continued, 'I have to say you do seem slightly more with it than the other day. How are you doing?'

'Just fine, thanks. I appear to have lost my husband and my dog though. Who by the way still has two perfectly intact front paws.'

'Oops, yes, sorry about that. With feet this big they should come with a government health warning, especially where small dogs are concerned.'

Rosa laughed. 'You settling in OK?' she asked.

'Kind of. Not all the locals are as friendly as you, sadly. It will get easier, I hope.'

'What is it that you do for a living?' Rosa dared to ask. 'Forgive me if you told me the other morning.'

'Nothing set up at the moment,' the big man said vaguely, then jerked a large thumb at the poster outside the pub. 'Fireworks tonight, I see.'

'Yes, and they are supposed to be good too. I think we are going to wander down.'

'OK, maybe I will venture out too.'

'Talking of my husband, you haven't happened to see a tall dark-haired guy wearing a green raincoat pulling along a disgruntled dachshund on your travels, have you?'

'Ah, that's your better half, is it? Yes, I have seen them. They're in the café where we met.'

'Hello, wifey.' Josh nearly knocked over his chair in his hurry to get up and greet Rosa. There was a blonde woman sitting opposite him. Hot, on noticing his mummy's arrival, also ran out from under the table and whined to be picked up.

Rosa glared at the pretty blonde – Sara, who ran the place. The last time Rosa had felt jealousy to this degree was when Josh had appeared in Cockleberry Bay with Juicy Lucy, his girlfriend before he and Rosa had got together officially.

'What are you doing?' Rosa tried to sound as normal as possible.

'Er, Sara and I were…'

'Hi there, Rosa.' Sara got up from her seat opposite Josh. 'We were just discussing what the "new look Ship",' she made inverted commas with her fingers, 'might be serving food-wise tonight.'

'Ah, right,' Rosa said – but why did she feel unconvinced?

Sara sauntered back to the counter as the café started to fill up with Saturday-morning customers.

'Sit down, gorgeous girl. Coffee? I've just ordered a bacon sandwich.'

'You have? OK.' Rosa sighed and began taking off her coat and hat.

'What's wrong?'

'I thought maybe we could have had breakfast together.'

'We can, now you're here. I was leaving you to lie in. Come on.' Josh put his fingers to either side of his mouth and stretched it into a smile. 'As you always say, "turn that frown upside down", my girl.'

Maybe she had imagined it, but Rosa felt that Josh had seemed startled and somewhat guilty when she walked in. She plonked herself down stroppily. 'Didn't know you were into cougars,' she muttered.

Josh laughed. 'What are you on about?'

'I mean she's pretty, but she's also pretty old.'

Sara Jenkins was very attractive for her age, and with a neat little figure and trendy blonde bob she could easily have passed for forty.

'Rosa, stop this. I was walking with Hot, it started to pour down, so we came in and had a coffee and Sara just joined me for a chat. Actually, what the hell am I explaining myself for?'

'Sorry.' Rosa's voice softened. 'I'm acting "crazy Rosa" again, aren't I?'

Josh nodded. 'Yes, you are.'

She tried to explain. 'It's just you were late, and I fell asleep… and, oh Josh, I miss you.'

'Bloody trains, it's making me think I might start driving again. At least if there is a traffic jam I can take a different route.

It was totally out of my control last night and you know that.'

Not daring to tell him the reason that she had been so tired was because she had been out the night before getting drunk and breaking promises, Rosa took one of Josh's hands across the table. 'I know. I just get excited to see you but was so knackered last night, I couldn't keep awake.'

'You were sleeping so soundly on the sofa and looked so sweet. I did try and wake you, but you were having none of it. I couldn't bear to sleep alone so I lifted you into the bed.' Josh lifted his wife's hand and kissed it. 'I love you, and only you, Rosa Smith. My precious wifey.'

A young waitress came over and took Rosa's order. Hot was now contentedly nuzzling a rubber kong with some hidden treats in it under the table. 'Sometimes I do wonder where my confident, bolshy girl has gone though,' Josh added, a little sadly.

'I'm always here, but maybe I just used to hide a little bit behind that bolshy, eh?'

'Never mind that. Just be yourself, Rosa. I married you, warts and all, as you did me.' He then beamed his sexy smile. 'Anyway, how nice is this? Breakfast overlooking a windswept beach, the Smith family all together again for two whole days.' Hot whimpered his approval from under the table.

'Yes, it's amazing.' Rosa smiled back. 'And Mary is covering the shop today, which is such a help too. I'm not sure how she'll get on selling the designer gear, but hey ho. She's not a believer in doggie coats. However, she does own a lead for Merlin Mad Cat, so go figure that.'

'My mother-in-law is a witch, there's no doubt about it.'

Rosa was open-mouthed. 'Josh! You can't say that.'

'I just did. I love her, she is wise beyond life itself, but also slightly weird, and you won't deny that either.'

'If we were to define both normal and weird, we could be

here all day and we are not all lucky enough to have been born with a silver spoon in our mouth, are we?' Oh no! Rosa knew she was carping again.

'Hardly. Granted, Mum and Dad have retired early, but they worked bloody hard to get there.'

Rosa rushed in: 'Anyway, I *love* the fact that Mary is so spiritual. She gave me a new crystal yesterday.'

'Yes, I saw it by the bed.'

The couple scoffed their bacon sandwiches with Josh sneaking titbits under the table to a happy Hot as they did so.

Sated with food, and feeling more settled, Rosa wiped her mouth with a napkin. 'So, shall we come down to the fireworks tonight then? I said to Alec that we might.'

'Alec?'

'Yes, I met him in here yesterday, he's new to the area.'

'Ah, did you now. Sit and have a coffee with him, did you?'

'Er. There were no other seats.'

'Ah, I see, one rule for one and all that…' And when Rosa stuck her tongue out at him, Josh said: 'Right, let's go.'

Before they'd even had a chance to scrape their chairs back and put their coats on, another couple were hovering over their seats. And in the kerfuffle of their cockapoo sniffing Hot and vice versa and the conversation that ensued, Rosa didn't notice the sneaky wink that Sara gave Josh as they made their way back out into the chilly November morning.

CHAPTER TWELVE

The rain had stopped, leaving a clear night sky, perfect for a firework display. Rosa made sure all the curtains were closed and that Hot was cosy with the radio on for company and distraction before they left him. She couldn't remember him reacting badly to fireworks in London, but she didn't want to take any chances.

'Aw, you are looking so cute.' Gazing down at his pretty wife, Josh kissed her nose. 'You had that hat on the day I met you, when you came round in answer to my ad in the local newsagents to rent out my spare bedroom.'

'And the rest is history,' Rosa said, pulling the blue bobble hat over her ears. 'Right – come on, let's go mingle with the natives.'

Sheila Hannafore was making the most of being back in Cockleberry Bay. She had rearranged the tables and benches on the front to create room for another live band, who were bashing out various favourite cover versions by the sound of it. She also had a BBQ set up which was already emitting amazing smells from home-made burgers and onions. Rosa cringed slightly as she could see Lucas prancing around with one of those great big white chef's hats on. At least he had a job to do so there was little chance they would bump into him.

Strings of coloured lights had been hung all along the beach wall and fairy lights that looked like rain hung down from the guttering.

'Anyone would think it was Christmas already,' Rosa said, blowing out a puff of steam into the freezing air.

'I forgot your hatred of everything Christmas,' Josh replied. 'But this year is going to be different. You're not on your own any more. In fact, we need to talk about what we are doing. Mum and Dad have obviously invited us if we want to go.'

'More planning, Josh, really?' Rosa didn't know why she couldn't stop bickering with Josh when their time together was so precious and so short.

The happy light in Josh's eyes went out. 'I hate to say it, Rosa, but that's what most families do,' he said coolly. 'And we have to be fair to Mum and Dad and give them some warning.'

Most families? Rosa thought back to Christmas at the different children's homes she had been placed in. They had been sad affairs on the whole. Yes, all the children had been given presents and a Christmas dinner, but Rosa could sense that half the staff didn't want to be there and she somehow knew that she was missing out on something more, something better – but didn't know quite what.

Last Christmas, she had been on her own at the shop and without her asking, Mary had plated up a dinner for her and brought it around. Although she had felt some sort of odd bond with Mary back then, she didn't have any inkling that the woman was her mother. Both Queenie and Mary had done their best to find her and do right by her when the time itself was right. So much had happened in such a short time. Was it any wonder she sometimes felt out of sorts?

Rosa took Josh's hand. 'Let's get a drink. Come on.'

'I'm not going anywhere near that pub, you know that. Not after the way that woman or her son treated you.'

'I know, I know. You keep saying!' Irked again, Rosa took his arm. 'Look, the Residents Association have got it all going on over there.' The big tent housed a very long table with a huge cauldron of hot punch on it and a barrel of real ale.

Making their way out to the beach with a pint of ale, a large glass of punch and a couple of big, tasty-looking pasties, the couple found a space on a bit of the beach wall and began munching and drinking.

'Blimey, this punch is knocking my socks off,' Rosa said happily. 'It's bloody lovely though.'

'Maybe just the one then, Rosa,' Josh cautioned. 'You know what happens when you get too drunk.'

'Oi, stop telling me what to do, Mr Smith. It's Saturday night and we are out to have some fun for once. Oh, my God, I so love this tune.'

The band must have been taking a break and Katy Perry's 'Firework' boomed out of the large speaker that had been put outside the pub.

'Uh oh – it's that real ale. It's gone straight through me. I really need a pee.' Josh was hopping from foot to foot.

'I think the café is open.'

'Yes, but look at the queue – bet that's for the loo too. I'll go in the back door of the pub.' Rosa nodded, drained her glass and went inside the tent to queue for more drinks.

Josh avoided eye contact with Lucas, who was now busily serving burger after burger, but on walking out, he heard his name being called.

''Ere, Smithy.' Lucas threw a slightly dented Halloween mask at him. 'Your missus must have dropped this here the other night.'

Josh replied with a curt nod and put the mask inside his jacket.

Noticing Rosa in the tent, Jacob and Raffaele waved wildly and walked towards her. 'Hey.' She kissed them both on the cheek. 'Sorry, I'd have got you both a drink. I thought you were going to text me.'

'It was all such a rush, darling, and the poor little Duchess hates the bangs, so my sister is keeping a close eye and we are literally going to run back up the hill as soon as it finishes. Ah, here's the big man.'

'Hey,' Josh greeted their friends and attempted a smile. Inside, his heart was far from happy. Feeling a rare anger rising within him, he was just about to pull Rosa aside and ask her what the hell was going on when with a sizzle, crackle and very loud bang the Cockleberry Bay Residents Association firework display began to fill the freezing night sky with light, colour and joyful explosions.

CHAPTER THIRTEEN

With her heart beginning to pound for all the wrong reasons, Rosa squealed and jumped back, causing one of her feet to go straight into the icy sea and soak her trainer. She could see Josh was shaking against the light of the big moon, which was beginning to re-emerge through the sulphur-filled air.

'You idiot,' she cried. 'Where did you find that?'

Taking a deep breath, Josh took off The Scream mask, screwed it up and put it in his pocket. He knew that shouting was not the answer where Rosa was concerned. That was all she had known growing up and there was never a good outcome.

'Oh, so you did lose it then?'

'I don't know what you're on about, Josh.'

'Rosa, don't bloody lie to me.' So much for him not shouting. 'Dear, darling Lucas said you left it here the other night.'

'I...oh...umm.'

'So you *were* here?'

'You don't own me, Josh.' Rosa started to walk away from him.

'I specifically said to keep away from him and his awful mother, Rosa. You promised.'

'It was Titch's idea,' she called back.

'Come back here!' Josh shouted. 'If she says jump, you don't have to say 'how high?'. I'm really disappointed in you, Rosa.'

The strong punch had begun to loosen Rosa's inhibitions. She put on a fake voice.

'"I'm really disappointed in you, Rosa"'. Then: 'Oh, fuck off then, Josh, and stop talking to me as if I am a child.'

Josh ran to her and swung her around. 'You are your own person – you can of course do what you want. But just one thing I ask of you, Rosa: don't lie to me.'

'I didn't lie to you. I just chose not to tell you. And maybe, just maybe, I was going to fill you in about it tonight.'

'Really?'

'Yes, really. Seeing as we never spend any bloody time together, *maybe* I was just waiting for the right time, because I knew this would be your reaction.'

With that she stormed through the crowd who were still getting food and refreshments and made her way up the hill.

Knowing there was no point in reasoning with her when she was like this, Josh walked down to the edge of the shore, bent down to pick a pebble up and skimmed it violently across the still, black sea.

Perhaps he should have listened to the sage advice of his mother. Lived together for a bit longer before tying the knot. Yes, love was a leveller and there was no doubt in his mind that he loved Rosa with all his heart. But if he was honest with himself, they were from completely different backgrounds. And even with his love and the security of the shop, his young wife had suffered a lot of anguish and neglect in her life – and there were a lot of broken cracks that still needed filling.

CHAPTER FOURTEEN

Josh looked back down towards the bay. The music had stopped, leaving just the low murmur of a jubilant crowd. Kids were laughing and running around with sparklers, and the smell of sulphur still hung in the clear air. It really was looking beautiful with all the twinkly lights and he couldn't deny that the refurbished Ship also looked smart. He trusted Rosa now that they were married, but his gut told him that her relationship with the wicked landlady's prodigal son had not been entirely platonic.

Just as he was about to make his ascent up the steep hill to home, a text came from Mary, who, despite Rosa's teachings was still not au fait with technology, in particular with predictive text. *Mary here.* This was how she started every message. *Rosa here, Joch. She's Drink! I talk to her.*

He was surprised and relieved that Rosa hadn't gone straight to the Lobster Pot and continued drinking. At least Mary would talk her down from her drunken high horse. And yes, his mother-in-law might not be 'normal' but, as Rosa said, what is 'normal' anyway? Mary too had had her share of heartache and loss. But she had overcome her alcoholism and was now doing as right by her daughter as she possibly could, with the life tools she had been given.

Josh acknowledged the light on in Seaspray Cottage and through the chink in the curtains could see two figures in the kitchen. Bless Mary, she was so thoughtful, leaving the curtains apart. He was sure they were normally shut tight to keep the heat in from the fire.

Pushing open the Lobster Pot door, he saw Jacob raise his hand over the busy throng of punters to mouth, 'Pint?' Josh nodded and went to the end of the bar so as not to upset any other locals who might be queuing. Jacob handed it to him.

'Hello, Josh, and sorry we didn't even say goodbye.' Josh got out his wallet, but Jacob waved it away. 'No, no, this one's on me. Where's madam anyway?'

Josh raised his eyes. 'Long story.'

'She's a little firecracker all on her own, that one.' Jacob flicked on the glass washer. 'But that's why we all love her so much. Right, better get on.' He went off to serve the queue.

'Seat?' A deep voice questioned Josh, its owner gesturing to a free place beside him.

'Brilliant, mate, thank you.'

'I must have been hiding it or people were too scared to acknowledge a stranger in their midst.'

Josh held out his hand. 'Josh Smith.'

'Alec, Alec Burton.'

'That rings a bell.' Josh turned his head to the side quizzically. 'Ah, yes! My wife, Rosa, mentioned that she'd met an Alec in the café.'

'Good lord, I'm that infamous already? I've only been down here a short while.'

Josh laughed. 'By now I should know your inside leg measurement and the colour of your bathroom suite.'

'Like that, is it?'

''Fraid so. I'm from Dorset originally, but for many years have enjoyed the anonymity that living in London brings.'

'Which has its plusses, I guess.'

'Yes and no. But a sense of community is also good. Anyway, cheers, nice to meet you.'

'Cheers.' They clinked glasses.

'So, what brings you down to Devon then?' Josh enquired.

'Your wife didn't tell you? That's a start; shows she's one who can be trusted.'

Josh coughed. 'Yes, she's a good 'un, my wife. There's far too much going on in that pretty little head of hers to bother with gossip – well, most of the time anyway.'

'Is she joining us?'

'Er, no. She wanted to pop into her mum's on the way back from the fireworks.' Josh had no wish to burden this fellow with a list of their disagreements.

'Were you down at the bay earlier?' he asked instead.

'I had every intention to go there, then got cosy in here with a drink and watched it all kicking off from the window.'

'Far more sensible.' Josh smiled, beginning to relax. He had taken to this newcomer.

'Seems like a good boozer.'

'Yes, we love it in here. Jacob and Raff are good friends of ours. They show all the live rugby games too, which is a bonus. It's England v. New Zealand tomorrow, if that's your thing?'

'Well, I'm a complete rugger bugger, so that's excellent news. Excuse me a minute.' Auburn Alec made his way to the toilet.

Jacob came over to the bar. 'Seems very nice, doesn't he? Not my type, duckie, but a looker in his own way.'

'Yes, he does seem nice. What's his story?'

'Divorced and looking to buy a place down here, apparently.'

'Ah, right. Has he got work down here too, then?'

75

'I didn't get that far, darling.' Jacob shimmied back to the other end of the bar to serve.

Josh was draining his glass as Auburn Alec returned to his seat. 'You off, mate?'

'Yes, good to meet you,' Josh said, shaking his hand.

'You too. Maybe I'll see you in here for the rugby tomorrow? I can fill you in on my sorry tale of departure from the shires.'

'Hopefully, but we'll see. I'm a bit of a part-time husband already.'

Auburn Alec smiled knowingly. 'Enjoy the rest of your evening.'

Chance would be a fine thing, Josh thought disconsolately to himself.

CHAPTER FIFTEEN

Titch waved at Rosa through the Corner Shop window, then pointed down the hill and held up both hands, mouthing that she'd be back in ten minutes.

Rosa started to do a stock-take. Last week had been amazing, sales-wise, and she now had to make sure the shelves were rammed tight for Christmas. She made a note to herself that she must find someone in the New Year to help with her website, as that seemed to bring the punters in. In the very beginning Jacob had helped her set it up, but now it was taking off, she felt she couldn't keep asking for his help. She would also have to see if she and Titch could manage packing the Christmas orders up. Rosa was proud of herself for all she had achieved in such a short time. What she wasn't proud of was the way she had handled herself with Josh at the weekend.

She usually hated Mondays but had to admit after the shaky weekend they had had, it was almost with a sense of relief that she had waved her husband off this morning. She had somehow managed to pacify him about her trip to the Ship, and to assuage her guilt, had even suggested he go and watch the rugby at the Lobster Pot with Alec Burton, whilst she took a much-needed siesta.

Josh need never know that she hadn't intended to tell him about it. For, as her mother had said last night, 'Before you say anything, Rosa, think: is it true, is it necessary, is it kind? And if it's not, then for goodness sake, *keep shtum*.'

Rosa went to the back kitchen and made herself a cup of coffee. Sitting on a stool by the cash register her relief turned to shame and sadness. If Josh had broken a promise to her, however small, she wouldn't have liked it one little bit. He always had her best interests at heart and she was a blinking nightmare when she was drunk. Knowing he was on the busy commuter train so he wouldn't hear her if she called, she texted him. *I feel sick with sorry. I love you Mr Smith (heart emoji) Counting the hours until you're home again.*

Ding! The shop bell released Rosa from her thoughts and woke Hot from his slumber. Both ran to help Titch who was struggling through the doors with Theo's pram.

'Here.' Titch handed Rosa a warm white paper bag. 'Your favourite, crispy bacon with a fried egg and ketchup in a white crusty roll.'

'Aw, thanks, mate.'

'Oi, Mr Sausage, that's not yours.' Titch bent down to stroke the hopeful dachshund. 'I know how much you hate Mondays, Rose, and I'm sorry I didn't even let you know about us not coming to the fireworks either.' She gently rocked the pram. 'The little man here was so tetchy, I thought it best to keep him in his own bed. Me and Mum just hunkered down with a take-out and watched crap Saturday-night TV.'

'I wish I had done that now.'

'Fireworks no good, then?' Titch walked through to the back kitchen to put the kettle on.

'I didn't even tell you this, but I saw bloody Lucas at the pub on Halloween. I must have dropped the mask or something.

Anyway, without going into all the boring details, I was busted for going down there.'

'Come on, Rose, you're a grown woman and should be able to go where you want.'

'I know, I know. But I didn't tell Josh and that's not funny when you make a promise to the person you love.'

'Do you still fancy Lucas, then? He obviously has the hots for you.'

'Oh, you know – bad boys make the heart beat faster and all that.'

'I hear you, but he's so not worth ruining what you have with Josh.'

'Titch – I know that. I can still look though, can't I?'

'Oh, come on, eat your roll before it gets cold and the masses start coming in.'

'It's Monday, so should be a quiet day. I've got to stock-take anyway, so I don't want it to be too busy.'

'I can help you for an hour, but then I must get back. I promised Mum I'd help her get on to the bus to Polhampton. It's easier for her now she has a motorised wheelchair.'

Rosa began to munch on her roll at the shop counter before suddenly exclaiming: 'I know what I meant to say! Mary is up for doing some readings for us – if you want one, that is?'

'Oh wow, yeah, of course I do. When can we see her?' Titch made a cooing sound to Theo as he began to stir.

'I think she's off today. The Co-op have messed her around with shifts because other staff are off sick. Should I call her?'

'Ooh, I love a bit of Tarot reading, I do.' Titch then stopped in her tracks. 'There's just the one thing though. I can't afford to pay her.'

'That's fine. You know she loves doing it anyway and she offered.'

Rosa put her thumb up as her mum answered the phone and they spoke. 'Wednesday at six?' She looked to Titch, who nodded excitely.

'That's a date then, girlfriend,' Rosa said, ending the call. 'I can come with you and mind Theo whilst you have your reading done, if you like.'

Feeling his phone vibrate, Josh put down his newspaper. The train was packed and silent aside from the obligatory station announcements. He could see texts from both Rosa and Sara. On reading both messages, he sighed and put his phone back in his pocket. He had been so certain of his intentions – until this weekend, that was.

CHAPTER SIXTEEN

As usual, Merlin shot out of the door when Mary answered it, nearly knocking both Rosa and Titch off their feet in his haste to get away from them.

'That cat is mad,' Rosa stated as she greeted her mother.

'"Misunderstood", I think he'd prefer,' Mary said, and they all laughed.

'How's your mum, dear?' Mary asked Titch as she put the kettle on and laid out three tea cups.

The girl yawned. 'She's really well, thanks. Zipping around in her new wheelchair as if she's competing for the Paralympics. She loves it.'

'That's good to hear.'

'Luckily, she's minding Theo for me for an hour, so we will get some peace.'

'I was quite happy to look after him,' Rosa added, yawning too until her eyes watered. It was catching.

Mary stifled her own yawn, chiding them, 'Look at the pair of you. Titch has got an excuse, but you need to wake up, daughter. Right, now let me sort these tea leaves.'

Titch raised her eyes to Rosa.

Getting the hint, Rosa asked: 'Can you do Tarot instead,

Mother?'

'No, just leaves today.' Mary's voice was sharp. *I'm in charge here,* it said.

Titch winked with understanding at her friend.

Mary Cobb sat down at the kitchen table, shut her eyes and began moving her hands over the tops of the now-full teacups.

'I read somewhere online that this is called something poncy, like Tasseography,' Titch piped up, only to be greeted with a hiss-like '*Shhhh*' from Mary.

'Sorry,' Titch murmured, echoing Rosa's thought that Mary was getting more and more like Queenie every day.

'Right, drink! But make sure to leave a dribble in the bottom.' Mary took a big puff on her inhaler, before adding a few seconds later, 'Put a log on the fire, Rosa duck. It's getting cold now.' Rosa did as she was told then took a seat in the front room, out of the way but in earshot of Mary's reading.

'Right, Patricia.' Mary strained Titch's cup with a saucer and began peering deep into the bottom of the cup.

'Nobody calls me Patricia.'

'Your dad used to though, didn't he?'

Titch took a deep breath. 'Yes, yes he did.' She thought back to that awful day when she learned that her father had taken his own life.

'Nothing to do with the leaves, this one. He came to me the other night. He wanted you to know it wasn't your fault. It really wasn't.'

Tears filled Titch's eyes. Her family tragedy had been extreme to say the least, with her brother, Ronnie, also dying as a youngster. Her mum always believed, along with the Coroner, that Ronnie had died in a motorcycle accident, but Titch knew different as she had found his suicide note and hidden it from her mother. She had, however, shown it to her dad, who was found the next day hanging in the garage.

'He says he loved you very much.'

'He left me and Mum.' Titch's voice wavered.

'I know, child, I know.' Mary reached over the kitchen table and put her hand on the young girl's shoulder. 'He was caught in a terrible moment. He just wanted the pain to stop. But it *wasn't* your fault. OK?' Titch nodded. Mary put the cup back down. 'Good. Now let's get on, shall we?'

Mary started making a funny guttural noise from her throat whilst moving her hands over the blue bone-china teacup. 'I see little Theo. He's a balanced Libra. That's nice.'

'Explain nice?'

'Well, one of his strengths will be diplomacy, duck.'

'So that must be from his father's side then,' Titch replied flippantly.

Mary chuckled, and hearing it, Rosa smiled in the front room.

'Mind you,' Mary went on, 'he can carry a grudge and sometimes be indecisive, but he will also be sociable and cooperative.'

'Aw.' Titch smiled. 'My dear little boy.'

'He also will like harmony and the outdoors, so Cockleberry will be perfect for him growing up.' She paused. 'Hmm...if you decide to stay here, that is.'

'Me? Leave here? No chance unless I win the Lottery.'

'Sssh, child. Now, you must keep an eye on your baby though, won't you?'

'Of course I will,' Titch said, slightly defiantly.

Mary put her hand to her stomach and screwed her face up in pain. 'I can see you at a hospital.'

Both Titch and Rosa, listening in the other room, were silent at this.

'I can also see you wrapping lots of gifts,' Mary went on.

Rosa, now sitting with her eyes closed, opened them wide. She hadn't yet told Titch of her plans to offer a gift-wrap service at the shop.

Mary's voice suddenly altered to a serious note again. 'I see a tall, dark-eyed man. A long train journey. BB, or maybe it's DD? I'm being told you must find him, find him soon.'

'How marvellous is that. Let's hope he's handsome too – and can't he find me instead, please? Trains make me feel a bit sick, if I don't face the right way, that is.' Titch put her hand through her cropped blonde mop. 'Anything else?' She wasn't a bit pleased with some of what she'd heard so far.

Mary's voice went childlike. 'It's hard without a daddy.'

'You don't have to tell me that, Mary.'

'For all of us…for all of us, Patricia.' Mary sniffed. 'That's enough now, enough! Find him, Titch. It's really important.'

Rosa had never really thought deeply about the fact that both she and Mary had been brought up without a father's influence. She coughed and stood up. She really didn't like it when, during a reading, her mum went a bit weird. Walking back into the kitchen, she said briskly, 'All done?'

'Yep. I'm to go and find a tall dark stranger on a train. Sounds very Miss Marple, I love it.' But Titch sounded uncertain.

Mary had quickly strained Rosa's leaves, but then she said unexpectedly, 'I'm tired, Rosa. I will do you another evening.'

'That's fine. I need to go and phone Josh anyway.'

'Yes, and I must get back home.' Titch picked up her bag. 'Theo will be screaming the place down. Thank you, Mary.'

Mary put her hand on her daughter's arm as she made to leave. 'Be careful, duck. I can smell burning.'

'What?'

'Just remember what I said. Goodnight, lovely ladies.' Mary opened the front door and Merlin shot back in, spitting in further discontent at his far too-busy household. 'I had best feed the Lord of the Manor. Off you go.' And with no further ado, she slammed the door shut on them.

Outside, Rosa looked at Titch, whose face said it all.

'Hmm. I know, mate,' Rosa nodded. 'Weird, eh. I hope it doesn't run in the family.' But then, remembering the burning smell, she bade Titch goodbye and raced back down to the Corner Shop to check that all was well.

CHAPTER SEVENTEEN

'Morning, morning, morning!' Jacob followed Ugly, Pongo and the Duchess into the Corner Shop, to both Rosa and Hot's delight. The pugs were looking smart in their fashionable coats, which were the same shade as their bulbous but enchanting brown eyes.

The three older dogs tore through to the shop kitchen and scrabbled at the door until Rosa opened it, allowing them to run around and play in the backyard.

Rosa picked up the Duchess and snuggled the adorable puppy into her chest, saying, 'Mmm, you smell so warm and clean.' The little dog, not enamoured by being half squeezed to death, started to wriggle furiously until Rosa was forced to put her gently back down to the floor.

'Not a lot of warm clean smells at ours, I'm afraid,' Jacob told her. 'More like pungent poops at the bottom of the stairs. Did Hot ever mess inside?'

'Oh yes,' Rosa nodded. 'These little beauties are renowned for it, evidently. He hasn't done it since I moved down here, as I'm with him most of the time, but when I left him in his crate when I worked in London, he quite often left me a little brown present – a protest poo as they're known – despite the dog-walker coming in at lunchtime and me walking him as soon as I got in.'

She advised, 'You've got to be fair but firm, leader of the pack Mr Jacob Sharp-Marino.'

'Message received. I'll pass it on to my co-leader of the pack, Signor Raffaele.' He held the Duchess's lead as the tiny creature danced around, her hindquarters waggling comically as she busily sniffed at the many fascinating smells in the shop.

'I'm not used to women at the best of times, as you know,' Jacob said, and they both laughed. 'By the way, I saw something in one of the Sunday paper supplements the other day describing the breed and thought I must tell you about it. The writer said that mini-dachshunds were "a fascinating blend of ferocity, entitlement and neediness", and that you should be ready to live with "a tiny clown".'

'That's probably how Josh would describe me now.' Rosa's voice was sad.

'Aw.' Jacob put a hand on her arm. 'When he came in to watch the rugby, he insinuated that you'd had a bit of a contretemps on Saturday night.'

'I wondered if he'd chat to you.'

'It wasn't for long as we were so busy serving. He was mainly chatting to Alec, the new guy in town. They even exchanged numbers. Well, fancy *that*...' He rolled his eyes and looked at her insinuatingly and Rosa burst out laughing.

'I'm happy to hear that. It will be nice for Josh to make more friends down here.'

'All OK now though? With you and Josh, I mean.'

'It's hard to tell on the end of a phone, but I think so. You know I'm a complete and utter nightmare when I'm drunk. And he did have a point about me not going in the Ship. It was all my fault, I expect.'

'Well, he didn't tell me that's what it was about, or I might have got stroppy with you too, girlfriend.'

'Ha bloody ha. My head is all over the place though, and I don't really know why. I never used to be this needy.'

'You never had this much to lose – not that you will, of course,' Jacob added quickly.

'You're right. I've gone from frightened little girl to having everything I ever dreamt of. That's why it's hard to work out why I'm still not completely happy.'

'Well, if you have a wobble you know where we are.' Ugly, Pongo and Hot were now all scratching at the back door waiting to be let back in. Jacob walked through to the kitchen. 'The next year will be over before you know it, and then you can both concentrate on whatever makes you happy, together.'

Ding! The shop bell rang.

'Hi there,' Rosa politely greeted the pretty blonde, almost falling over the counter as the four furry friends barged their way to the front door. 'I'll be right with you. Hot!' she raced out to stop him from getting out onto the street. 'You're staying with me.'

Shutting the door behind her, Rosa stood against it and smiled, until another *Ding!*

'The new coats!' Jacob popped his head back around the door. 'That's what I really came for.' He handed her two £50 notes, and hugged her before lifting the Duchess into her special carry bag and being pulled backwards out of the door by the two determined pugs, straining on their shared leash.

Becca Fox was one of those women who, despite having had four children, and one of them recently, still had the most perfect figure and skin. Her long blonde hair was mostly in a pony tail and her jeans always fitted her five-foot ten frame in all the right places. But despite her outward beauty, it still hadn't stopped her low-life husband from cheating on her with Rosa.

Rosa had always seen herself as very streetwise. But she'd never been in love before and this had removed her 'gut radar system'. Joe had played a good game, helping her set up the shop-opening event and then getting her on the radio to promote it. But underneath all his charm and helpfulness, he was not only having his wicked way with her but was also extracting as much information as he could about the hit-and-run incident. All for his personal gain as editor of the *South Cliffs Gazette*.

For all her past promiscuity, Rosa had retained a strong 'girl code'. She also had never forgotten a particular predatory male carer at one of the children's homes, whose greedy eyes for the teenage girls, including herself, had made her feel sick and scared. After breakfast every day he would tell them, 'Luke chapter six, verse thirty-one: *Do unto others as you'd have them do to you* – and never forget that now, will you?' Although the evil man was using the sacred words in completely the wrong context, the philosophy behind them had stayed with her.

She had only found out, just last year, that she was in the midst of a marital affair when Mary deliberately sent her to Joe Fox's address to collect a fictitious television. She was greeted by a heavily pregnant Becca, as well as their teenage son, the five-year-old twin boys and Suggs the Great Dane. She could have just outed Joe as a love cheat there and then, but instead she walked away. Why ruin five lives – seven including the unborn child and the dog. But she took comfort from the words of the great Bard himself, and subsequently Mary Cobb: 'The truth will out'. And she was sure that in Joe Fox's case it most certainly would, one of these fine days.

The truth had definitely been outed for her, as Mary and Queenie had 'seen' what was going on and thought the only way Rosa would face the truth was if she walked into it. She had been heartbroken afterwards. Joe was the first man for whom she had ever had true feelings – until Josh, that was. Who with his forthright and loving presence had transformed her life.

'Oh, you're working today, then?' Becca sounded surprised.

'Yes. Most days I'm keeping the pet population of Cockleberry and surrounding areas happy. I have cover when my husband's around, that's all. On your own today, I see.' Rosa said, and started tidying her counter.

'Er, yes – why?'

'It's just you either have your little one or Suggs with you, that's all.'

'Ah, Rosie's at nursery today.' Then softly, 'My husband has taken Suggs.'

Rosie? This was the first time Rosa had heard the baby's name. How weird was that? Joe had been seeing her when his wife was pregnant, and their baby's name was almost the same as her own! And he had taken Suggs where? Rosa wondered. That was how the aptly named, wily Joe Fox used to be able to spend so much time with her during their affair. Their meetings had consisted of a dog walk and a quick bunk-up – in the flat usually, with Joe blaming the pressures of work on never staying over. Once a cheater, always a cheater. He was probably on to his new temporary source of extra-marital sex already.

Thinking back on it, she couldn't believe that she hadn't suspected anything. How could she have been so stupid? But as Titch said to her after it had happened, 'Love is blind, deaf and dumb, Rosa, so just get over it.'

Close-up, Becca looked tired today. She hadn't even put any make-up on which was rare for her, Rosa thought.

'Sorry, but could I use your toilet, please?'

'Of course. It's just through the kitchen on the left.'

The woman was back within minutes. 'Too much coffee.' She

seemed slightly flustered. 'I didn't realise you had a back gate. Could I park in that space in future, maybe? It would be so much easier to leave Rosie and the dog in the car, out there. If that's OK, of course?'

'Yes, if it's free, no problem. Although a lot of my deliveries come in that way. You just need to ring the bell so we can come out and unlock the gate.' Hot, tired from his earlier playing, let out a little snore from his bed. 'So, what I can get you today? Food for Suggs?'

'Um. Actually, do you do coats for Great Danes?'

Rosa was slightly bemused as she had already told her on a previous visit that she didn't stock them but could order them in.

'Here, take this catalogue and let me know which one you want. It will take three to four days to get here though.'

'Perfect. Er, do you mind if I take your number so I can just call you rather than driving over from Polhampton again?'

'Of course.' Rosa gave her a flyer with her mobile on it. Inwardly cringing that this poor woman had no idea what had happened between her and her husband, she willed her to leave – and soon.

'Right, bye then.'

'Bye, Becca.'

Rosa's thoughts about how strangely Becca had been acting were instantly forgotten when her mobile started ringing.

'Rosalar!' Josh sang down the phone, causing Rosa to experience the old tingle she used to feel when she had first fallen in love with her gorgeous husband. 'You all right?'

'I am now. It's nice to get a call in the day from you.'

'It's just a quickie.'

'Ha! I wish.'

'Soon, soon. Yes or no, I need to ask if there is anything in the diary I don't know about happening this Thursday?'

'I don't think so, why?'

'No questions.'

'Ooh, what are you planning?'

'What part of no questions did you not understand?' Josh laughed.

'Is it exciting?'

'Rosa!'

'OK, OK. I'm forgiven then?'

'I've gotta go. Love you. Big kiss for Hot and I'll see you Thursday evening.'

Rosa did a little jig and scooped Hot up in her arms, wincing as his tongue slapped around her face. 'What's your daddy up to then, eh?'

CHAPTER EIGHTEEN

In true Josh style, Thursday's treat had been arranged with military precision. Titch had arrived at the shop with Theo and her overnight bag at midday.

'I can't talk to you, Rosa, 'cos you know how bad I am at keeping secrets, but you're to go upstairs and get yourself ready. Take my bag up with you, can you, please? I'm staying for a couple of nights with meladdo here, then your mum is coming in on Saturday, so we can both mind the shop and him.'

'Come on, Titch, tell me what's going on.'

Titch pulled an imaginary zip across her mouth, then got on with sweeping the shop floor, tidying up the stock and dusting the shelves. There was always plenty to do.

'Aw, you look amazing!' she exclaimed as Rosa clunked back downstairs later, carrying her own overnight case. 'I love that red jumper; it so suits you, and look at you with high-heeled boots for a change.'

'Do you know, whilst I was getting ready, I realised how few times I do get dressed up these days. I should do it more often or Josh *will* be running off with his secretary.'

'Shush, you. Right, Jacob's here.'

'Lady Smith.' Jacob put Rosa's case in the boot of his car and

93

held the front passenger door open for her. 'Go get Hot and his lead, darling, as he's coming too, for the ride, but then he's got a play date with the boys and the Duchess.'

'Dartmouth?'

'No.' Jacob turned left just as Rosa spotted the sign.

'Dittisham? Ooh, I've never been here before. What's it like?'

'Listen, you townie, it's pronounced "Ditsum".' Jacob said no more for fear of letting the secret out.

After a few minutes he told her, 'Right, this is us. I'm dropping you here, young lady. Your instructions are that you need to walk down the hill and ring the bell at the end of the jetty next to the Ferry Boat Inn.'

'Are you sure?' The road down to the quaint little village seemed endless to Rosa. Patience had never been her forte!

'Behave! Course I'm sure.'

As Rosa gave Hot a tickly kiss goodbye on his black whiskers, Jacob got her case out of the car. 'Toodle-pip, sweetie,' he said and gave her a big hug. 'Have an amazing time.'

Rosa pulled her coat tightly around her. It had been one of those lovely winter days, crisp but bright, and the sun beginning to set over the estuary in front of her made for a perfect vista. Empty boats clinked and creaked as they bobbed up and down close to the jetty that loomed in front of her. A man with a brown woolly hat and pipe acknowledged her as he came out of the pub. Sweet smoke now joined the laughter and loud voices that carried through the chilled gloaming.

'There it is,' Rosa said to herself, beginning to realise that there was so much more to Devon outside of Cockleberry Bay.

'Ring it, lass, it's fine. Then walk down to the end of the jetty. The boat will come.' The pipe man then wandered off to the left, across the wet seaweed-laden sand, and disappeared.

Rosa did as she was told, then jumped from foot to foot to keep herself warm. Within minutes she could see a boat approaching the wobbly wooden jetty.

'Surprise!' Josh appeared from behind the huge bouquet of old-fashioned red roses he was carrying. It was just him and the ferryman on board. Helping her onto the boat, he brushed her lips with his. 'About time we had a little honeymoon, don't you think, Mrs Smith?'

They sat down on the bench seat, watching the wide River Dart flow by in the afternoon sun.

'Here we are, mate. Greenway.' The boatman pulled up against the jetty. 'Watch out for the ghosts.'

'What?' Rosa held on to Josh tightly as he lifted her up on to terra firma.

'Yes, rumour has it that Agatha Christie roams the grounds by night, telling everyone whodunnits.' The boatman laughed heartily. 'You've got the key, haven't you?'

'Yep, all set. And here – thanks so much.' Josh handed the man a fiver tip.

'Oh my God, Josh, are we really staying in the Queen of Crime's house? That is amazing! I've heard people talk about it in the pub before, but I didn't realise it was here.'

'Well, not quite in the main house, but hopefully this will be to your satisfaction, madam.' Josh pointed to the Lodge House, a quaint little stone building set in the magnificent grounds of Greenway, Agatha Christie's home.

Rosa placed the roses gently in the sink then ran from room to room. 'Oh, I love it here!' she cried excitedly. Secretly, she was also relieved that her period was not due for another two weeks.

'It's basic, but it's what we need. I got the fire going.'

'So I can see. Oh, it's so cosy.'

'I sensed we could do with the lie-in, hence Jacob minding

the sausage too.'

'Aw, you thought of everything.'

'I sure did.' Josh went to the fridge and pulled out a bottle of champagne. 'Even got someone to fill the fridge for us so we don't have to move a step out of here the whole weekend if we don't want to.'

'You are amazing.'

'I try my best.' Josh put his arm around Rosa. 'We can have a really naughty Fifty Shades of Mr & Mrs Smith night.'

Rosa giggled as Josh lifted and carried her like a baby into the bedroom, telling him, 'Now hurry up, get naked and give me some red-hot loving, you big hot hunk of husband.'

A while later, they were sat up in bed munching pizza and drinking champagne. The silence and serenity of the place was bliss after the comings and goings and endless seagull chorus of Cockleberry Bay.

'I'm sorry it's been so hectic, Rosa. This little break was much overdue,' Josh said tenderly. 'And over Christmas, let's book a real honeymoon. I was thinking maybe Bali or the Maldives. You will just love it there, I know.'

Rosa took a slurp of champagne and put the crystal glass back down carefully on the bedside table. 'I still can't believe I've never been abroad.'

'No. But that's all going to change.' Josh stroked her cheek.

'Saying that, Cockleberry is just as gorgeous on a summer day, I'm sure.'

Josh smiled at his unworldly wife. 'When you see beaches elsewhere, you may change your mind.'

'Well, whatever I think, the Bay is still a wonderful place to be in, come rain or shine.' She paused. 'You're not getting bored of being down here already, are you? Please say you're not.'

'No. I love it down here too. But I do think we should keep the London house for when the kids get older. It would be good to open their horizons a bit.'

'Blimey, how many are we having?'

'Oh, hundreds.' Josh kissed her forehead.

'OK. In which case we will have to think of some pretty special names to go with Smith. Longer names like Elizabeth or Jennifer would work, I reckon.'

'Hmm. I want boys, a rugby team full. William and Jackson, I like.'

'How very public school.' Rosa put on a posh voice. 'They'd probably be shortened to Jack and Will though, but that's OK, I guess.'

'So, what are we waiting for?'

'There's so much to do with the shop still, and like I said before, seeing Titch with Theo – well, I don't think I'm ready to give up that sort of freedom yet. She says it's harder than any full-time job.' Rosa brushed crumbs off the bed. 'Talking of Titch, I hope she's getting on OK. I can't even call her to check.'

'She'll be fine. Your mum's going to work with her on Saturday too and we can call her when we go out tomorrow.'

Rosa leaned over, hugged Josh and sighed, 'This is so lovely. I want us to be just us for a little while anyway. We've only just got married and we couldn't be doing luxury holidays when little ones come along.'

'You do want kids though, don't you, Rosa?'

Rosa let out a faux scream. 'Josh, not again!' She then had a thought and grinned. 'I bet our boy is causing havoc at the pub.'

'He's such a character, isn't he?' Josh cuddled into her and let out a big loud sigh. 'Mmm, this bed is so comfortable.' He hadn't been sleeping at all well since last weekend, with its turmoil.

Wriggling herself free, Rosa cleared the empty plates and

glasses, went to the bathroom, got her make-up off and slipped on the silky lingerie she had worn on her wedding night.

'Ta dah!' Ever the insatiable, Rosa paraded into the bedroom to be met by the gentle snoring of her husband. She recognised just how handsome he was, with his muscly chest on show above the crisp white duvet. Not wanting to disturb him, and realising that she would have to wait until morning for another passion fix, she contentedly snuggled up against his broad back and drifted into a peaceful slumber.

CHAPTER NINETEEN

'Thank God.' Titch went straight to put her coat on. 'Sorry, Rosa, I'm going to have to get straight off. Theo has been a little angel up until lunchtime today and then he just wouldn't stop screaming. Bless your mum, she's taken him home to try and soothe him.'

'I'm so sorry, mate. I know we said we'd be back at four, but the traffic was awful. I did send you a text.'

'I haven't had a chance to check my phone, it's been manic today. I've cashed up Thursday and Friday and put everything in the safe.' She paused to ask, 'You did have fun, I take it?'

'It was just what the doctor ordered, thanks, now off you go and we'll catch up later. Thank you *so* much.'

Josh was busy chatting to someone outside. Rosa noticed the towering figure of Auburn Alec. 'I'm just going to go and get Hot from the pub, love,' Josh told her.

'And a pint of something to go with that, I expect?' Rosa smiled at the pair of them.

'Well, if you don't mind?'

'Course I don't. I'm going to finish up in the shop and then have a soak in the bath. Here, give me the bags. You OK, Alec?'

'Yes, great, thanks.'

'Aw, and this must be Brown. Hello, boy.' Rosa bent to stroke the placid brown Labrador. 'He's adorable. And what a good dog.'

'He's only quiet as he's an old boy and has just been acting like a teenager down on the beach.'

Josh ran upstairs to put the bags in the bedroom, then went off with Alec and Brown up the hill to the Lobster Pot.

A customer had just come in to browse through the dog-lead rack when Rosa heard the ringing of a mobile in the back kitchen. It was a different ring to either of their usual tones. Realising it was Josh's phone, she glanced to see who was trying to contact him. The words *1 missed call from Café Sara* stared back at her. Shaking, she picked up the phone to try and see if she could look at his call log or messages, but his password had also been changed. Sara had no reason to be ringing Josh, surely? And why a different ring-tone? They weren't even friends, just acquaintances. Remembering back to the café incident last weekend, Rosa was about to run up to the pub and ask what the hell was going on, when she was suddenly overcome by a vision of her great-grandmother, repeating her last words to her. 'Sometimes in life, if you don't know what to do, do nothing, say nothing and the answer will come to you.'

A tingly feeling went right through Rosa. Queenie was right. She was being ridiculous. She would wait until Josh was back home and she would ask him calmly, face to face.

It was late when Josh appeared in the lounge of their flat; he was slightly the worse for wear. Rosa had managed to calm herself by lying in a hot bubble bath and having a large glass of wine. He noticed his phone on the coffee table.

'Ah, there it is. Phew. I had visions of having to drive back to Agatha's place.'

Despite all efforts, Rosa felt her anger rising. She twirled her hair through her fingers. 'Why would Sara from the café be calling you? And more importantly, why does she have a special ringtone?'

'I…er…It's a new phone. I…'

'Don't lie to me, Josh. She's in your phone as *Café Sara*, so you obviously consciously put her number in there.'

'Oh, I remember now, sorry. I'm a bit drunk.' He grinned and pushed his hip into hers in a comedic fashion. 'It's coming back…that's right – she wanted me to send her the number of a good freelance marketeer I know. Yes, that's it. She asked me the other morning. Phew!'

'What is "phew" supposed to mean?'

'Phew, that the Rosa rage can now stop.'

'Well, maybe you should call her back right now and tell her?'

'Leave it, Rosa. I'll speak to her tomorrow. I forgot to get it for her, and frankly I can't be arsed. Now, come here, don't be silly.' He pulled his wife towards him. 'We haven't finished our weekend yet.'

Rosa pushed him away and headed to the kitchen. 'I need a drink.'

'You don't, but if you're going to be ridiculous…' Josh lay on the sofa and clicked the TV on. Within minutes he was lying on his back snoring like a wart hog.

Rosa left him there and after a couple of hours without being able to settle down, she slid out of bed, pulled on her dressing gown and tiptoed past a now sleeping Hot in his basket and her still snoring husband and went and sat out on the roof terrace. It was freezing but she didn't care. Soothed by the waves crashing on the shore in the bay down the hill she tipped her head back and took in a big breath of cold clear air. Why oh why, did this love business have to be so complicated? Why did it have to hurt so much? Josh had never given her any reason to feel like this before, but she was so scared of losing him that her mind was working overtime.

What if he was beginning to think that they had married too soon? That she wasn't enough for him? Sara was successful, about to retire, much more of a catch than her. But, on the other side, Josh had just treated her to the most amazing weekend away. Hang on – what if that was a cover, so that he could have his cake and eat it down here. But if that was what he wanted, having an affair in London would be a lot easier. She hadn't even thought of that before. Maybe he was doing that too! Rosa tried hard to rid herself of these irrational thoughts. But men were clever. Look at Joe Fox, for instance. He had hoodwinked her for months.

A wet tongue suddenly licked her ankle, causing her to nearly jump out of her skin. She hadn't shut the balcony door properly and her furry mate had come to see what she was up to.

'Hello, boy.' Thinking it was breakfast-time, the little sausage dog started to leap around excitedly and bark. 'No. Shush! It's late, darling.' She ushered him back into the lounge, locked the French windows behind her and was just about to go back to bed when she heard a loud knocking on the door. She checked her watch – it was gone midnight. Josh was still out for the count, so she grabbed a big torch and went downstairs.

Pulling the front door blind up, she was greeted by a frantic Titch, who was looking the colour of snow.

'Thank God!' she gabbled. 'Rose, you must come with me, please. It's Theo. He's really ill. Mum's staying at her sister's and I don't want to go to the hospital on my own.'

'Let me get the keys.' Rosa opened the door hurriedly. 'Oh, the poor little mite. What's wrong, do you think?'

'I don't know, he just won't stop screaming and he keeps

102

pulling his legs up in a funny way, and his nappy's been dry for ages so I know he's not peeing much and he's hot and . . .'

'OK, OK, calm down, sweetheart, where is he now?' Rosa suddenly heard the little one's pain-ridden cries.

'In the fish and chip van. Ritchie said he'd drive us.'

CHAPTER TWENTY

It was still dark when Josh was awoken by a face lick from a hungry dachshund.

'Hello, sausage.' Josh flailed out his hand to stroke the impatient hound. He shivered and groaned. His mouth dry from too much beer. 'Where's your mummy?'

Eyes still half-closed, he eased himself off the sofa and let Hot out on to the roof terrace to relieve himself; he then went to the bathroom to do the same thing.

'Rosa!' he shouted downstairs, thinking maybe she had got up and gone to do something in the shop.

Hot came scuttling in from the cold and went straight to his bowl. He'd done a poo outside, but Josh didn't notice. Instead, yawning hugely, he leant down and played with the little hound's ears, telling him, 'Come on, mate. You must be hungry. I'll get your breakfast ready and we'll go out in a bit, I promise.'

After pouring out some of the special dry food designed for small dogs, Josh picked his phone up from the coffee table. Rosa had worked herself into a dreadful state last night about Sara's call. But surely not enough of a state to leave the flat and go somewhere else for the night? Mind you, this was the first time he had ever woken up on the sofa. Whoever said marriage was easy was lying.

He was so glad he had managed to hold his drunk tongue and not tell the truth. Things weren't quite sorted yet and it was such a brilliant Christmas surprise for Rosa that he wanted everything to be perfect. He would have to tell Sara that it would be better if they avoided texts but met face to face next time. He could easily pop down to Coffee, Tea and Sea with Hot for a walk again and have a chat, plus they could email when he was back at work to make sure everything was finalised, and all systems go for the Friday in December when he finished before the festive break.

It was so sad that Rosa couldn't just trust him. She didn't realise how rare and beautiful a soul she was, albeit a troubled one. And sometimes also very trying. He would never hurt her. He loved her too much.

No message, that was strange. With a worried feeling in his stomach, Josh phoned his wife's number. She replied straight away with a whispered, 'Hang on, hang on, I need to go outside.'

'Rosalar? What's going on?'

'It's Theo, he's had to have an operation. He's still in surgery.'

'Oh, no. That's awful – the poor little chap. What's wrong with him?'

'Something to do with his digestive system. We'll get the full details when he comes out. Titch is in a right state.'

'Of course she is. You at Ulchester General?' Do you want me to come?'

Rosa's voice was raspy with tiredness. She'd obviously forgotten all about their row the night before, since this was far more serious. 'Oh yes – you drove down this weekend, didn't you. It would be great to see you, but please don't rush. Why don't you go back to bed for a bit? I'll call you when I need a lift.'

Josh made himself a cup of strong coffee, had a quick shower and got dressed. He took Hot out for a fifteen-minute walk to stretch his tiny legs, then put him upstairs with the radio on, closed the lounge door and set off for Ulchester.

It was the least he could do, to get over there and do anything he could to support his exhausted wife and friend in their hour of need.

CHAPTER TWENTY ONE

Ding! The Corner Shop bell announced the arrival of Mary.

'Morning, duck.'

'Morning, Mum.' Rosa was on her knees on the floor. 'Quick, put the blind down and turn the key, can you? I want to get all this Christmas stock out before opening.'

Hot started to run around in the packaging that Rosa was pulling off and throwing to one side on the floor. 'I'll get this lot recycled later,' she promised.

'All this plastic,' Mary tutted.

'I know, I know. Last night I watched a programme about what it's doing to the planet. I just hope the manufacturers were watching too and took heed.' Rosa opened a box and said, 'Look, I'm starting to do my bit for the cause.'

She handed her mum a brown paper carrier bag. It had a cute little dachshund on one side and *The Corner Shop, Cockleberry Bay* printed in blue on the other.

'They're really nice, love, and good on you. The angels can do only so much to make things right in this world, you know that.'

'I've just put the kettle on. Fancy a cuppa?'

'Yes, please. But I can't stop long, I'm afraid. I'm due at the Co-op nine till three today. I was just wondering how Titch's little lad was.'

'Well, I spoke to her last night. They are back home now.' Rosa knew that Titch was very shaken up, and she felt the same. What if it happened again?

'Remind me what it's called. I know you said it was something to do with the little lad's intestines.'

'Oh, I've forgotten – it sounds something like vulva.'

'Ah, I know, Volvulus. Kitty Trenon's girl had it, way back. It can be very serious, I believe.'

'Yes. Good on Titch having the sense to take him straight to hospital. Poor little mite. They had to put him on a drip and rehydrate him before the operation, that's why we were there so long.'

'And what happens now?'

'He was very lucky as the damage to his bowel was minimal. There is a slim chance it can happen again, so she's obviously got to keep a good eye on him now.' Rosa stirred sugar into her mum's tea. 'You saw it, didn't you?'

'The angels sent me something, yes. Tummy ache!'

'I think Titch will realise how important it is to find his father now.' Rosa carried on opening boxes. 'Theo has a Ro subtype of Rhesus blood, which is rare, evidently. Luckily the operation was straightforward, but they did explain that if he'd had to have a transfusion, supplies of the blood he would have required are not plentiful.'

'Yes, it's worth her finding out for sure, if she can.'

'It's not guaranteed he will be a match, but I think she has to try and locate him if she can.' Rosa yawned. 'The dark-eyed man that you mentioned – could that be him?'

'Maybe. I was told for Titch to find him soon.'

'Hmm, dark eyes and a long train journey and the letter B or D would even be difficult for a Scotland Yard expert, I should imagine.' Rosa stopped and then gasped, remembering the initials her mother had spoken of. 'Actually, yes – his name is Ben. Big Ben, that's right. That's our Mr BB.'

'Big Ben? What's that all about?'

Rosa reddened slightly. 'Oh, that doesn't matter, but how amazing that you were sent that message. I will talk to Titch.'

Mary shrugged. 'I'm not sure I run to nicknames, duck. But if I get anything else, I will tell you.' Taking a deep puff of her inhaler, she stayed silent and held her breath, then breathed out and made her way to the door. 'Right, have a good day, my Rosa. Where's that Peridot stone I gave you?'

'On my bedside table, why?'

'Keep it on your person, love.' Mary unlocked the door. 'Right – see you later.'

CHAPTER TWENTY TWO

The next few weeks passed in a flurry of Christmas preparations: ordering in stock, items flying off shelves, and time spent gift-wrapping customers' purchases. Titch turned out to be very good at that. Rosa was really enjoying her life as a shop-owner, and now that she'd got some help in the shop again, even Josh being away didn't seem quite so bad. She was so busy in the daytime that she would be tired in the evening and spent her nights happily chilling. She loved meeting all the pooches too, and made sure that the shop was always a completely dog-friendly environment, with a dish containing free bone-shaped dog treats on the counter and a big bowl of fresh water outside the door. Even Hot was behaving himself. A brisk early-morning walk meant he was happy to snooze until lunchtime, when Rosa closed the shop to have a snack and take him for another little trot, occasionally leaving him for a play-date with the pugs and the Duchess. With Titch concentrating on Theo's recovery Josh would also help her in the shop on Saturdays now it was so busy, and this arrangement was working out well.

Today, Rosa was just belting out the crescendo to the chorus of her favourite Christmas song, when the shop bell rang. Without looking down from the ladder she was standing on in order to dust the top shelving, she warbled, 'Won't be a second.'

'Mariah Carey has got nothing on you, girl. Best get yourself down to a decent pub and do some karaoke.'

Taking a deep breath, Rosa straightened her jumper with one hand and reversed down the ladder. Hot stirred momentarily, then recommenced gentle snoring in his basket in the corner.

Lucas Hannafore scanned Rosa's neat little figure before saying, 'Check *you* out. You really are the best thing that's ever happened in this dump.'

'Oh, it's you. And you are neatly filed away forever in my Wanker Bank.'

Lucas laughed out loud. 'I don't think you've got the concept quite right.'

'Oh yes, I have.' Rosa nodded her head vigorously as she said it. 'Anyway, when are you going back to London?'

'Worried you are going to miss me, are you?'

'Do you ever give it a rest?'

'No.' Lucas was highly amused. Rosa fought a smile and then struggled not to mention the fireworks. As usual, her mouth won. 'Thanks very much for getting me into trouble last month, by the way.'

'What do you mean?' Lucas said, pretending not to know. Then, 'Ah, you hadn't told lover boy you'd been drinking with the enemy – thought as much. Not as innocent as everyone thinks, are you, Mrs Smith, and don't I know that for a fact.' He picked up a studded dog lead. Whipping it gently against the counter, he murmured, 'I don't know why you play games with me, Rosa. I know you still want to.' He looked her right in the eyes, then placed the lead in her hand. 'I'll have this too…thank you very much.'

'Jesus, that was close. I nearly bumped into Lucas.' Titch was slightly breathless. 'I literally dived into the Co-op and hid behind a magazine rack.'

'He was just in here, flirting outrageously. Despite everything, and I wish I didn't, I still find him so bloody attractive.'

'I hear you.' Titch raised her eyebrows, as Rosa immediately changed the subject, saying, 'How is our boy Theo?' And on hearing that he was doing OK, she went on, 'You know what, Titch? You will eventually have to stop this hiding away as Sheila will soon find out that Lucas is not the father of Theo – and Cockleberry Bay is too small a place for you to be able to avoid her forever.'

'I told you at the fireworks, she's not going to bother making a fuss. They know already, I reckon,' Titch said gloomily. 'Ritchie's mum, who cleans the pub, is the biggest bloody gossip. She will be delighted to tell everyone. Make herself feel important.'

'Yes, they'll all be shocked that you didn't go for the usual inbreeding and dared to mate with anyone from outside of the Bay.'

'I don't care. As I said, old Ma Hannafore won't want the trouble. Three grand is nothing to her and she's probably over the moon that Lucas is in the clear, as I'm sure he will be too.' Titch ran a hand through her blonde crop so it stuck up in spikes.

'I still can't believe she paid you off to get a termination. Actually, I still can't believe you had the gall to hoodwink her and get the money in the first place!'

'Well, I didn't know who the father was, did I? Anyway, Rosa, I don't give a toss about any of that. My only concern is Theo's health and finding his real father.'

'I'm glad you are addressing that, Titch. I didn't want to push it when Theo was so ill, but it does make sense to try and find him.'

'Oh Rosa, I don't know what to do. It's opening such a big can of worms. But after the night at the hospital, just imagine if more blood had been needed. I have to do right by my son.'

'Yes, you do.'

'But what if I go to all the trouble of finding him and one, he doesn't want to know and two, he isn't the same ruddy blood-type?'

'It's a chance you've got to take. He can only say no, but I think it would take a man with a heart of stone to do that, especially when he meets the little fella.'

'I guess so.'

'You can put it to him that you don't want anything from him, just his blood.' Then realising what she had just said, Rosa started to laugh. 'Maybe don't actually say it quite that way.'

Titch laughed too. She put on a dramatic voice, like a gangster in a film. 'We are after your blood, man. Say nothing, do nothing and nobody gets hurt.'

'You're crazy.' Rosa touched her friend's arm. 'We need to think how we do this. If it's any help, Mary spoke about a long train journey.'

'I've already scanned every social media medium I can think of for a Ben or Benjamin in Wales, and nobody is springing out at me, which is hardly surprising. I don't remember him having an accent, but the groom definitely had a strong Welsh one, as I remember being cheeky with him about it. My lad's name was definitely Ben though. BB – Big Ben.'

'Yes, a needle in haystack is what we are looking for here without having a last name.' Rosa bit her lip. 'Are you sure you can't remember it?'

'Rosa, mate, the state I was in, I doubt if I even asked him for it. They were a random group anyway, supposed to be doing a pub crawl in the area, so there wouldn't have been any written booking made that we could have somehow followed up.'

'Is there CCTV in the pub?' Rosa asked suddenly.

'Yes! Genius. At least, I know there used to be a camera on the front door.'

'So, not quite a genius, as how are we going to get at the footage? I mean, it was a year ago. It could have been wiped. The pub's been totally refurbed since then too, so it might not even be the same camera.'

'I know exactly how.' Titch moved her full lips about in comical fashion. 'You say that Lucas still fancies you . . .'

'No way, Titch.'

'You don't have to do anything, silly. Just a bit of a flirt and fact-finding mission, that's all. And it is for the baby.'

Rosa let out a big sigh. 'If it's for Theo and you, OK, but Josh must never find out.'

'This is different. And if Lucas does drop you in the shit again, then I step in and tell Josh that I really needed the information and it was all my fault. Lucas is going back home after the New Year anyway, isn't he?'

'I dunno – is he?'

'Yes, Ritchie's mum was on about it in the chippie the other day.'

Ding! The shop door opened.

'Oh hi, Mrs Rogers,' Rosa said pleasantly.

'Talk of the devil,' Titch whispered under her breath.

'Where's that little one of yours today, then?' the older woman asked nosily.

Titch winked at Rosa. 'With his granny. I'm just zooming back home to feed him. Bye now.' And the young mum hotfooted it out of the door.

'Not often we see you out and about of a lunchtime, Mrs Rogers,' Rosa said.

'Good, innit?' The woman grinned. 'Freedom. I don't smell of cooking fat today either. Been to the fish-market in Brixham and then realised I'm totally out of food for our own fishes.' She coughed. 'Now, I know this is a bit random, but I just wondered if you stocked Koi Carp pellets?'

'You're very lucky there as I do have a customer in Polhampton who asks me to order them in, so I have one spare pot.'

'Brilliant.' Edie Rogers reached for her purse. 'I do wish she'd sort herself out, that one.' She nodded her head towards the door. 'My Ritchie adores her, always has, but a bastard kid and one that's…well, not from round here, makes all the difference, doesn't it?' She pursed her lips in disapproval.

Rosa was just about to spill her indignation at this implied bigotry, when Hot decided to wake up.

Rosa bent down to stroke the sleepy hound and to hide her angry face. 'Have a good afternoon, Mrs Rogers.'

'Thank you, dear.'

When the door closed, Rosa scooped Hot up in her arms. Breathing in his warm doggy smell, she confided to him, 'She's brave, saying that in front of me, I'll give her that, Mr Sausage. But if she dares to ever say it again…'

CHAPTER TWENTY THREE

Rosa gave a sigh of ecstasy as she fell back into the steamy hot bubbles and laid her head against the edge of the bath. It had been a busy day, as the private school kids had broken up already for the Christmas break and the holiday homes in the Bay and surrounding areas had started to fill up. She had made the shop window look particularly festive and appealing, causing people to stop and take note that she sold little gifts and trinkets, as well as pet products. She could feel rather proud of herself, Rosa thought, for being able to manage a shop on her own and without any formal training. Mind you, she had so much to thank Jacob and Josh for, since they had put her on the right track from the start.

Christmas this year didn't seem so foreboding either. It had been all set that they would close the shop on Christmas Eve at 4 pm, then drive to Josh's parents for a couple of days. Audrey Smith's roast dinners were legendary, so Rosa was more than happy about that. Her mother-in-law had also kindly extended the invitation to Mary. And despite Rosa's pleading with Mary to come, as it would be their first proper Christmas together, Mary was quite happy to stay at home with Merlin and spend Christmas at Seaspray Cottage. 'It's just a day, duck, and we can catch up anytime. It's not like we don't see each other now, is it?' she had said, both secretly knowing full well her social skills would not extend to a house full of posh strangers.

'Damn,' Rosa said aloud and tutted. She'd forgotten to order some more of the crackers with doggie treats inside. With one more weekend of selling before the break, she must do that tonight, as the items had already proved a bestseller.

Hot made a little creaking noise of pleasure as he made his customary flop down onto the bathmat. Rosa put a wet hand out and stroked his head fondly, saying, 'Hello, Mr Sausage.' He then shook his head violently to get rid of the damp bubbles on his coat.

Josh had his works Christmas party in London tonight. Couples weren't invited, which had aggrieved Rosa slightly. She had even put the Peridot crystal next to the bath to try and keep her jealousy at bay. Despite her husband's outpourings of love and continual reassurance of her beauty, the little – or in her case – big green-eyed monster was always lurking. Josh had sat down with her and had a serious chat about her suspicions re Sara and assured her that there was nothing going on and never would be – not in a million years.

Tonight, his company were hiring a nightclub in London somewhere, with burlesque acts, magicians, et cetera and then a live band. She pushed to the back of her mind the thought of him getting drunk and chatting to female co-workers who were dolled-up to the nines for the party. Lying back in the hot bubbles, she tried to think of other things.

She had to work out when she could corner Lucas and what on earth she was going to say to him with regards to finding out about the CCTV camera. Sudden inspiration dawned and she sat up immediately, creating a tsunami of warm bubbles.

'Yes! Yes, that's it – I've got it!'

117

Hot started barking.

'Sorry, my little wiener,' Rosa apologised, but she looked jubilant. 'Mummy's had a brilliant idea and it's all thanks to you.'

Singing to herself, Rosa pulled on her cosy velour dressing gown and filled the kettle. She fired up her laptop and cranked up the radio, and with a steaming hot chocolate by her side, she reached for her supplier catalogues. The laptop hadn't shut down properly and she was just going to reboot it, when she opened her eyes and mouth wide in shock.

For right in front of her eyes, Josh's email was open for all to see – and there, right at the top of his inbox, was an email from Sara from the café with a linked reply. Knowing that what she was doing was wrong on many levels, Rosa's heart began to race as she clicked to open it. She knew she was being ridiculous, since it had to be Josh just sending the marketing contact he had mentioned. Hmm, but why would it be at the top of his inbox, when that was ages ago?

With the email link now open, Rosa stared at the screen, then looked away, in the hope that if she looked back again, what she had just read would have disappeared. No – it was still there. Jealousy reared up inside of her and she began to shake.

Dear Sara

You cannot ring me or text me at the weekend again. Honestly, it was so close that Rosa could easily have found out what we were up to.

I will of course mail you from London in the week. We need to work out how we are going to tell her.

I literally can't wait until next Friday!

See you then.

J :)

Rosa poured herself a glass of wine and drank it down in one, then began to pace around the flat. Not knowing what to do with herself, she paced and paced until she was dizzy, sure she could feel a burning pain in her heart.

Clawing her hand through her wild brown curls she began to make little whimpering noises. Not her Josh. No. He wouldn't do this to her. Or would he? Her inner voice had told her something was going on. Why hadn't she just listened to it earlier?

She refilled her glass and reached for her phone.

Josh answered immediately. 'Rosalar!' Loud music and voices boomed in the background. Then someone was saying knowingly, 'Oi, oi, it's Josh's missus checking up on him.' Followed by girls laughing. Rosa's hand was shaking so badly she could hardly keep hold of the phone. 'Josh, you must tell me what is going on between you and Sara right now or so help me I will kill you.'

'Rosa?…Rosa? I can't hear you, sorry. We're in a basement. Just sitting down for the meal. Promise to call you after. I love you.'

It sounded as if he was surrounded by women there too! Rosa drained her glass then slumped down on the sofa, her head in her hands. The alcohol was beginning to take effect. Why oh why, did Josh have to be so far away? If something was going on, she had to hear it from the horse's mouth. And she certainly wouldn't want to give Sara the satisfaction of knowing how hurt she was by their duplicitous actions. I mean, the woman was more than twenty years older than her. Sensing her distress, Hot scrambled up the dog steps they had bought him so he could climb up and down from the sofa, and rested his snout on her lap, rubbing his long jaw up and down her dressing-gown to comfort her. 'Oh Hot, what am I going to do?' she sobbed.

Memories of the pain she had experienced when she found out Joe was married came flooding back to her. She had vowed then that she would never let a man hurt her again. How could she have read someone so wrong?

Hot was now fidgeting and had a look on his face that she recognised. 'OK, OK, I know you need to go out. Hang on.'

She lurched to the bedroom and without even bothering with underwear or a coat, pulled on joggers and a sweatshirt and grabbed her keys.

Rosa's breath plumed like an angry dragon against the freezing-cold night air. She had to clear her head, to try and make sense of what she had just read. Hot moved as fast as his little legs would carry him as his mistress tore down towards the beach. With tears streaming down her face, she made her way to the sea's edge. Somehow being so close to nature made her feel better.

Letting Hot off the lead, she pulled her bobble hat down over her ears to protect herself from the wind that was now rushing towards her. Even the waves crashing at her feet had trouble masking her cries, which came from a place deep within her. Hot, not used to being off the lead in the dark, kept running around in circles, as if he knew that their world was about to be split apart. She tried to call Josh again, but there was no reply. How long did it take to eat bloody dinner?

Shivering with cold and with Hot now yapping at her heels, she made her way back to the beach wall. Just as she was clipping on Hot's lead, her phone rang. In the haste to get it out of her pocket, it flew through the air, catching on a jagged rock as it did so and smashed into pieces. She scrabbled about on the wet sand trying to find all the missing bits. '*Nooo!*' With her knees now cold and sodden, she let out a massive sob.

'Here. Let me help you.'

With bubbles of snot coming from her nose, Rosa looked up.

'Blimey, Rosa, what's wrong? I came out to have a fag; I didn't realise it was you out here freezing your tits off and bawling like a baby.'

'As if you care,' she said bitterly.

Lucas took her hand and helped her up onto unsteady feet. He caught the whiff of alcohol on her breath. 'Maybe that's where you've got me wrong then.'

Rosa found a used tissue in her pocket and blew her nose. 'My phone,' she snuffled and started crying again.

'Bloody hell, girl, it ain't Oscar season for a while.' Lucas turned the torch from his phone towards the sand and picked up as many broken pieces as he could see. 'Here's the sim card, that's what matters.' He took off his jacket and put it over her shoulders, telling her, 'Wait here a sec.'

'This is posh.' Rosa lifted Hot into her arms.

'Shush.' Lucas put his finger to his lips and struggled to open the big red front door of the mansion on the sea-front. An assortment of bottles and cans rattled in the bag he was carrying. A grand holly wreath with little sparkly lights nearly flew off as he managed to open the door. 'Quick, come on in.' The handsome plumber ran to tap in the alarm number that he had written on his arm, before shutting the door.

'Take your shoes off,' he whispered.

Lucas then led her in darkness to the conservatory at the back of the house. He pulled down the blinds and put on the twinkly lights of the massive tree in the corner so they could see what they were doing.

'Take your joggers off.'

'No way! What are you playing at, Luke? That's it, I'm going.' Rosa tried to push past him and get to the door. She was shaking and half-delirious with cold and alcohol. Hot, too, was wet and shivering non-stop. He looked scared stiff.

Lucas took Rosa by the arm. 'You're soaking wet, girl! Sit on the bloody floor then. Here.' He got a can of Pina Colada out of his bag and handed it to her. 'This and a few lagers were all I could find in the back fridge at the pub.'

Rosa started to sing and jiggle around. 'If you like Pina Coladas and getting caught in the rain, at a bar called the Ship Inn, we can plan our escape.' She then giggled. 'You could have got a towel for me to sit on too.'

'What is that song?'

'Queenie – that's my great-grandmother – she used to sing it sometimes.' Rosa laughed again. 'But Lukey boy, I'm not escaping with you. And it didn't say the Ship Inn really.'

'Rosa, you're drunk and not making sense. You need to calm down a bit, darlin'.' Weirdly, she found that his familiar London accent soothed her slightly.

Rosa hiccuped, opened the can and took a slurp. 'You,' she pointed a wobbly finger at him, 'have kidnapped me.'

Hot, totally bemused at the whole affair, started to run around barking.

'Put a sock in it, Mr Sausage.' Lucas opened the bag and brought out a packet of crisps. 'Here, wrap your laughing gear round these,' he said kindly and took a couple for the little dog to eat. He told Rosa, 'Look, no more messing around: you both need to get dry.' He left the conservatory and knowing his way around from working in the house, came back with two big warm towels. He made a note to himself that he must remember to put them back in the airing cupboard. He then opened a beer for himself, grumbling, 'The trouble you cause me, girl. From the very first time we met. I dunno.'

Hot ran to Rosa and jumped up at her legs. She plonked

herself on one of the towels on top of the slate tiles and patted her lap for Hot to jump up. He immediately calmed down as she dried him and snuggled up in the cosy warm towel; she then used the end of it to dry her face and hair. When she'd finished, she tipped her now spinning head back and exhaled.

'What are we doing here?' she asked. 'Whose house is this anyway?'

'It's somebody my old woman knows; it's their holiday home. They wanted their boiler serviced before they came down for Christmas. Don't worry – I'll come back and clear up like a good boy.' Lucas drank from his bottle, then plonked himself next to Rosa on the floor. 'Now, pretty thing, tell me what's wrong. Don't tell me you've had a row with lover boy?'

Remembering the email, Rosa began to cry.

'Oh, Jesus. Not again. I can't deal with drunk women at the best of times, but when they get emotional… Oh Rosa, please don't cry. Look, you're upsetting both me and Mr Sausage, here. Just tell me what the matter is.'

'I can't tell you.' Rosa continued to sob.

'All right, don't tell me then.'

Rosa sniffed, blubbered, then took another gulp from her can. 'Do you think Josh would have an affair?' she eventually asked in a small voice.

Lucas's ears pricked up. 'Quite frankly he would be mad to.' He loosely put his arm around her. 'With someone down here, you mean?'

'Sara,' Rosa announced.

'From the café? Sara without an H Sara, you mean?' This was Lucas's chance. 'Do you want me to be honest?'

'I know that will be a first for you, but if you've heard anything, Luke, you have to tell me.' Rosa's words slurred and her head rolled into his shoulder.

'I've seen them together a couple of times chatting in the café and once walking with Hot on the beach, yes.'

'Really?'

'But that doesn't count for an affair, Rosa. As much as I don't want to say this, he loves you, I can tell.'

'It does count with what I've just discovered.' Rosa started to ramble. 'I don't know what to do. And my phone is smashed, and he was supposed to call and…he didn't tell me about a walk on the beach. And I'm so drunk, Luke. 'S not good.'

Rosa turned to Lucas and looked directly inside his soulful hazel eyes. He placed his finger on the little lightning-shaped scar on her left cheek, and his voice was husky when he said, 'The minute I saw you, you took my breath away.' He bit his bottom lip. 'You still do, Rosa.'

'Ha!' Rosa tilted her head then patted Lucas's nose with her index finger. 'Now don't you be getting soft on me, Luke Hannafore. I know what you're after.'

'Me, soft around you? Never, missus.'

'Oi. You are so damned rude.'

'You love it.' Lucas smirked.

Rosa stared right at him again and with a head full of pina colada and a mind full of revenge, she whispered, 'Kiss me.'

CHAPTER TWENTY FOUR

BANG! BANG! BANG! Rosa sat up in bed with a start. Sluggish from her heavy, drunken slumber, she couldn't fathom where the noise was coming from. Her mouth was tinder dry, and she appeared to be wearing nothing but her sweatshirt.

'Rosa, will you come and open this door this minute!' The angry Devonian twang of Mary Cobb's voice could be heard coming from the French doors of the roof terrace.

Rosa pulled on her dressing gown and sloped over to let her mother in, mumbling resentfully, 'You have a key.'

'Not to these doors I don't, and you've bolted the shop one.'

Rosa turned her back on Mary and shambled back to the bedroom, her head banging.

'Where have you been, Rosa? Why is your phone turned off? What's going on?' Mary's hips wobbled as she pursued her daughter.

Rosa's mind started to wake in her still-sleeping body. 'Fuck.'

'Josh is at his wit's end. He said he's been trying to call you all night. I even came up here at one in the morning and knocked as loudly as I could. What the hell are you up to, my girl? I was worried. And stop that foul mouth of yours.'

'I'm a grown adult and twenty-six years old – and Josh doesn't

125

give a shit, so stick that in your pipe and smoke it.'

'You may be that age, young lady, but you're acting far worse than any teenager.'

'And how would you know what a teenager is like then, Mother? You wouldn't because you were probably still drinking yourself stupid whilst I rotted in another bloody children's home.' Rosa fell into bed and covered herself with the duvet.

Her voice cracking, Mary used all of her life experience and compassion to deflect the blow.

'We all make mistakes, Rosa,' she said quietly. 'I am doing what I can, with all I have now.'

'Yes, we all make mistakes.' Rosa looked to the ceiling and her eyes filled with tears. Frantically trying to remember the sequence of events after kissing Luke, she delved deep but that was all she could remember. A lovely soft kiss. 'Fuck!' she said again.

'Rosa!' Mary sighed. 'What on earth's the matter, duck? Granted I haven't known you long, but it's been long enough that I know when something is really wrong.'

'I don't know if I can tell you,' Rosa wailed.

'Of course you can, I'm your mother. And I am here for you now until the day I die. I can promise you that.'

'Woah.' Rosa struggled up from under the duvet. 'I can't take this right now. I don't want to be horrible, but please go home. I will see you later. I need to clear my head.'

'Oh Rosa.'

'It's fine, it's all fine.' But the young woman's voice held panic.

Mary put her hand on her daughter's arm. 'Do you want me to take Hot out for a walk?'

Rosa's face suddenly whitened.

Mary's voice was now stern. 'Rosa, where is he?'

With no care that she might flash her bits to all and sundry,

Rosa leapt out of bed, checked her best friend's three different dog beds and then charged down the stairs, nearly fainting with relief when she heard the little mutt's scratching paws and yaps of anguish at the back-kitchen door. He flew in, almost knocking her over.

Mary came down to the shop, grabbed his lead and a tin of dog food and put the freezing cold pet under her arm inside her coat.

'You should be ashamed of yourself,' she managed as she unbolted the front door to the shop and let herself out.

'Morning,' Titch said breezily as she arrived for her Saturday-morning shift and crossed a seething Mary at the shop entrance. A ravenous Hot barked as if saying hello, whilst Mary carried on without acknowledgement back up the hill to Seaspray Cottage.

'Oh, OK – and a very good morning to you too, Mary Cobb.' Titch locked the door behind her, checked the Closed sign was down and made her way up to the flat.

'Shit.' Titch had to take a step back to get a proper look at her friend. 'You look dog rough.'

'That really doesn't help me. Pass me some knickers, will you.'

Titch threw over a pair of pink pants from the dressing-table drawer. 'What's happened? I texted you this morning twice.'

Rosa wiggled into her knickers under the covers, then pointed to the phone pieces on the bedside table. She had no recollection how they had got back here either. However, her voice when she spoke was now calm and matter of fact. 'My phone is broken, and I think I may have slept with Lucas.'

Titch's eyes widened. 'How? Why? Rosa! I mean, I said flirt with the guy to get the CCTV footage, but not . . .'

'I know, I know, I know.' Rosa put her hand to her head, jumped out of bed and started pacing. 'But worse than that, I'm ninety-nine per cent sure that Josh is having an affair.'

'Have I just walked into some sort of soap opera here? I just don't get it.' Titch shook her head. 'Put some bottoms on and I will make us some tea.'

'I don't want tea, I need lemonade. There's a bottle in the fridge.'

The girls sat in the lounge with Rosa gulping back the sweet cold liquid; the flashing lights of the Christmas tree doing nothing to lighten their spirits.

'There has to be an explanation.' Titch reread Josh's email to Sara. 'I don't buy this at all. He loves the bones of you, that man. He truly does. Why on earth would he play away?'

Rosa sighed. 'I don't even know what time he's going to be home. It's so annoying, not having a phone.'

'There's a mobile phone shop in Ulchester. You could put the SIM in mine, but I think it needs unlocking or something.'

Rosa ran her hands through her unwashed hair. 'I can't even think about practicalities at this moment, Titch. Oh shit, what if I did shag Lucas, though? He will not think twice about telling Josh.'

'I know this is gross, Rosa, but did you notice anything this morning, as in – well, you know…like wet between your legs?'

'I did check, yes. Oh God, this is like my worst nightmare times ten.'

'I should be saying that I can't believe you allowed yourself to get in such a state. But look what I did with Big Ben from the valleys, or wherever he comes from.'

Rosa made a laugh-type noise that turned into a sob. 'I remember kissing him.' She groaned. 'I kissed him! I was so angry with Josh.'

'We can deal with a kiss, it's fine. Josh need never know. In fact, he need never know about any of it.'

'I just don't remember what happened next. How I got home,

how I got into bed, how my knickers came off…maybe I didn't wear any knickers. Yes, I sort of remember that, just pulling on my joggers and stomping down to the beach without a coat on.'

'Then what happened?' Titch took a slurp of tea and stuck her hand in the biscuit tin for the third time.

At that moment Josh came running up the stairs and into the lounge.

'Yes, then what happened, eh Rosa?'

Titch jumped up and gulped. 'Look at the time. I must get down those stairs and open up. Hi, Josh.' And she fled, leaving them to it.

Rosa opened the French doors and walked out to face the sea. She needed a second to plan her attack.

Josh went on, his teeth gritted, 'So, I've driven all the way from London, when I could be having breakfast in the Wolseley with the rest of the gang, and here you are, bold as brass, completely fine. Your mum tells me now that you dropped your phone and broke it. You could have told her that, so she could have just messaged me.'

Rosa turned around with fire in her eyes. Her words came out in slow motion. 'Message you? Is that what you said? Message *you.*'

'Rosa, what is it? You're being weird now.'

'Why the fuck should I message you when you've having a fucking *affair*!' Rosa screamed the word 'affair' at the top of her voice.

'Rosa, what are you on about? And will you stop swearing please.' Josh placed his big arms firmly on her shoulders to try and pacify her.

'The email!' She shook herself free from his grasp. Having read it so many times she knew it off by heart. '"Dear Sara," ' Rosa put her fingers to her throat and mimicked retching. '"You

129

cannot ring me or text me at the weekend again. Honestly, it was so close, Rosa so easily could have found out."' How am I supposed to react, Josh? You tell me that.'

Rosa went back out to the roof terrace, her body now almost floppy with distress. 'I love you so much, Josh. I've never loved anyone like I love you. And now…now you've not only broken my trust, you've broken me. I can't recover from this.' She sobbed, 'I might as well be dead.'

Titch could hear everything in the shop below. Luckily there were no customers in yet. Praying that Rosa would keep her head, she gulped and carried on putting stock out.

'No, no, no, no no! You've got it all wrong. Oh, my darling girl.' Josh ran towards her.

'Get away from me,' Rosa screamed. 'I hate you.'

'Rosa, my love, calm down.' Josh took her hand and said, 'I'm not having an affair and I can prove to that to you right now.'

But Rosa's anger had taken away the power of rationality and she threw her first verbal punch. 'But it's fine, Josh, because I was with Luke last night. Yes, I was. He was actually really nice to me and we…'

Downstairs, Titch put her hand to her head and whispered, 'What have you done, Rosa?'

'Stop it! Don't even say that out loud. That's too low a blow.' Josh was now shaking. 'You're lying. Please, please, say you're lying. You wouldn't do that to me, to us?'

Rosa bit her lip and looked away.

Josh grabbed her by the arm and threw her Puffa jacket and trainers at her. 'Put these on,' he snarled. 'You're coming with me.' And when Rosa made no move, he shouted: 'NOW!'

130

CHAPTER TWENTY FIVE

Lucas turned the radio up in his van and began singing along to George Michael's 'Careless Whisper', swearing as he nearly missed the London-bound junction. His mum wouldn't be happy he was leaving before Christmas, but he didn't care. There was no way he could stay in the Bay now. He would have to make up some elaborate lie about a plumbing emergency. He had cleared up in the conservatory of the big house, turned off the Christmas tree lights, then washed and dried the towels and put the door key back in the key safe for the James family, and hoped he'd got rid of any evidence of last night's shenanigans before they came home for Christmas.

The plumber sang along with George's sad lament. Yes, they could have been so good together, he and Rosa, but she was never going to dance with him, was she? He whacked his steering wheel, annoyed with himself. He'd told her she'd taken his breath away. When did he ever get so soppy?

When Rosa had asked him to kiss her last night, he had felt so happy. What was it with that girl? She ticked every damn box and more. If he was honest with himself, from the minute he'd met her, when she'd just arrived in the cold and shabby Corner Shop and he'd been able to put on the heating and hot water for

131

her, she had put a spell on him. Maybe it was the cockney in them both? No, it was more than that. She had courage, she was quick-witted, funny and so sexy without even realising it. Yes, he'd been with loads of women since he had slept with her last year, but none of them were as beautiful or zany.

'The kiss' had been better than any before that, probably because he had been waiting so long to do it again. He was sure that she fancied him, but in Rosa's own words *you can't kid a kidder* and at that moment he knew that all she had wanted to do was punish her husband, while all Lucas had wanted to do was make tender and sensational love to her.

For her sake, he hoped that no one had seen him piggy-backing her home up to the Corner Shop or heard her drunken laughter. It had taken all his strength to get her up the steep stairs, and allowing himself a final peek at her toned body as he peeled off her still-damp trousers, he had put her into bed and laid her gently on her side in case she was sick in the night.

He hadn't dared stay with her or leave a note as he guessed Josh could be home anytime from now.

She had been in such a state he could imagine her not remembering what had happened, and with her phone broken, she couldn't even reach him to find out. Maybe that was a good thing now.

At least with him out of the picture for Christmas, it wouldn't be awkward if they bumped into each other. And if truth be told, he couldn't bear to see her again, not for a long time anyway.

Not now he realised that he was properly falling in love with her.

132

CHAPTER TWENTY SIX

Intent on his mission to prove his innocence, Josh marched Rosa down to the bay, ignoring both her chattering teeth and cries of protest.

The café was already quite full of Saturday-morning beach walkers and Christmas visitors getting their fill of the scrumptious cakes and breakfasts on offer.

'I don't want to go in the bloody café,' Rosa seethed as Josh led her around to the front of the old building. Catching a glimpse of Sara coming towards the window, he discreetly motioned her back away from it.

A cold wind was blowing off the sea and Rosa moaned, 'I want to go home, Josh. I don't feel well.'

'You apparently felt well enough last night. Now pull that,' he commanded her.

'What?' Rosa looked at him as if he was going mad. 'Pull what?'

Hanging down from the edge of the whitewashed café walls there was a piece of rope to which was attached a star fish and a piece of tinsel. Josh handed it to her. 'Just pull it, will you,' he said.

She did so, then screamed loudly as a green tarpaulin fell

to the ground, just missing her head. 'What the…? That could have bloody killed me.'

Josh tilted her head upwards. If Rosa's mouth had opened any wider, she could have caught a passing basking shark. Tears started to roll down her anguished face. For there, above her in beautiful red sign-writing were the letters RO, with a space for more letters, followed by a sweet painting of little Hot wearing his tartan jacket and with a string of sausages in his mouth.

'You did this – for me?' She put her hand to her heart. 'Don't say you have bought the café…for me? Oh, Josh. No.'

'Yes, yes, I did. I thought it would make you happier. Prove to you, in your silly little head, that I love you more than anything in the world.' He stopped to explain in a hoarse voice, 'It just needs the SA'S painted on there and it would have been ready for you as the perfect Christmas gift that I was planning WITH Sara, FOR you! FOR YOU, ROSA! My wife, my one and only.' Rosa squirmed in front of him. 'But if it's true what you just told me, then I don't think even the real SAS could help me with my decision now.' Josh's eyes filled with tears. 'How could you?' he said in a low voice that the wind almost blew away.

Rosa felt sick with the enormity of what she had done. She began to gabble. 'Calm down, come on. Let's talk. Josh, you know I love you. I love you so much. You don't even know what happened.'

'You are telling *me* to calm down?' Josh roared, and nearly shook the glass in the café windows. 'Maybe it's time you took a good look at yourself, Rosa.'

'What do you mean?'

'Look at you and your drinking, that's what I mean. You moan if I'm late home, then get drunk and don't even bother waiting up for me. You lied about being down at the Ship with Lucas at Halloween. Drunk again! And it's the reason you have fallen asleep before I got home many times before. And then last night you get so pissed that you don't even know if you had sex with someone – and that someone is a man who has no respect for anybody, least you. You're a bloody joke, Rosa No better than your mother used to be.'

'Josh, no! That's too cruel.' Tears of anger and sadness engulfed her.

But he hadn't finished. 'And as for running a café, what was I thinking? You're only doing so well with the Corner Shop because I bloody helped you from the start.'

'Josh, stop this.' Rosa put her hand to her head; she was sobbing profusely.

'Go home, Rosa. I'm sick of the sight of you.' Josh turned his back on her. 'And maybe I'll come back and find you one day when you decide you like yourself.'

'Where are you going?' Rosa asked, frightened. She'd gone too far now and was terrified of the consequences.

Josh whirled round. 'Just get out of my sight!' he screamed at her.

'What are you looking at?' Rosa snarled through the window at the few nosy onlookers in the café, tears and snot running down her face. 'The show's over.'

Then, on seeing the lone figure of her beautiful husband walking towards the sea, his shoulders shaking with grief, a knife twisted in her heart.

CHAPTER TWENTY SEVEN

Joe Fox didn't like children much. In fact, if he was honest, he found the whole 'bringing up baby' thing extremely tedious. Now that Sam, his eldest, was coming up to eighteen, at least he could relate to the boy at some sort of watching football and drinking level. It had disturbed Joe recently when he realised that he had been the same age as Sam was now when he had got Becca pregnant. He had felt so grown-up then, but so obviously wasn't. What a drama that had been. Yes, he had loved Becca in the way that teenagers do, but if he had had his way, then Sam wouldn't be here, and he very much doubted he would have even thought of marrying Rebecca. But give his wife her due, she had put Sam in nursery and gone out and worked so that he could study for his journalism degree. This was the reason he had agreed to her having another baby after Sam, now he could afford to be the sole breadwinner. Of course, if he had known it was going to be twins, he would never have agreed. Becca *was* a great girl, but he was with her more by necessity than need now. Mainly as it would be too bloody expensive to leave her!

He put his key in the door, expecting to hear the usual turmoil that a house consisting of a tired wife, young baby, boisterous twins and a teenager would bring, to be greeted by a subdued woofed hello from Suggs the Great Dane, who remained sprawled out across the whole sofa. Strange. Becca hadn't mentioned she was going out.

The newspaper editor took off his scarf and coat and checked himself in the hall mirror. At thirty-seven, he was attractive in a geeky sort of way. Tall and skinny, with a little bump on the top of his nose, he wore horn-rimmed glasses. His blond hair was cut short with a trendy little Tintin quiff. His lips were full and his eyes light blue and almond-shaped.

Just then, Suggs let out an almighty bark, jumped off the sofa and followed Joe to the kitchen. 'I'll walk you in a minute, boy,' he promised. Opening the kitchen door, he patted the big dog on his back and let him amble outside.

Joe picked up a scribbled note next to the kettle.

Have decided to go to Mum's for a few days with Rosie and twins. Sam staying with mate. Rosie is teething. Need a break before Christmas madness. Tried to call. B X

'*Yesss!*' Joe punched the air, grabbed a can of Coke from the fridge and turned on the radio. Freedom to do just what he wanted. Surely it was a bit drastic, though, his wife deciding to go all the way to Spain – and without discussing it first. His mother-in-law had moved there many years before, which was great on one level for free holidays, but not so great for Becca where support with the children was concerned. He wondered why she hadn't even mentioned it to him, but that was Becca for you. Independent to the core. And her mum would have paid for the flights as usual, as the woman was loaded and guilt-ridden, so he had no worries there either.

Poor little Rosie and her teething. Despite his aversion to babies as a rule, she *was* a little precious. A real Daddy's girl. He was glad she hadn't been another boy – mainly for fear of Becca wanting to try again. The only disconcerting thing was the kid's name. He thought back to the day when Becca had told him that 'Rosie' was top of her list. He was doing all he could to hide his affair with Rosa Larkin at the time, so he just went along with everything his pregnant wife was saying. But after the baby was born, every time the name Rosie was uttered, his thoughts would immediately turn to his feisty ex-lover.

Oh, how he had loved his time with Rosa. She was just so wild, not only in bed but in every other way. Not intellectually clever per se, but just so much fun to be with and so wise beyond her years about many things. He had been genuinely sad when she had ended it. How on earth had she had found out about him having a wife and kids? And how lucky was he, that she hadn't confronted Becca, as most women would have done. But Rosa was not 'most' women. It was half Becca's fault anyway. She wasn't putting out as she was pregnant, and a man has needs, and all that.

'Due to low pressure in the south-west we can expect some snow flurries in higher areas this weekend,' the radio weather presenter declared.

Joe drained his can of Coke and reached for the big dog's lead. He opened the back door.

'Come on, Suggs, mate. Let's get up those cliffs before the weather changes.'

CHAPTER TWENTY EIGHT

'He's gone? What do you mean, he's gone?' Titch continued to tweeze her eyebrows in front of the mirror.

Rosa cradled a sleeping Theo in her lap. The church bells were ringing in the pre-Christmas Sunday service and Hot snored gently in his bed in the corner of the lounge, twitching as he dreamed about chasing the Siamese cat which had moved into the cottage a few doors down.

'Did you really think he'd stay after I told him that I might have slept with Luke?'

'I can't believe you told him about that, when you don't even bloody know for sure that it happened.'

'I know, Titch, I know, but once I'd actually half-said it…what could I do? Even if I'd just said I'd met up with Luke, I don't think Josh would have stayed. And, quite frankly, I don't blame him. He said the only chance I might have of him forgiving me was if I told him the whole truth. That if I didn't tell him and something came to light afterwards that he didn't know about, he just wouldn't be able to trust me ever again.'

'So, there is a chance then.'

Rosa laughed bitterly. 'I mean, how can I not know whether or not I have slept with someone? That was what hurt him the most. That I could allow myself to get in that state. Not only is it complete whore-like behaviour, it's bloody dangerous.'

'Well, you need to talk to Lucas and find out.'

'No! I don't ever want to see him again.'

'You don't mean that.'

'Josh is likely to kill him anyway. And Luke's not going to tell the truth, is he? And if I *have* slept with him and he says so, then it's game over – or in my case, marriage over.'

'Oh Rose, don't be so bloody dramatic.'

Tears started to trickle down Rosa's pretty face. One dripped onto Theo's hair, causing the baby to stir.

'Ssh there, ssh.' Rosa rocked him gently until he was asleep again; her piercing green eyes now glistening with wet.

'Look, I'm sorry. That was harsh.' Titch peered at herself in the mirror and carried on plucking. 'Where has he gone anyway? I assume you are spending Christmas together.'

'You assume wrong.'

'Oh shit, it's that serious?'

'Yep, he's gone back to London and then will be spending Christmas as usual with Mummy, Daddy, his siblings and Great-Auntie Deirdre – if she's still alive.' Rosa sighed. 'I expect he'll find some excuse for why I can't be there.'

'But he'll be back for the New Year, right?'

'I don't think so. He is hurting so badly. I need to give him time. He took hold of me...' Rosa's voice started to crack. Titch went and sat next to her as her sorrowful friend continued, 'And he said that he loved me with his whole heart, but wasn't sure if he could keep on dealing with my reckless behaviour and my jealousy. And that maybe I should think before I drank so much as it obviously didn't agree with me.'

'And what did you say?' Titch reached over and wiped a drop of dribble from her baby boy's mouth.

'I ridiculously told him that I could do what I wanted and that he didn't own me.'

Titch shook her head. 'That poor man. You're the one who should have been begging forgiveness. You do realise he thinks you've slept with Lucas, the man he forbade you to see? That's heavy shit. Imagine if he *had* been sleeping with Sara, you would have had him bloody castrated by now.'

'I know, I know. And now the café too…he was putting all his life savings into it. They evidently haven't exchanged yet. Sara had agreed as a sign of goodwill that he could sort the signwriting in advance so that he could do the big reveal as a Christmas present for me.'

'So basically, he could back out on that if he wanted to.'

'In theory, yes.'

'What a dreadful mess.' Theo started to cry. 'Here, let me take him, he's hungry.'

Rosa handed Theo to his mum. 'Thank goodness I didn't say anything to Sara. I just hope that Josh didn't tell her about Lucas. It will be a repeat of the same time last year.'

'What do you mean?'

'As in the whole of Cockleberry Bay will be talking about me AGAIN. Not about me being a new shop-owner this time, but about my pending divorce!'

'You know that's not Josh's style and anyway, he has to face everyone too, you know.'

'What sort of woman am I, Titch? I arrive in the Bay, have an affair with Joe, who turns out to be married, and now all this with Luke. Why can't I just be happy with what I've got?'

At that moment the phone rang; it was Mary. Titch signalled that she was leaving.

'Hang on a minute, Mum,' Rosa said. 'I'll call you back. I just need to say goodbye to Titch.' She turned to her friend, saying,

'You don't have to go, Titch.' The thought of spending another night alone was beginning to play on Rosa's mind.

'Sorry, but I do.' Titch noticed her friend's face fall. 'I'm in the shop with you tomorrow. Let's have a good old natter then over a large cup of coffee.' She put a consoling hand on Rosa's arm, whispering, 'This will blow over, just you see. Everything will be OK.'

'What if it's not?'

'Then we deal with it, like we always have, together.'

CHAPTER TWENTY NINE

Rosa put on Hot's tartan coat and lead and braced herself to go out onto the streets of Cockleberry Bay. They made their way up to the Co-op, and she tutted as the naughty dog decided to do a poo right where the small row of trolleys started.

'Terrible when they do it on their own doorsteps, isn't it?' Edie Rogers said meaningfully, and smirked as she made her way out of the mini-supermarket.

Rosa fumed. She tied up Hot, binned his mess, then marched into the shop. 'Mary, did you just say something to her?'

'To whom?'

'Mrs Rogers from the chippie.'

'Of course I didn't, Rosa. I may be a gossip, but if it's something that concerns my own family, you should know by now I'm loyal as a lion. Anyway, say something about what? You've yet to tell me anything. Apart from, I must confess, I did see Josh go off in his car last night and it's not back this morning.'

'This is why I wanted to see you face-to-face and not just call you back.' At that moment three people came up to the counter. 'I'll go, Mum. I'm just taking Hot for a walk and I'll pop over to Seaspray after, if you're about?'

'I'll be home around three. You got that phone of yours

sorted yet?'

'I've ordered a new one. It's being delivered to the shop tomorrow.'

'Good girl. Come for dinner, I'm cooking your favourite.'

'Ooh yes, that will be lovely, thank you.'

Rosa grabbed three miniature bottles of wine on her way out and, thank heavens, they went through the self-serve without asking for an assistant to check her age. Maybe Josh was right, she thought; perhaps she was drinking a bit much, so if she allocated a small bottle per night, that would be just one glass. And the thought of getting through a weekend night without Josh *or* wine was too much to bear.

Popping the bottles in her handbag, she untied Hot and started to walk down to the beach. The little fella trotted jauntily in front, his tail waving happily, sniffing and pausing to cock a back leg and leave his doggie scent now and then.

The shops and eateries all looked so gorgeous with their colourful and sparkly window displays. The council had even pushed the boat out and put garlands of lights across the buildings in the narrow Main Street. No expense spared, it seemed. Shame they couldn't just spend the money on some decent street lamps.

Rosa was relieved to see that the beach was empty aside from a lovey-dovey couple at the water's edge. Seeing them embrace made her feel even more hopeless. What if Josh didn't ever come back? Letting Hot off the lead, she made her way to the bench – the same bench that had been witness to too much drama for her and Titch, and over such a short period. This time last year, she wasn't even in a relationship with Josh and now she was not only married to him but could potentially be divorced before too long!

There was something quite comforting about not having a

phone, Rosa thought. It meant that nobody knew where you were, and you didn't have to answer to anyone. It was very liberating, in fact. Also, she didn't have the anguish of waiting for Josh to *not* call her!

An icy blast of wind caused her to stand up and pull her hat down further over her ears. Mary had said that because the forecasted snow was rare down here, when it did come it was usually quite bad.

Just as she was about to summon Hot, she caught sight of the Ship Inn door opening and the familiar figure and white hair of Sheila Hannafore striding towards her in fighting stance.

'Hot, Hot! Time to go home,' Rosa frantically called her little pet, hoping that she could get him on the lead and start walking up the cliff path before the dodgy publican reached them.

'Hello, Rosa.' Sheila's perfect white smile belied the bile that was about to come out of her mouth. 'I believe I've got you to blame for my lad clearing off back to London.'

Rosa felt at first relief on confirmation that Lucas was out of the picture, then mortified at what his mother might know.

'I don't know what you mean.'

'You got me in trouble with your lies before, missy. So don't you be trying that on again. I saw you with him.'

'You did? Hot, come on.' The little brown sausage at last did as he was told. 'I'm sorry, Sheila, I've got to go.'

'Not so fast. Sit down for a minute.'

'No, I'm…'

Sheila pushed Rosa's shoulder down, forcing her to sit back on the bench. Furious, she jumped up immediately. A now-distraught Hot ran around the bench until Rosa managed to grab him and secure his lead.

'Don't you ever touch me again,' Rosa hissed and headed towards the edge of the beach and the cliff path.

'So, you seeing him the other night, laughing, joking, getting a piggy-back off the beach has nothing to do with him going away for the whole of Christmas then?' Sheila bawled after her.

Rosa turned. 'Ssh now.'

'Oh, I can shout louder than that, my fine lady.'

Rosa walked back to her, sighing.

'Do you want the whole of Cockleberry Bay to know what a slut you are, Rosa Larkin, or whatever your name is. Or just your husband, maybe?'

'Look, I chatted to your son, yes – but so what? I've no idea why he has gone back to London. And quite frankly, I don't care.'

'Don't you think it's a bit strange that he's just upped and left?'

'I don't know, Sheila.' Rosa shrugged. 'And that's the truth.'

'Well, did he say anything to you?'

'I don't remember. And before you think of starting any trouble, Josh knows I was with your precious son.'

'Drunk again, were you?' the woman sneered. 'If him not spending Christmas with the family is down to you, there will be hell to pay. You know that, right?'

'Everybody is responsible for their own actions, Sheila. Including you.'

'What's that supposed to mean?' And when Rosa ignored her: 'You're nothing but a little tyke.' The formidable woman then turned on her heels and strode furiously back towards her pub.

Shaking slightly, Rosa reached into her handbag, pulled out one of the miniatures of wine and started to gulp it down. The cold liquid soon began to relax her. She pulled Hot close and began her ascent to the cliff top, drinking to console her aching heart as she climbed. The wild wind, the sea crashing on the rocks below and the rolling grey clouds bringing bad weather further darkened her mood.

Thoughts began to chase through her head. Why on earth would Lucas go back to London? Maybe he was worried that Josh would find out about her being with him, but that was her problem not his. After all, she was a big girl and hadn't done anything against her will. Or maybe she had? That was the most terrible thing. She had no idea. Maybe Lucas felt guilty?

Mortified at what she might have said or done, she finished the small bottle and unscrewed the top of a second. Forgetting it all seemed the best option at this moment in time. At the top of the cliff path, forgetting how dangerous it was, she let Hot off the lead and looked down at the stunning view of the bay, where she could make out the twinkly lights along the beach wall and adorning the exterior of the Ship Inn.

A little tipsy now, she raised the half-finished bottle to the sky. 'Happy Christmas, Great-Grandad Ned, Happy Christmas, Great-Grannie Queenie, Happy Christmas, Granny Maria. Meet me where the sky touches the sea.' She sang the last sentence and then her voice broke.

She bent down to pick up Hot and cuddle him for comfort, telling him, 'It's OK, boy. Mummy's just sad that Daddy has gone away for a while and nasty old Sheila Hannafore just scared her a bit.'

Loudly hiccuping, she looked at the ominous sky. 'Right, come on, mister. We need to get home; it looks like that snow is about to start falling.' But suddenly Hot was no longer at her feet. She heard a deep bark and further commotion, and saw a ball heading at speed to the edge of the cliff top, hotly pursued by a speedy dachshund and his flailing ears.

Rosa's *'Nooo!'* was lost in the wind as her beloved dog suddenly disappeared. With the alcohol dulling the danger and with no thought for herself, she raced towards the edge, then on peering over and seeing a whimpering Hot shivering on a ledge about ten feet down, and with a trickle of blood coming from his mouth, she ditched her handbag at the top and started to clamber down.

As she got halfway towards her beloved pooch, Rosa suddenly realised that she had made a dreadful mistake. The cold wind had made her gloveless hands numb, and the effects of the alcohol caused her feet to be unsteady. As she tried with all her might to cling onto the slippery jagged rocks with her hands, one suddenly gave way under her foot, causing her to let out a bloodcurdling scream as she fell.

CHAPTER THIRTY

Mary had got in from work and was just putting some logs on the fire in the kitchen when the lights went on and off three times.

'Queenie?' Mary said aloud. 'Come on – stop that.' Merlin then came bolting in through the cat flap and started being unusually affectionate. Mary got a sudden shooting pain in her right arm which made her wince.

She checked the clock. It was only three-thirty but with the sky heavy with snow it seemed a lot later. She would get the fire going, have a nice bath and put a small roast beef joint in the oven that she could share with Rosa when she came in if she fancied it.

She shivered violently as she lit the fire, only warming up as the logs began to crackle and the oven started to heat.

CHAPTER THIRTY ONE

'Suggs, what is it, boy? Oh no – did your ball go over the cliff?'

With his fear of heights, Joe Fox didn't dare venture too close to the edge. The wind really was getting up and the light was fading fast. He was sure he had just felt a snowflake land on his cheek, too.

'Come on. We've got loads more balls at home.' He nodded for the Great Dane to follow him, but the animal wouldn't leave the cliff edge. 'Suggs!' Joe was getting irritable now. 'Will you come.' The dog started barking a deep warning. When he eventually stopped, Joe thought he could hear a faint cry; cocking his head to the side he suddenly heard it again.

'Help, help us, someone, please!' And then came the yap of a little dog. Still too scared to walk so close to the edge, Joe got down to ground level and slithered his way across the grass. With his stomach churning with fear, he kept calling out, 'Hello, hello,' as he went.

'Help! Please help us!' It wasn't just the voice he recognised, but the bark. He had been on so many walks up here last year with both Hot and Rosa, how could he not?

'Rosa?'

'Joe, is that you? I never thought I'd say this, but I am so pleased you're here. You've got to help us. It'll be dark soon, and this ledge is so small.' Her voice went into a panicked screech. 'I've done something bad to my arm too. I'm in agony. And I'm so scared that Hot will fall over the edge.'

Trying not to show fear in his voice, Joe took control. 'OK, OK, keep as calm as you can. I'm not going to risk coming down, but I'm going to get help, all right?' The ledge they were both perched on can't have been more than three feet wide; it was a miracle, in fact, that they had both managed to land on it. Joe felt extremely fearful for the pair of them.

'Don't leave us,' Rosa whined.

'I will stay right here, it's fine. Just keep very still, the pair of you.'

Joe could see the tide below was coming in fast. Just as he was about to call for help, the snow started to fall. Not just tiny, romantic, floaty flakes but those great big wallopy ones that would probably even settle on the sea.

'Oh my God, oh my God.' Rosa experienced fear like never before. She crouched down on the ledge to try and settle her balance. Hot was now cowering between her legs on the little ledge. They were both shivering badly.

'Try not to panic, Rosa. The coastguard has got the rescuers out. They are saying fifteen minutes max. Try and keep moving if you can to stay warm. Actually no, don't move!' Joe felt panic rising in his throat.

Rosa shouted up, most of her words getting lost on the wind. 'If something happens to me, please tell Josh I'm sorry and that I loved him so much.' She let out a funny little wail. 'I'm *so* cold.' Even Joe could hear her teeth chattering.

'Nothing's going to happen, it's all OK. Just hold on.' Joe managed to stand, pulling Suggs into his side, for warmth more than anything. The intuitive hound knew something was badly wrong. He let out a regular deep bark as if to show both Rosa and Hot he was there for them.

'OK, I can see the boat coming, Rosa. Hold on, girl, it won't be long now.'

Joe carefully wound his way back down the coast path with a powerful torch sent up by the coastguard crew. Rosa lay back in the boat, wrapped securely in a tinfoil blanket, moaning softly. Hot's cut had been cleaned up with an antiseptic wipe and he had tucked himself close into his mistress's side, occasionally making his special creaking sound that showed his joy. Apart from having suffered a fright and a tiny cut on his lip where he'd bitten it when falling, he was fine.

'You were both extremely lucky, Rosa,' the bald crew member said to her. 'The tide was coming in fast and if you hadn't been found in that snow, well, anything could have happened. Good job that fellow was on the cliff, eh?'

'If he hadn't been on the cliff, he wouldn't have thrown a bloody ball. Ouch! I don't feel very lucky with this pain shooting through my arm,' Rosa croaked. And a hangover was kicking in.

'There's an ambulance waiting for you at the lifeboat station. We'll soon get you checked out.'

'Oh no, what about my dog! Can he come with me?'

'Is there someone you can call?' He looked at her wedding ring. 'Your husband, perhaps?'

Rosa began to well up. 'No. I haven't got a phone…or a husband, at the moment.'

'It's fine. Can you remember any numbers?'

'There's Jacob. Yes, please call Jacob at the Lobster Pot in Cockleberry, he'll know what to do. Ask him to tell Mary too, please.' Rosa wailed again. The pain in her arm was becoming excruciating. 'Can I have some painkillers, please?'

'Let's wait until you see a doctor, eh?' he said.

'I need the toilet badly,' Rosa moaned. 'And I feel really sick.'

Before either of them could reach her with a bowl, Rosa sat up and vomited all over the deck, splattering Hot as she did so. The force of her vomiting also caused her to empty her bladder. She began to sob uncontrollably, then wailed, 'I'm so, so sorry, and I've wet myself now too.'

CHAPTER THIRTY TWO

'Oh Rosa.' Jacob went to hold his friend's hand. He noticed a bruise and small cut fixed with butterfly stitches on her forehead. Her arm was being supported by a collar and cuff-type sling. She was extremely pale and had been very fortunate to be put in a private room in the hospital as it was the only bed that had been available for an emergency.

'You haven't rung Josh, have you?' she asked.

'No, I haven't. I thought I'd wait and see you first as your mum said you'd been having problems and I didn't know who you might be with, up on the cliff. The lifeboat guy did say that somebody saved your life up there.'

Rosa put her hand to her forehead and felt around the stitches. 'Yes, it was Joe.'

'What – Joe Fox, that bastard? Really?' Jacob was horrified.

'It's all innocent with him, honestly.'

'OK. If you say so.' But Jacob's face was grim. He forced himself to relax. 'So, when your mum said she wanted to come here, I told her you'd talk to her later as I was calling her from the car and was driving at a hundred miles an hour to reach you.' He heaved a sigh. 'I was so worried about you.'

'Good job somebody was.'

'Don't sat that. You are loved, and you know it.'

'Quickly text Mum for me, can you?'

'No. You must call her yourself, Rosa.'

As Rosa reached out to take the proffered phone, the realisation sank in that she would just have one hand for a while, as there was a chance that she had broken her dominant, right one.

On seeing the look on her face, Jacob dialled the number and handed the mobile back to her.

'Drunk? Is that all you care about, whether I'd been drinking?' Rosa went to give the phone back to Jacob, but when he shook his head she held on. 'Look, I'm fine, Mum. I'm waiting for a doctor to check over an X-ray. They think I may have broken my arm. They want to keep me in for observation overnight as I hit my head too. Just please don't tell Josh. You haven't already, have you?' Jacob could hear Mary's concerned voice in the background. 'Good, good, please don't. And yes, Hot is fine. Raff followed Jacob down and took him back to the pub. My knights in shining armour had it covered as usual.'

She finished up, handed Jacob the handset and then winced in pain.

'I can't believe how much it bloody hurts. Off the scale, even with painkillers, honestly.'

At that moment the doctor appeared. 'Mrs Rosa Smith?'

'That's me.'

'You were very lucky not to have broken your arm, Mrs Smith. It is just very battered and bruised. You still need a sling to protect it, and it will take a good couple of weeks before you are pain-free, I should imagine. So, keep taking paracetamol regularly to manage it.'

He looked at her kindly. 'Now, how are you feeling, apart from a headache, I should think?'

Tears pricked Rosa's eyes. 'Horrible, I feel horrible.' She began to cry.

The young doctor put his hand on her good arm. 'We can give you something to help you sleep.' He smiled at Jacob. 'You staying here for a bit? At Jacob's confirmation, he added, 'Ah, that's good.' And he went off, consulting his clipboard.

'How am I going to cope in the shop?' Rosa worried. 'It's the busiest time right now.' She then switched to survival mode, something she had been used to for much of her life. 'It's not so terrible. I can supervise, I'm sure, I just won't be able to lift much. Titch wanted extra money anyway and now the little one's on the bottle, her mum can babysit a lot more. It'll be fine. I'll be fine.'

'It's all right not to be fine sometimes you know, Rosa,' Jacob said.

'I've messed everything up.' Rosa began to cry. 'What if Josh doesn't come back?'

'Tell me what's happened. I can maybe help.'

'It's so messy and so ridiculous. Did you know that Josh was in the process of buying the café?'

'No! He didn't say a thing. Wow, that's amazing. Why? When? How? Are you giving up the Corner Shop then?'

'Too many questions,' Rosa moaned. 'And no, I can never give up the Corner Shop. I need to leave that to somebody who deserves it, not just sell it or pass it on to any Tom, Dick or Harry. If all I can do to honour my receiving such a gift is follow Ned's wishes, then that's what I'm doing.'

'So, Coffee, Tea or Sea – what was that all about?'

'I don't know what was going through his head. I had mentioned before that I would love to run a café, and Josh being Josh, thought that by buying one for me would make me happy.'

'Josh being Josh, showing you that here is a man who is so

much in love with you that he would do anything for you.'

Rosa bit her lip. 'I thought he was having an affair.'

'You what? That's like saying to me that I love kissing girls or something.' Rosa managed a faint smile as Jacob added firmly, 'Josh is a decent man, Rosa. He just wouldn't.'

'Well, I bloody know that now.'

'How many times do I have to tell you that he loves you. Why can't you just believe it?'

Rosa ignored her friend's kind words, lamenting, 'I should have just confronted Josh, instead of acting like a child and throwing my legs open for the first man who showed a bit of interest. It was a pathetic attempt at revenge.' She dramatically threw her good arm up and then winced in pain as the muscles were affected on her other side.

'Oh, princess, please be careful – and who did you spread-eagle for?' Jacob camply brushed his hand through his fringe. 'Please don't say it was that little bitch Lucas Hannafore.'

'Yep. I went back to a holiday house with him.'

'No.' Jacob let out a big sigh. 'What were you thinking, Rosa?'

'I *wasn't* thinking, was I?' she muttered in disgust at herself. 'I think I kissed him, which is bad enough – and I have no idea if we did anything else. Because yes, I had been drinking.' Yawning, she added, 'Anyway, I'm bored of talking about it now.'

Rosa's flippancy annoyed the usually unfazed Jacob. 'Don't you think Josh needs to know what has happened to you today, at least?'

Rosa roused herself. 'No, no way – and promise me that you won't tell him. He needs to come back because he wants to, not because he feels that he should out of pity.'

'You put me in such a difficult position, Rosa. Where is he anyway?'

'He's gone to his mum's to think things through and no doubt be encouraged to find a decent woman this time, not some street urchin with the morals of an alley cat.'

'Street urchin?'

'Yes, I looked up the word "tyke". Sheila called me it earlier.'

'Well, I hope you responded with "dyke" – horrible woman – and I'm sure she is one, despite having been married to some poor man before.'

Rosa began to laugh quietly, but then the memory came back, in full Technicolor, of that horrific moment on the lifeboat when she had vomited then wet herself, a double disgrace. She fell silent. It was as if all bravado and fervour had been sucked out of her.

'Jacob?' she whispered.

'What is it, honey?'

'I think I might need some help.' She reached her good hand out to him and he took it in both of his. 'I can't keep mucking things up like this.'

Jacob leant forward and kissed her on the cheek, and with eyes full of tears and compassion, he replied softly.

'I understand.'

CHAPTER THIRTY THREE

Rosa was filling the counter bowl with bone-shaped dog biscuits with her left hand when Titch breezed into the shop and put her handbag down on the counter.

'Happy New Year, Rose. Oops, probably the wrong thing to say to you.'

'Yes, thanks for that. I'm not a big Christmas fan as you know, but funnily enough, I have had better ones.'

'Yes, funny that.' Titch took off her coat.

'New Year's Eve with Mary, Merlin and Jools Holland's *Hootenanny* wasn't exactly a barrel of laughs.'

'Well, it's all over and done with now. How's your arm?'

'Still sore and I can't do a lot yet, but I can feel it's on the mend now, thanks.'

'Good. Well, I've decided that now I'm Acting Manageress of the Corner Shop in Cockleberry Bay, not only do I have a new job, my New Year's resolution is to find a new knob.'

'You really are quite disgusting.'

'When did you get so bloody serious?'

'When I catapulted myself down the side of a bloody cliff; that's when.' Rosa put the empty box under the counter ready for recycling.

'Aw, it's shit, isn't it? But I'm here every day now, so if you need me to do anything at all, then just ask.'

'Yes, thank goodness. I do, in fact, need help putting some orders through on the laptop. It really is amazing how we take it for granted, having two working hands.'

'Poor you, let me put the kettle on. I've got some biscuits too. We can have a right old catch-up, as I can't imagine it's going to be very busy today.' Titch picked up her bag and headed to the back kitchen.

Ding! Rosa looked up from the laptop and gasped. For there in front of her was the lanky figure of Joe Fox.

Following her accident, she had been reliving the moment over and over in her mind, trying to remember if he would have noticed that she had wet herself. She remembered seeing him at the harbourside returning the torch to the lifeboat crew and hoped with a passion that the crew would have kept her dignity behind that silver blanket.

'Hi,' he said awkwardly. 'I just came in to get some treats for Suggs – and of course to see how you are.'

'Yeah, good thanks.' Rosa managed a half-smile. 'Apart from doing a mini-skydive without a parachute, that is.'

'Is your arm broken?'

'No, thank goodness, but it hurts quite a bit.'

Joe fidgeted while his card transaction went through. 'I hope it gets better soon. I feel so bad about throwing that ball.' He looked very uncomfortable. 'So I'll…um…be off then.' And he turned to leave, forgetting both his card and the package on the counter.

'Joe?' A now slightly flushed Joe turned around as Rosa handed him his stuff and began to speak. Her words rushed out. 'Thanks for saving me and Hot.'

'Time I stepped up and did something right by you, isn't it?'

He gave an apologetic shrug and left. Just as he was closing the door behind him, Becca Fox appeared and there was a heated exchange between the two of them outside on the street. Rosa gulped hard.

'You look like you've seen a ghost.' Titch dropped the packet of ginger biscuits from between her teeth and plonked two steaming mugs of coffee down on the counter.

'No, just a fox.'

'Shit, it's him,' Titch said, spotting Joe through the window. 'He's got some balls, coming here. Glad I was out the back.'

'It's fine. In a way, I'm glad I've seen him. I was thinking I should thank him personally somehow, and it's done now. Without him Hot and I could have died, what with no phone and the weather and tide coming in.'

'Yes, but if he hadn't been throwing that ball…'

'Oh Titch, what is it your mum says? "If ifs and buts were gold and silver, then we would all be millionaires".'

'True enough. Ritchie's mum was telling me the other day she didn't think that Joe and Becca were very happy.'

'I saw them have words outside just now actually.'

'She never found out about you and him though, did she?'

'No, there's no way Becca would still come in here and give me business if she did, I'm sure.' Rosa moved her arm about in her sling to try and get comfortable. She then threw a blister pack of Paracetamol at Titch. 'Can you just press a couple of these out for me, please?' Titch handed the tablets to Rosa and went out the back to fill a glass with water.

'Here.' Rosa washed down the tablets, then managed to clumsily place herself onto one of the high stools behind the counter as Titch babbled on. 'Anyway, my mum says that waiting for an ex to come back is like waiting at a red light with a sign that reads *This light might never turn green*.'

'When did I ever say I wanted Joe Fox back?' Rosa looked puzzled. 'And I'm not sure it was a big enough relationship to even classify him as an ex, to be honest.'

'You didn't, but you did cry a bloody river over him when he left. Such a bastard.' Titch jumped up on the stool next to her and began dunking biscuits in her coffee.

Rosa sighed. 'Yes, Titch, he was and is such a bastard. And one who I will forever keep at arm's length from now on, despite his heroics.' She took a slurp of her drink. 'You do realise the seriousness of my situation, don't you? I had one stilted message from Josh, all over Christmas. That's it. And that was asking more how Hot was than me. I even missed his birthday. He isn't replying to anything.' Her expression was pained. 'I know what I did was terrible, but if he loved me, surely he'd come to me now. I miss him so much. I actually don't know what to do.'

'I know, Rose. I think every day you must text him a loving message and say how sorry you are. Have you tried to get hold of Lucas?'

'No, there's no point. I mean, having to ask someone if you slept with them or not wouldn't be my finest hour, now would it? And it's gone beyond all that, I think. I normally would just get on a train and go to Josh, but although I can't believe he doesn't want to talk to me, I can feel he needs the space too.'

'But, maybe if…'

'No, Titch. Just leave it. How was your Christmas, anyway?'

'Quiet. Just me, Mum and Theo.'

'Have you thought any more about finding Theo's dad?'

'No, because with Lucas out of the picture to help with the CCTV, short of putting an ad in a national newspaper, I don't know where to start.'

'Is the little lad all fine now?'

'Seems to be. I took him to the doctor the week before

Christmas and everything was as it should be.'

'Such a relief, eh?'

'Tell me about it. I wouldn't want to go through that again in a hurry.' Titch looked suddenly worried. 'Having said that, Rose, he did have a strange little crying turn on Boxing Day and I freaked out, thinking he was ill again. I called the emergency doctor and everything, then it turned out I'd probably eaten too many gherkins with the cheese board.'

'You're still feeding him yourself then? I thought he was taking the bottle now.'

'Half and half, it works well like that. But now I'm looking for a *real* boyfriend, I can't be having leaky boobies, now can I?'

'There was a boy at one of my children's homes who used to have a thing about lactating women.'

'Ew. That's weird.'

'I know, we were all a bit weird there. There was another girl who collected owls.'

'That's quite sweet, like toys and ornaments of them, I guess?'

'No.' Rosa laughed. 'Real stuffed owls.'

'Hilarious!' Titch nearly spat out her mouthful of coffee. 'What on earth did *you* collect?'

'A selection of STDs mainly.'

'Rose!'

'Says the girl who doesn't know who the father of her child is.'

'All right, you win.'

'I *was* only joking,' Rosa sighed. 'I think we should try and have a peaceful January though, don't you? I can't take any more dramas.'

Hot, frustrated at not being able to jump up on the high stools, started barking his discontent below them.

'And that includes you, Mr Frankfurter,' Titch told him, throwing him a piece of broken-off biscuit.

CHAPTER THIRTY FOUR

'This is it, 35 Fore Street.' Jacob took Hot's lead out of Rosa's hand as they reached the terraced cottage with a black wrought-iron gate and two stone lions at either side of the yellow front door. 'You OK?' Rosa nodded, as her friend continued, 'It's what you wanted and need right now.'

Rosa exhaled deeply. 'I know.' She could barely speak for nerves.

'I'll be right here waiting outside with Hot in exactly fifty minutes. You'll be fine, go on.'

Jacob kissed Rosa on the cheek. He looked back and waved as she knocked on the door, and then reached for his ringing phone.

'All right, fella?…Yes, I've just walked her there and will meet her as she comes out…Yes, she seemed nervous, but that's to be expected…Yep, that's all in hand too… I know you do, and I promise I will be looking out for her, as always.'

'Alec?' Rosa put her hand to her head. 'So you're Dr Burton? Alec Burton, of course! I didn't dream it might be you. I'd totally forgotten your last name.'

The big man remained expressionless. 'As we have met before,

164

I need to check first that you are happy to work with me. From now on it will be a therapist/patient relationship, so we will not be able to be friends on a deeper level, whilst you are seeing me in this capacity.'

Rosa listened intently as Alec continued: 'Whatever is discussed in this room is strictly confidential. The only time this ever goes outside is if your case is discussed with my third-party professional peer group, but your name will never be mentioned.' He smiled. 'How does that sound, Rosa?' Despite his large stature, his demeanour was very gentle.

'It sounds fine,' Rosa nodded. 'We barely know each other, and I already feel comfortable with you.'

'That's good to hear. I have drawn up a contract, which you can take home and read and then sign. You're initially booked for six sessions, but there is no time limit if you did want to continue. OK?'

'OK,' Rosa replied quietly.

'There's water and tissues on the side if you need them.'

'I thought it was only weak people who had to have therapy,' she blurted out nervously, then shifted her bottom to the back of the comfy armchair she was sitting in. Alec sat in a matching one directly opposite her.

'It takes a massive amount of strength to walk between those two lions, I can assure you,' he responded, causing Rosa to immediately well-up. 'All the time you are here, I want you to feel safe, respected, accepted and as comfortable as you can be, considering we will be delving deep into your mind and feelings. In your own time tell me why you are here, Rosa. We can then have a general discussion today and see where the session takes us.'

Rosa reached for the glass of water and took a sip, then grabbed a tissue from the box and held it tightly in her good hand. 'I'm here because I seem to muck up relationships, especially my most recent one.'

'OK.' Alec nodded encouragingly and waited.

'I drink to mask my feelings and I keep putting myself in danger by drinking too much. And I can't understand why, because even though I have a lot of good things and people in my life now, I'm still not content. I still think everyone will either let me down or leave me.'

Rosa then started to cry. Not just any old cry but a full-blown howling wail of a cry that would have competed with one of Merlin the cat's tantrums. Every time she lifted her head to try and say sorry, she began to blubber even more.

All the while, Alec sat quietly until she eventually finished her sad outpouring of anger and emotion.

With her breath hitching, she managed to stutter, 'I d-didn't think I would cry.' She wiped her swollen eyes and stood up shakily. Then grabbing her bag and lurching towards the door, she looked back and said, 'I'm sorry, Alec. I can't do this right now. It's too hard. I just can't.'

It was now dark, and Jacob's face was lit by the emails he was checking on his phone when Rosa came tearing past him. Hot was being remarkably quiet as he crunched a doggie treat on the pavement at his feet.

'Rosa! Wait!' Jacob shouted, stopping her in her tracks. Hot jumped up and began to bark.

Walking slowly back towards them, she managed to stutter, 'I'm s-sorry, Jacob, I know you took the tr-trouble to sort all this out for me, but I'm not ready to talk out l-loud about my past or how shit I am at r-r-relationships.' Sounding like a Dalek, she then sniffed loudly and wailed, 'I just want my Joshy back,' and she began to weep on his shoulder.

'I know you do, darling, but believe me, everything will be

all right.'

She lifted her head. 'You promise?'

Jacob held the young woman away from him and looked right at her. 'Are you absolutely sure you don't want to go back in there? You've barely given it a chance.' Alec had come out to stand at his front gate. Then, on seeing that Rosa was safely with Jacob, the big man went back inside.

'How will talking to a stranger help me?'

'The way I see it, you need to be ready to delve deep – and from the many people I've faced across the bar, if you do these things before you are ready, then there is little point, to be honest.'

'But I thought I was ready. Oh, I don't know. But thank you for being so understanding.' Whatever would she do without Jacob, Rosa thought. His support throughout had been amazing. How could she ever repay him? She would love him and Raff forever.

Arm-in-arm, the friends walked slowly down to the Corner Shop, Hot waggling along beside them. Scrabbling for the front-door key in her handbag, Rosa cursed Titch for not leaving an outside light on.

Jacob's phone started to ring. 'That's probably my hubbie,' he said. 'We're almost full with early dinner bookings tonight.'

'Quick, you go, then. You've done more than enough. I'll be fine, honestly.' Rosa put the key in the shop door.

Jacob placed Hot's lead in her free hand, blew her an air kiss, and just managed to catch the incoming call as he started to power walk up the hill to the Lobster Pot.

'Literally just left her,' Jacob panted. 'Sorry, mate, but she doesn't want to do it. Ran out before the session ended, in fact. She's just not ready, that's what it is.'

Josh, sitting in his study in the house off the Whitechapel Road in London, rubbed a hand through his hair. 'Oh shit, that's a shame. OK. I need to press on to Plan B then. Is she all right?'

'She misses you – a lot.'

'Good.' Josh sighed. 'But apart from that?'

'She's doing as well as can be expected. The shop has been open every day so that's a positive sign, and I see Titch is spending a bit more time with her too. So she's not too much on her own.'

'OK. Can I leave it for you to settle whatever with Alec?'

'Sure, sure. At least you can stay on a mate's level with him now.'

'Yeah, always a silver lining and all that. I'll be in touch. Love to Raff. And thanks so much, J. I honestly don't know what any of us would do without you.'

'I know what I'd do with *you*, given the chance,' the handsome publican flirted, causing Josh to laugh, hang up and look to the contacts directory in his phone.

This was the hardest thing he had ever had to do in his life, but if his marriage was to stand any chance of survival, he knew it was necessary.

CHAPTER THIRTY FIVE

Rosa fed Hot and ran a deep bubble bath. Relaxing back in the warm, soothing water, she heard the little dog waddle into the bathroom, and put her hand over the side of the bath so he could administer his customary lick. Flopping down onto the bathmat, he wiped the bubbles off his coat by rubbing his jaw several times over the soft material. If Josh could just appear in the doorway and tell her he loved her, then everything would be back to normal, Rosa thought dreamily. Or would it? Had she ruined everything irreversibly? She prayed not.

Bless Jacob for organising a therapy session for her. She obviously wasn't as ready as she'd thought, to look at herself from within. Maybe the fact that she had admitted that stuff was wrong was a start, at least. Mind you, lately she had gone from being so outwardly resilient for so long to crying at anything! What on earth was wrong with her? The social workers, of whom she had seen many when she was in care, had never really helped her, in fact they'd made her worse to a degree, but now she knew she could do with some help. Falling from the cliff path had been a big wake-up call: it had made her realise just how low things had become for her. She cringed at the thought of that ledge not being there; it could have been a whole lot worse – and imagine if something had happened to Hot too. She couldn't even bring herself to think about that. And as for wetting herself, she cringed every time she replayed the scene in her mind. But the prospect of sitting and baring her soul in front of Alec…no, she just couldn't handle that. Maybe in time it would become easier.

She tried with all her might, as she had done so many times before, to remember what had happened that night with Lucas…but nothing. She must have had a black-out again; how terrible was that! And the fact that he had gone away over Christmas too surely meant that something must have taken place. Maybe she should just call him, but on the other hand she quite liked not knowing, since if they *had* slept together then the guilt would be appalling.

She was just drying herself off in the bedroom, when she heard a familiar voice. 'Rosa, what's going on? Are you all right?' Titch appeared in the doorway. Theo was sound asleep up close to her chest in a baby carrier.

'Bloody hell, Titch. Haven't you heard of using a doorbell? I could have been doing anything up here.'

'Like what? I've been calling you off the hook. I was worried about you.'

'Titch, I'm fine. I was having a bath.'

'Your eyes look like piss-holes in the snow.'

'Charming. Thanks for that. And whilst we are being so nice to each other,' Rosa made a face, 'please remember to leave a light on somewhere when you finish in the shop. I had a right old game trying to find my keys in the dark earlier.'

'Sorry! I was in a rush to get home and feed this little fellow.' She ran one finger gently over her sweet baby's forehead. 'How was the counselling, anyway?'

'Dr Burton only turned out to be big Alec.'

'No way!'

'Yep. I guess that's why he wasn't always open to telling us what he did for a job.'

'How did it go?'

'I don't want to talk about it.'

'Are you sure?'

'Titch, I'm sure.'

The young girl handed her an envelope. 'Anyway, I'm not stopping, I just popped out from home to get fish and chips. Want me to get you some?'

'No, ta, I'm not hungry. Anything to get a chat in with Randy Ritchie, eh?'

Titch ignored her comment. 'Here, this was on the mat.'

'What is it?'

'A letter. Anyway, gotta fly, I'll be here and open up with you tomorrow.' She glanced at Rosa standing there in her towel. 'Your arm's looking much better.'

'Yes, it feels better, thanks. I'm ditching the sling now, just a bit of swelling to go down and I'll be back to normal.'

'You'll never be that,' Titch riposted, then, 'Rose?'

'That's my name – well, nearly.'

'I'm not very good at sentimental stuff, but you know you can talk to me about anything, don't you?'

Feeling herself welling up again, Rosa replied, 'Get to the chippie. I'll see you tomorrow.'

With a cup of hot chocolate by her side and Hot sleeping on her stretched-out legs, Rosa remembered the envelope and pulled it out of her dressing-gown pocket. She recognised her mother's shaky scrawl on the front.

Dear Rosa. I couldn't get you to answer earlier and you know I don't like leaving messages on those recorder things. Rosa screwed up her face. She was sure she hadn't missed a call, but Mary's use of a mobile phone was dubious at best. *Let's have a chat tomorrow. Meet me by the cafe at 11. Love Mum x*

Rosa decided to call her, but there was no answer. She checked the time: 9.30 pm. Her mother liked her early nights, so was probably in bed asleep already. She was such a funny old stick, although there was something rather nice about receiving letters or even a note like this in today's age of technology.

As she always did just before bedtime, Rosa phoned Josh. It made her heart physically hurt to know he had probably blocked her, as without fail it went through to his answerphone. And even though she knew that would happen, she still did it. Purely so she could listen to his lovely well-spoken voice on his voicemail message and tell him every night that she loved him.

In his last message, a stilted one at Christmas, he simply said that he still loved her, but just couldn't be with her at the moment. That he needed time to think. How long did he bloody need to think? Rosa thought fiercely, then groaned aloud. How could she even be harsh on him in her thoughts? She was the one who had most likely slept with another man. All Josh had done was to try and make her life better by buying the café. A vision of Lucas came into her mind. Yes, he was handsome, yes, he was exciting, yes, she felt a spark with him – but she didn't love him. And if she was offered the chance to put things right and not have that night happen, she would pay a million pounds to do so. Josh and she were meant to be, she was sure of that.

She hadn't even thought twice about the café until then. Or even looked to see if the new sign had now been removed. That would just be too painful. Josh was sensible, he wouldn't chance his life savings, she didn't think. She was surprised that the Cockleberry Bay rumour mill hadn't reached Mary yet and let her know what was happening. There was no way she could ask Sara – that would be too mortifying. The poor woman hadn't done anything wrong at all. Was just helping to make the gift of the café a delicious Christmas surprise. And now she probably had to start all over again and find another buyer.

Rosa let Hot out on the balcony for a pee and went to the kitchen. Noticing a half-full bottle of wine open in the fridge she poured herself a glass, drank it down in one, then got herself a pint glass of water and made her way to the bedroom. She hadn't touched a drop of alcohol since her fall, but suddenly in her woe of missing Josh, self-medication seemed like the only answer.

Sighing loudly, she threw her dressing gown to the end of the bed, jumped in and pulled the covers up to her chin and then began to cry.

CHAPTER THIRTY SIX

Rosa woke to Hot whining to be let out. She picked him up and he started licking her face with smelly dog breath. Pleased that she had slept for a good eight hours, she opened the French doors to the balcony roof terrace and let him out. 'I'll take you down to the beach in a minute, darling,' she cooed, and waited until he had watered the usual plant pot and came running back in, bringing the feel of cold with him.

Ding! The shop door opening downstairs caused Rosa to smile at Titch's punctuality for a Saturday morning. How that girl had changed for the better since having little Theo.

'Making a bacon sarnie if you want one,' Rosa shouted down the stairs.

'No, thanks, Mum's packed me up some warm scones. Enough for two if you fancy one for your afters.'

Back from his beach walk and still full of boundless energy, Hot was now chasing a growling Jack Russell round the shop back yard. Keeping one eye on the shop and the browsing dog-owner, and one on the goings on outside, Titch and Rosa tucked into the homemade scones with butter and blackcurrant jam in the back kitchen.

'You OK to man the fort for a bit at eleven?' Rosa asked Titch. 'Mary wants to see me for a chat. She said to meet her by the café, but not in it, thank goodness.'

Licking her lips, Titch loaded more jam onto her second scone. 'Have you seen Sara since your massive row outside there?'

'No, I've made a point of keeping my head down, although it's hard to do that, as she's right on the beach.'

'I'm fine to look after the shop,' Titch mumbled through a huge mouthful of scone, 'but I do need to pick up Theo after lunch and bring him back here though. Mum's got an appointment this afternoon. Once I've fed him, he can sleep upstairs in the carry-cot for a while.'

'That's fine. If I'm not home by then, just put the *Back in 20 minutes* sign up. And thanks so much.'

Rosa was cleaning down the back kitchen when a very white-faced Titch came running in to her. 'Rosa, oh my God, you have to go out there. I can't. I just can't.'

'OK, OK.' Rosa wiped her hands on a tea towel and tentatively made her way out to the shop.

'Hello, Rosa,' the cleanshaven red-head greeted her.

'I didn't recognise you without your beard on,' Rosa replied, unsmiling.

'I bet you say that to all the boys,' the man creeped. 'How are you?'

'I'm OK.'

'And Titch and her new ankle-biter?'

'None of your business really, is it, Seb?'

'Not sure why the attitude, Rosa. I haven't done anything wrong in the eyes of the law now, have I?'

'You were lucky to get off and you know it. You ran that girl over.'

'And from what Sheila tells me, *you* ran her son out of

town,' Seb smirked, highlighting the wrinkles on his thin and weathered face, which so betrayed his thirty-something age tag.

Rosa felt sick at Sheila Hannafore spouting about her business. 'What do you want, anyway?'

'Nothing from you. Just wanted to check on the blonde pocket-rocket; that's all.'

'She's not here.'

'I thought you were better at lying than that, Rosa. Anyway, if ever she wants to chat, I'm back now. Living in one of the rooms at the Ship for a bit.'

'Back from where exactly?'

'I do have a passport, Rosa. Needed a little break, you know?' He tapped the side of his nose.

'Went away for the dust to settle; clever old you.'

'Sarcasm doesn't become you, love. I happen to know there is life outside of Cockleberry Bay. But Sheila needs some help now Lucas has gone and it's warmer working a bar than down at the station kiosk this time of year.' His tone changed. 'Now stop being stupid and fetch Titch for me.'

'She won't want to chat.'

'She has her own tongue, Rosa. Last time I looked she could make her own decisions too.'

'And her decision was no! Which you ignored, you...' Rosa was now red with anger.

Before she could say the word 'rapist', Seb Watkins turned, slithered out of the door and back down the hill.

'This is too much. I had hoped he would never come back to the Bay.' Titch appeared from the back kitchen, a smear of jam around her mouth. She looked as if she was about to be sick.

'I know, same here – but he has come back, and we need to deal with it. OK, so you told the police that he ran that girl over, but if he hadn't raped you, you wouldn't have done that, would you?' Rosa frowned. 'If Seb Watkins has any brains, he will let it lie. I reckon he just wants to test the water with you. Check he's totally in the clear. Although to my mind, I reckon he should be bloody castrated.'

'Rose, are you mad? I grassed him up.' Titch shuddered. 'He only got off because Sheila Hannafore bribed a magistrate. I reckon he's furious.'

'Maybe you should go to the police about what he did to you, then?'

'No way!' Titch shouted.

'All right, calm down.'

'There would be no proof or evidence now, anyway. It happened over a year ago. Even the van was crushed that it happened in to cover tracks of the hit-and-run. And to be fair, with my past reputation there wouldn't be many good character witnesses.'

Rosa cringed. 'It's all so wrong, but I do understand where you are coming from.'

'I don't want Theo knowing either, and if it went to court, he would eventually find out when he's older. I shall just have to keep out of Seb's way.'

'I daresay you're right, and even if he is angry, he won't dare do anything, as the police will have their eye on him. No smoke without fire and all that.'

Ding! An old lady appeared through the door, pulling a wheeled basket with a scruffy, blind miniature poodle snuggled up inside.

'Hello, Mrs Tregor,' Rosa shouted. 'I'll leave you with Titch today, as I'm popping out.'

'Ditch? Who's in the ditch, dear?'

Rosa winked at her friend, placed a treat under the little blind dog's woolly mouth, and went to fetch her hat and coat

CHAPTER THIRTY SEVEN

The Seven Lessons
One: Fear

After the couple of days of snow down in Cockleberry Bay, the weather had turned particularly mild for the time of year. Ever aware that the wind sometimes took on a mind of its own up on West Cliffs, Rosa pulled her blue bobble hat down over her ears and set off.

Now that her sling was off it had been easy to put a jacket on; better even than that was the fact that she at last felt pain-free. Titch had convinced her to leave a soundly sleeping Hot behind with her and Theo in the shop. It felt a little bit strange to be out and about without the dachshund at her side.

Reaching the edge of the beach, Rosa looked across to the café and then at the steep path that led up to West Cliffs. She dreaded bumping into Sara, so every beach walk had become a kind of stealth mission to avoid encountering either her or Sheila Hannafore.

Realising her mother was nowhere to be seen, she reached for her phone only to find a text from Mary saying sorry but the Co-op had literally called her in as she was setting off and asked if she could do a shift. With a sigh, Rosa was just putting her handset back in her pocket when she felt the presence of somebody close behind her.

'Rosa? Rosa Smith, isn't it?' It was a tall, bald man in his early fifties who was addressing her.

Rosa spun around. 'Er…yes, who wants to know?'

'I'm Darren, Darren Pitt. Remember me? I'm a crew member for the Polhampton RNLI, and we met a couple of weeks ago. Not in such great circumstances, if you recall.'

Rosa wanted to thank him for saving her life and Hot's and for putting himself in danger to do so, but all that came out was: 'Well, this is embarrassing. I…er…' The vision of herself being sick and then weeing all over the boat would forever haunt her.

Darren gently put his hand on her shoulder. 'Rosa, life throws us some bloody curved balls sometimes.'

'And some bloody round ones too,' she quipped, cheering up. 'And look where that got me!'

The lifeboat man laughed loudly. 'And there was me, trying to be serious then. But joking aside, I just saw you as a human being in front of me who needed help. No need to be embarrassed, honestly. It's all part of the job.'

'You really are being a bit too kind here, Darren. I mean, if you brought a pizza and chips up all over me, well…'

He stopped her, asking, 'How are you and the brave little doggie, anyway?'

'I'm much better than I was, thank you. And Hot Dog is in the pink, thanks to you and the crew.'

'That's good to hear.' The bald man's face lit up with a smile. 'Where are you off to on this fine day?'

'My mum was supposed to meet me, but she's just let me know that she can't make it. Hot was lying doggo at home and it's easier to chat without him being the centre of attention.'

'True. Dachshunds are little dogs with great big attitudes, eh?'

Rosa laughed. 'You've got it. And yes, it's such a lovely day that I think I will have a walk anyway.'

'Up the cliff?' Darren pointed to the start of the cliff path.

A feeling of panic suddenly descended on Rosa. She felt herself go pale. 'Er…maybe not today. I'm stupidly feeling a bit scared, as it's the first time I've been near here since my accident.'

'Well, that's totally and absolutely understandable. Here, take my arm and we can walk together, if you like. It's good for me to look down from the top and see where we can pull in with the boat, et cetera, especially whilst it's such a lovely calm day.'

'But didn't you just come down from there?'

Darren ignored her comment, saying instead, 'Your accident made me realise that I don't know every nook and cranny of this coastline yet, so let's just say we are doing each other a favour, eh?'

Rosa linked arms with her rescuer. As the path got narrower and the drop deeper, she started to breathe a little faster. 'I don't think I can go any further,' she managed to say, and grabbed Darren's arm tighter.

'The fears we don't face become our limits, Rosa, and how sad would it be not to be able to go to the top of these beautiful cliffs again? You told me yourself you were a bit drunk that day, yes?'

'Yes,' she admitted quietly, still holding on and not looking out to sea.

'I doubt very much if you will be drunk alone on a snowy afternoon up here again; in fact, I could put a bet on it.'

'Yes. It wasn't my finest hour, that one.'

Darren continued, 'And being brave isn't the absence of fear, anyway. Being brave is having that fear and finding a way through it. Come on, trust me.'

Rosa took a deep breath and carried on. The gulls circling overhead cried out as if willing her to put one foot in front of the other to get her to reach her goal.

'All right?' Darren could feel her grip loosening slightly. He carried on talking as Rosa lengthened her stride. 'Even now when we are out on a tricky shout in the lifeboat, I still see fear in the lads' eyes; it's human nature, isn't it, but I say there's no point letting your fear of what might happen let nothing happen. We have a job to do out there.'

'You are all so brave and I am *so* grateful to you.' Rosa felt tears pricking her eyes. Darren was such a decent man; she could feel his heart through his words.

'Brave? Not sure about that. Probably stupid, more like. I quote this poem to the crew too. It's called "The Reality of Fear".' The lifeboat man cleared his throat and addressed the horizon.

'You are not scared of heights – you are scared of falling.
You are not scared of the dark – you are scared of what's in it.
You are not scared of the sea – you are scared of drowning.'

His voice softened. 'I don't always quote this last line…'

'Go on.' Rosa urged.

'You are not afraid to love – you are afraid of being loved back.'

Darren stopped, moved away from Rosa and carried on looking out to the expanse of ocean below them. The sea was perfectly calm, aside a few small breaking waves on the rocks below.

'Life is for living, Rosa. For feeling the fear – and I know already that you are wiser and stronger for what happened to you. Just look at that horizon.'

'Where the sky touches the sea,' Rosa murmured, taking in the expansive horizon in front of her.

'What was that?'

'Oh, just something my great-grandparents used to say.'

Rosa then stepped nearer the edge. 'Just hold my arm a sec again, Darren.' The big man held her tightly as she tentatively looked down. She noticed a small piece of rock sticking out of the main cliff. 'Was that the ledge we landed on?' She clung to Darren, open-mouthed. 'It's tiny.'

'Yep. You were a very lucky young lady. As was that little pooch of yours. He could so easily have slipped.'

'We were lucky, weren't we? It was obviously not our time to go.'

'To where the sky touches the sea, you mean?'

Rosa smiled. 'Exactly that. Thanks so much, Darren. One for saving my life, and two for this. I couldn't have done it on my own today.'

'I know you couldn't have.' Darren's voice was soft again. It then lifted, became brisk. 'Anyway, I need to get a move on. I'm interviewing for a new recruit in half an hour. Our second lady for the crew, hopefully. Shall we go down?'

'No, you go. I will be fine. Fear of what might happen will let nothing happen, and all that.' She laughed.

'There's a girl,' Darren smiled. 'And it was good to meet you...' he paused, '...on your way up, Rosa.'

When he'd disappeared down the cliff path, Rosa moved away from the edge, perched herself on a rock and thought back to Darren's poem recital.

Maybe that was it? That she was afraid of being loved back.

CHAPTER THIRTY EIGHT

Rosa rested against her mother's soft but undeniably wheezing chest.

'I don't know what to do without him,' she sobbed.

'Well, on a positive, Rosa, Kahlil says love knows not its own depth until the hour of separation. What he means is, at least you know you love him.'

'I've never doubted that. I want him home, now.' Rosa castigated herself: 'And if I love him so much, why did I even think about going off with Lucas?'

'Because unlike the eyes that see and the ears that hear, the heart pretty much has its own agenda. We are all different, duck. And even when our head tries to tell our heart what to do, it ain't listening, sunshine. That heart of ours has two fundamental goals, one to keep beating and the other to keep loving, the best way it can.'

Mary went to the cupboard and got some crunchies down for Merlin, who was nowhere in sight.

'I don't think it was my heart and certainly not my head that was veering towards Luke, that night.'

'Oh, pet. You were at a low – and the demon drink was involved. True love means you are joined by an invisible cord.

Even if Josh is in Timbuktu right now, you are still together. He will be feeling it as much as you. Right here.' She put her hand on her tummy. 'Give him some time. He will come back, Rosa, he will.'

'Have you heard from him?'

Just then, Merlin screeched in at a hundred miles an hour through the cat flap with a mouse jiggling about in his mouth. Mary quickly opened the back door and shooed him back through it with a mop. Slamming the door shut and locking the cat flap, she then reached into her apron pocket, pulled out her inhaler and took a big puff.

'Well, Mum, have you heard from Josh? You didn't answer.'

'Right, lunch-hour over, a quick wee and then I must get back to work.'

And with that, a slightly breathless Mary made her way to the bathroom, leaving her daughter staring after her, slowly shaking her head.

CHAPTER THIRTY NINE

Upstairs in the lounge at the Corner Shop, Hot woke from a horrible dream in which the Siamese cat from down the street was chasing him… He opened his eyes and instantly smelt smoke. Hot had always known that his sense of smell was far superior to any human's. His nostrils were highly sensitive scientific instruments. Whiffling hard to detect the source of the smell, he coughed and sneezed, flapped his ears wildly about to wake himself fully, then sat up when he heard a cry which he recognised. Trotting to the sofa cushions which were always put across the doorway, to create a barrier and stop him from getting through to the bedroom when Theo was put down to sleep in there, he dug his long snout beneath them and pretended he was digging into a badger's sett, growling with the effort.

Fierce and determined, the little dog finally broke through and trotted out onto the landing, where a pungent black smoke was drifting towards Rosa's open bedroom door. Seeing the carry-cot lying on the floor by the big bed, with Theo crying and thrashing around inside it, the small dog climbed inside, nudged the baby over to give himself room and dug around with his long snout until he had managed to lift the lacy blanket over both their heads, to keep out the smoke and create a pocket of air. Then, while the baby quietened and went back to sleep, comforted by his doggie warmth, and with a tiny arm flung over Hot's shiny brown coat, the dachshund tried to stay awake to guard his human. However, exhausted from his morning run on the beach, he too fell asleep, one fat brown paw resting on Theo's cosy Babygro.

The scene in Rosa's bedroom was one of total peace, neither dog nor baby stirring as the smoke spread and thickened, and toxic fumes filled the air.

Rosa opened the door from her mother's cottage on to the street, only to smell smoke. When she looked down the hill, her heart almost stopped as the smoke appeared to be coming from the back of the shop. She started to race off towards the Corner Shop as an out-of-breath Jacob caught up with her.

'Didn't Titch call you?' he panted. Rosa felt for her phone and couldn't find it; she must have left it in the flat. 'There's a fire at the shop. The fire brigade are on their way.'

'Oh my God, Titch, Hot and Theo are in there.' Rosa then heard screams, and realised they were coming from her friend.

Ritchie came out of the chippie, and as soon as he heard Titch's distress he started running too.

The young mum was standing at the front of the shop, coughing. 'I tried to get up the stairs, but the smoke is so bad,' she told them frantically. 'Theo's up there. I put him up in your bedroom for a nap, Rosa, but I can't see or breathe enough to get through . . .' She started sobbing and pulling at her hair.

Rosa panicked. 'Where's Hot?'

'Yes, he's upstairs too, in the lounge.'

Ritchie took off his top and put it around his face. 'Just one flight, yeah? Which room?'

'Yes, and turn first right for the bedroom.' He set off and Rosa shouted, 'I'm coming too.'

Jacob put his arm out to stop her. 'No, stay here.' He ran to the back of the shop with the fire extinguisher he had grabbed from the pub kitchen.

At that moment the fire engine arrived, blocking the narrow road; two of the firemen already had breathing sets on. 'How many unaccounted for?'

'A baby, a dog – and a man's just gone in to rescue them. Quick. Please be quick.' Rosa was now trying to restrain a hysterical Titch, who wanted to get back inside and up the stairs again.

The two other firemen ran out their hose and pushed their way through to the kitchen.

In what seemed like hours, but was probably only a matter of minutes, a spluttering Ritchie emerged with a screaming Theo, wrapped in a reeking white blanket.

Both Titch and Rosa were crying. 'He's screaming, Titch, he's screaming, that's good,' Rosa said feverishly. 'He's alive! But where's Hot? Where's my darling boy?'

An ambulance had now arrived on the scene and immediately took Theo and Ritchie on board to see how they were doing. Titch went with them.

And then, as if all the prayers she would ever say in her whole life had been answered, there in the doorway, with Hot clinging precariously to her shoulder, was her mother, choking through the smoke. Rosa ran over and hugged them both, leading them away and into the fresher air, then she took Hot from Mary. The little dog was quivering feverishly, his heart racing. 'Mum! How? When? Oh, never mind that. Quick – let me get you to the ambulance.'

Mary spluttered. 'He had somehow managed to get in the

carry-cot with Theo and had made a tent to keep out the fumes. He was licking the baby's face as if to keep his nose clear. It was the sweetest sight. I reckon that Hot may have saved Theo's life.'

'Oh, Mum!' Rosa said hoarsely, tears pouring down her face and onto Hot. 'I can't believe you did that. I didn't even see you come past us.'

'I told you the other night, I could smell burning.' And that was when the strength in Mary seemed to dwindle before her daughter's eyes and she had a bout of coughing that nearly brought her to her knees.

Cuddling Hot as if she would never let him go, Rosa helped her mother over to the beckoning paramedic, who immediately put an oxygen mask on the distressed woman.

'You should never have gone in there with your condition,' Rosa wailed. Then she reached out with her free hand and held tight to her mother's.

Mary Cobb locked her beautiful green eyes onto those of her daughter and managed to gasp, 'You saved my life years ago, duck.'

Rosa leaned forward and kissed Mary's forehead. 'I love you, Mum.'

A lone tear furrowed its way down the woman's face. Shakily pulling the mask away from her nose and mouth, she said, 'I have never stopped loving you, Rosa.'

Even the paramedic appeared affected by the emotional scene as he had to clear his throat before gently replacing Mary's mask and beginning to take her blood pressure.

Rosa pushed her nose into Hot's smoky-smelling coat. 'And we'd best go and ask Vicki to check you out too,' she mumbled into his side. 'My best boy, my hero, Mr Sausage.'

She laughed and cried at the same time as his tongue came out and started to slap at her face, to lick the tears away.

A black-faced Jacob also appeared. 'The fire's out and thank goodness it isn't as bad as you might think. I reckon it was all the smoke that made it seem a lot worse.'

One of the firemen overheard him and said, 'But if it had happened in the middle of the night, fella, then it would have been a very different story.'

Rosa handed Hot to Jacob. 'Sorry, my arm's too sore to hold him any longer and bless you, just look at you.' She stroked Hot's silken head gently, looked into his brown eyes and then said to her friend, 'And you, my other hero, will need a once-over in the ambulance too.'

Jacob shrugged. 'Oh, I'm fine,' he said, recovering some of his usual swagger. 'I was more concerned about ruining my Armani jacket, darling.'

CHAPTER FORTY

The Seven Lessons
Two: Self-esteem

It was late on Sunday morning, and Rosa was clearing up in the back kitchen when the shop bell rang. Feeling a bit miffed at being disturbed, she came out holding a cloth and then saw a familiar figure waiting outside.

'Hi, Raff,' she said, unbolting the door. 'Come on in. Is everything OK?' It was so unlike him to come to the shop – without Jacob anyway. 'Aw, love her.' She noticed the Duchess peeking out from his coat.

'Yes, I've just finished my lunchtime shift and Jacob has taken the boys to the vet's. Neither of us can bear putting their flea stuff on as they hate us when we do it and play up for at least a week afterwards.'

'He's gone to the vet on a Sunday? I thought they were usually closed then.'

'Well, this vet is called Vicki and Jacob is a friend of hers. They're going to have a late lunch together. Brad and Alyson are working the pub tonight so I said I will meet him later at home.'

Rosa remembered now. 'That's right – Jacob told me that Vicki Cliss is the only vet in Devon who can touch Pongo and Ugly without them having a hissy fit. I must make an appointment with her soon, as she said she wanted to see Hot again after the fire to double-check on his lungs. I still can't believe how he climbed inside that carry-cot to shelter Theo.'

'He's a plucky fella – like his mum, that's why.'

'Or just plain stupid, maybe. I've already told him he could have ended up a proper Hot Dog.'

At that point, the Duchess made a little whining noise and Raff made a fuss of her, saying, 'I was just popping out to get some fresh air with this one and was wondering if you and Hot might want to meet me at the South Cliffs path when you're done. It's a beautiful day.'

'Sounds like a fantastic idea.'

'How's the kitchen coming on after the fire?'

Rosa beckoned him out to the back. 'Come and see. Mary, Titch and I have scrubbed away at it for hours, and we've left a bowl of vinegar and a bowl of ground coffee in all the affected rooms. Mum's idea, of course, but it seems to have done the trick to get rid of the smoke smell. Also, every time it's not too cold I leave all the windows open. Thank goodness the weather should get warmer soon.'

'*Mia cara ragazza*. My darling girl.' The handsome young Italian grabbed her and kissed her with force on the forehead, nearly squashing the Duchess, who squeaked. Raff flailed his arms about dramatically. 'This is not fair.'

'I know. But sometimes life isn't. And anyway, I've put in an insurance claim, so we'll have to wait and see. I just wish I knew how it had started.' *And I wish that Josh had been here too,* were her unspoken words. 'Right, let's get out of here. Walk time, mister.' At the W word an excitable Hot impatiently stayed still to have his lead put on and then trotted jauntily to the door, his every movement watched closely by the little Duchess.

On reaching the beach, Rosa breathed in the invigorating sea air and lifted her face to the winter sun. 'I can't wait to go up this path. It's crazy that I've been here over a year and never been up this side of the bay.'

'It is less of a slope for the Duchess and there is more grass to run around on, so she loves it up there.'

They headed towards the South Cliffs path. 'Going back to the kitchen, do the police think that somebody started it deliberately?' Raffaele asked.

'Not necessarily. There were investigators crawling all over the place afterwards, as it did look like something could have been thrown in the bin which caused it to catch fire. The smoke was dense as the actual plastic bin was burning. Nothing else caught alight. Thank goodness.'

'So, it wasn't Titch having a mad cooking moment?'

'She tells me not, anyway.' Rosa laughed.

'Scary though, especially with Theo, Titch and Hot in there.'

'I know. The police are going to come to me once a full investigation report has been written. Seb is the only person I can think of who would even consider doing such an awful thing.'

'No, I don't think even he would be that stupid as to commit arson, would he? Not after just getting off with the hit-and-run?'

'That is very true, Inspector Clouseau.'

'*Dio mio!* Not a Frenchman, *per favore*. Inspector Montalbano, maybe.'

'I'm trying not to think that someone may hate me so much that they might try to burn down the Corner Shop. In a bittersweet way though, Raff, missing Josh overrides most of my other thoughts.'

Her friend was sympathetic. 'Rosa, how are you coping with your man not being here?'

'I go through phases. Today I feel angry.' Rosa's voice lifted. 'Really angry, but that's ridiculous as I don't want him to know about the fire. I don't want him back because he's sorry for me or thinks I can't cope. But why, oh why, is he being such a stubborn bastard?'

'You are both being the stubborn bastards, I think. And why so angry?'

'I want his support; he would help me.'

Raff shook his head. 'But you just said you didn't want his pity. Rosa, I don't understand you.'

'I don't understand myself.' She breathed deeply. 'Part of me wants his big arms around me. To tell me that everything is going to be all right.'

'But it might not be.'

'Ever the bloody realist, you.'

'The reality is, we don't ever know if anything is going to be all right – the patient with cancer, the mum who's due to give birth, a woman slipping on a cliff path – so saying the words "everything is going to be all right" is quite often futile.' He shrugged. 'Of course, more often than not, it *will* be all right, but it might not be. Do you see what I am saying?'

'I don't know.' Rosa's brain was now whirring.

'Is my English good enough?'

Rosa tutted. 'It's nigh on perfect, silly.'

'And if we can get *ourselves* strong enough to process these thoughts, we don't need a Josh to put his arms around us. You can put your arms around yourself and support just you…and of course each other when you need to. It's a two-way street, this relationship thing, Rosa.'

'I'm so tired of having to manage things myself.'

193

'So, if you don't want Josh because he's sorry for you, how do you want him?'

'I want him to tell me how much he loves me, that he forgives me for whatever I did with Lucas.' She paused. 'Which still bothers me so much, because I can't remember.'

The Duchess and Hot were now scurrying around, play-fighting and chasing each other amongst the bushes and boulders which created a safe boundary from the beach far below.

'Why don't you call him then?'

'Because part of me is too scared to know the truth.' Rosa groaned. 'I know, let's change the subject. Guess what, Raff? The other day I bumped into the lifeboat man who saved us.'

'Ooh, was he big and hunky?'

Rosa smiled. 'What are you like? He recited a poem to me about not being afraid to love, but afraid of being loved back.' She felt tears starting to run down her face. 'I was so scared that Josh would leave me, that I wasn't good enough for him – and he has left me. But it was as if I…' Rosa's voice began to crack.

Raff took her hand. 'Take your time,' he said gently.

'It was if I wanted…' She blubbered. 'As if I wanted to ruin it and I don't know why. Why would I even consider sleeping with Luke? But then again, I thought Josh was cheating on me.'

'But he wasn't, was he?'

'I know that now,' Rosa wailed.

'So, *are* you afraid of being loved back?'

'Oh, I don't know. But what I do know is I can't bear the thought of him leaving me for good.'

'Like your mother left you, you mean?'

Rosa put her hand to her forehead. 'Raff, this is heavy shit. I hadn't even thought of that.'

'We need to smell that shit sometimes. Have it smeared right in our faces to make us understand why we act the way we do. Rosa, you've never really talked to me in depth before.'

'I'm sorry.'

'Don't apologise; we are all guilty of it.' The handsome Italian checked his watch. 'We had better go back down; it's sunny now, but will be dark before we know it. I can't believe I'm saying it, but I love this weather. Crisp and sunny.' He laughed. 'It's not quite the same as my natal Roma, but this place can still be as warm in the summer.'

'I just love living in Cockleberry Bay,' Rosa said wistfully. 'I feel as if I belong somewhere for the first time in my life.' She sighed. 'Raff, tell me that Josh will come back.'

'As I said earlier, I can't do that. I do think to get the best out of people you should love them without an agenda. And Josh loves you without an agenda and I know that for a fact.'

'What, with my nasty temper and vileness when I'm drunk?'

'We are a sum of many parts, Rosa. You just need to boost that self-esteem of yours and realise how great you are.'

'He could have anyone he wanted,' she said moodily.

'Could he? Really? And even if he could, he chooses you. He has given up a lot to be with you. Yes, he works away in the week, but he loved you so much, he changed his whole life and followed you down here. He married you, for goodness sake!'

'That's what I'm worried about as well. What if he gets bored?'

'What if *you* get bored?' Raff challenged her. 'Just start living your life, Rosa, and stop worrying. Start believing you are amazing.' He put his arm on Rosa's good shoulder. 'I'm going to tell you a little secret,' he said.

The waves in the bay below rose and fell, and seagulls screamed their Sunday lament as the afternoon wore on and the sun began its orange and red descent. Rosa pulled her coat in tighter around her. 'Go on.'

'I am adopted. I was just a baby when I was introduced to my adoptive parents – the most beautiful couple you could wish to meet. I never met my real mama or papa. I don't feel I want to either.'

'Wow. You never said.'

'It doesn't define me, that's why. Don't get me wrong – I have my insecurities. There's nothing like knowing that the woman who gave birth to you doesn't actually want you, eh?' Rosa nodded as he carried on.

'I came over here to make a living, and when I met Jacob, he was older, so cool, so wise, so good-looking. And I was still just a boy really, in my early twenties, a bit like you, Rosa. I wondered why on earth he wanted me – the young, unsophisticated Italian chef. Was it just because I was young and handsome? I mean, look at me, I am pretty gorgeous,' he added to amuse Rosa. 'Maybe, of course, at first it was the passion which kept us together, but it soon became clear that he loved *me*, the whole sum of me. He admires my work ethic and cooking skills. I admire his passion to succeed, and as you know, Rosa, he is the kindest man. We are a true partnership. Equal. He believed in me and my capabilities from the start. At first, I wanted him to tell me how much he cared for me, how good a job I was doing… all the time. But eventually I came to accept that it's actions that count and which define us, not words or our backgrounds. He truly respects me. I'm very lucky.'

'You both are lucky to have each other.' Rosa was so moved. She was so lucky too, to have Jacob and Raffaele in her life.

'Yes, we are. We work well together, we play well together and most importantly, we love well together.'

Rosa had tears falling down her cheeks; she hugged him gently, murmuring, 'Thank you so much, Raff. I needed to hear that.'

'I know you did. It's easy to say and hard to do, I know, but if you love yourself, then everything and everyone just seems to slot into place. And when life does throw up its inevitable challenges, you're ready and strong enough to handle them. By yourself, if need be.'

'Thank you, Raff.' Rosa gave him a watery smile. 'Thank you so much.'

Suddenly there was a commotion in front of them. The Duchess was squealing as an excitable Hot had chosen to jump on top of the tiny bitch and get just a little too up close and personal for comfort.

'Talking of respect . . .' Rosa ran towards them. 'Oi, Hot! Get off her this minute.'

CHAPTER FORTY ONE

Titch was wandering down the hill, singing to herself, when Ritchie appeared out of the chip shop, cloth and stepladder in hand, ready to clean the front window. On seeing the pretty blonde his thin face lit up and his arms took on a life of their own; he nearly dropped the ladder on her feet.

'Hey, Ritchie. I've been meaning to call you.'

'You have?'

Was Titch imagining it, or was he blushing? 'Yes,' she said. 'You saving Theo from the fire, it was just the most amazing thing, and on the day, I was so stressed with it, I didn't thank you enough.'

'It was nothing.'

'It was everything.'

'Actually, Titch, I was wondering if I maybe could take you out for dinner. Next Thursday. The Anchor Inn in Polhampton is really nice, I hear.'

Titch's face went into a wide smile. 'Are you asking me on a date, Ritchie Rogers? And outside of the Bay too? Wow. I do feel honoured.' She took in Ritchie's long face, messy curly hair and gangly body. He might not be the best-looking man hereabouts, but he certainly was one of the kindest. And he had just saved her son from a burning fire. 'Let me see if I can get a babysitter. I'll call you, OK?'

'OK.' Ritchie's grin belied his attempt at being cool. 'Right, better clean this window before the old dear starts creating. How is Theo, by the way?'

'Fortunately, he's got humungous lungs like his mother's.' Titch winked. 'One cough and he was all clear.'

'Shame that doesn't apply to me.' Mary caught the edge of the conversation, taking a big glug of Ventolin inhaler and turning bright red as she tried to hold her breath for a count of ten.

'Oh, poor you.' Titch put a hand on Mary's arm while Ritchie nodded politely then turned to get on with the task in hand so the two women could talk in peace.

'Yes,' Mary wheezed, 'that ruddy smoke didn't help at all.' She banged her chest and coughed.

'You shouldn't have rushed in like that.'

'Hot is family too, Titch, and Rosa would have been destroyed without him.'

Titch hugged the older woman. 'Well, look after yourself now, Mary.'

'Oh me, I'm fine, duck. You heading down to the Corner Shop now?'

'Yep.'

'Can you tell Rosa that Jacob said Vicki the vet is dropping by to see him later and she's happy to do Hot's check-up at the flat, so they don't have to travel to Polhampton to see her.'

'Oh, that's great. I'll get her to call Jacob, yeah?'

'Please. Have a good day.'

'You too, Mary.'

Rosa was running around the shop with a feather duster on a long stick when Titch arrived. The radio was blaring.

'I love a bit of spring-cleaning,' Rosa said, humming along to the music.

'But it's not spring yet, it's still only February,' Titch said. Then, the truth dawning, she muttered, 'Oh shit!'

'What's the matter?' Rosa turned the radio off and stopped what she was doing.

'What date is it next Thursday?'

'The fourteenth – Valentine's Day. Why?' Rosa noticed her friend's pained expression.

'Ritchie asked if I wanted to go out for dinner. I didn't realise it was Valentine's Day.'

'Yep, and it marks a year since the grand opening of the shop. I had better think of some sort of raffle or special offer to celebrate.'

'Blimey, where has the year gone? That only seems like yesterday.'

'I know. It's been quite a year. I've moved from London, I've got married, I've opened a shop, I've fallen down a cliff, potentially slept with someone else out of wedlock and now am probably getting divorced.'

'Don't say that, Rose.'

'Anyway, it was sweet of Ritchie to ask you. I do like him.'

'I like him too, but we've always just been mates.'

'You should go. Just please don't tell me he's taking you to the Ship Inn for chicken and chips.'

'No, the Anchor Inn at the Sands, actually.'

'Wow, I went there with Joe the unmentionable and it's lovely. And do you know what, nothing has to happen romantically. Just go and have a nice time.'

'I need to ask Mum to babysit first.'

'I bet he hasn't asked *his* mum if he can take you out, you unmarried-mother harlot.' They both laughed. 'If your mum

200

can't do it, I will. It's not like I'll be doing anything myself, is it?'

'You never know. Josh might turn up on a white charger and say all is forgiven.'

'I doubt it.' Rosa's smile vanished.

'You still leaving him a message every night?'

'Yep, every night.'

'I also meant to ask if you'd heard from Lucas at all.'

Rosa sighed. 'OK, I have a confession. I tried to call him after a glass of wine the other night. You see, I finally felt I was ready to find out and cope with what happened, and to ask him why he had left Cockleberry Bay so suddenly.'

'And?' Titch was wide-eyed. 'What did he say?'

'His number is unobtainable. Must have changed it or his phone supplier.'

'Unless he's blocked you.'

'Oh, I didn't think of that. Charming! My husband and him both not wanting any contact. That's just great – not!' Just then, her phone rang. 'Jacob, hi. No, I haven't seen her today yet. OK. Yes, that's fine, Titch is here, yes. That's so kind of her. Thanks, and I may pop up for a drink later. What time? I hadn't even thought about it, six-ish maybe. OK, see you later.'

'Oops, sorry, was that about the vet? Your mum told me to tell you to call Jacob. She's still not right after the fire with her chest, you know.'

'I know, it's such a worry, but she's got a good doctor looking after her now. I don't know what else we can do. It's not like we can even send her somewhere by the sea to convalesce, like they used to do in the old days.'

Rosa's phone rang. 'Hi there, it's Vicki Cliss, Supervet and friend of Jacob here.' She laughed lightly. 'I was going to check on Hot today, but an emergency rang in and I'm on my way back to the surgery. Sorry to be a pain.'

'Don't worry at all. It was above and beyond what I expected anyway. Don't worry about us.'

'Can you meet me on Polhampton Sands one day this week, maybe? We can look at Hot then. Any excuse for me to walk on the beach.'

'Wednesday morning would be good for me.'

'Great, great – I will text you a time once I'm back home.'

Ding! The shop bell caused Hot to tear out from the back kitchen, barking. It was the detective who had interviewed Rosa straight after the fire.

'Have you got a minute, Mrs Smith?'

She glanced at Titch, who nodded immediately, saying, 'It's fine, I'll be here.'

'Yes, of course. DC Clarke, isn't it?'

'Well remembered. Look, Mrs Smith, I have some news – is there somewhere private we can go?'

CHAPTER FORTY TWO

'Did you put two sugars in it?'

'Yes, I remembered this time. Anything else for you?'

'No thanks, Katie. And can you shut the door behind you, please?'

Josh let out a big sigh and reached for his mobile from the large desk in front of him. If the worst his new assistant did was get his coffee order wrong, then he would be pleased. The screensaver of Rosa and Hot always made him smile. Katie was twenty and very pretty. How Rosa would hate it if she knew about her. Her insecurities wouldn't be able to take it.

It was such a shame that she wouldn't commit to seeing Alec, as Josh was sure that it would have helped her greatly, especially on the low self-esteem front. It pained him that she was so broken sometimes but her will was strong and her heart and mind would be open to getting better soon, he hoped. If only she would accept that he literally didn't have eyes for anyone else. He had fallen under the Rosa Larkin spell, the minute he had met her. She had a way of making you fall in love with her. Was it her energy? Her integrity? Her generous heart? For one who had had to be streetwise growing up, she was also quite naïve, where men were concerned, anyway. Maybe that was what love was. A combination of every little bit of that person.

Josh was so pleased when Mary told him that Lucas had left the Bay. Surprisingly, she had not been able to find out why, but Josh didn't need to know that really. All he cared about was that the dodgy Londoner was away from his wife. Josh kept wondering if it would make him feel better if he did know the full story of the night Rosa had spent with Lucas. What if she and Lucas had had sex – how would he feel? He grimaced. But knowing Rosa so well, he could imagine how hurt she must have been, thinking that he and Sara were having an affair. Her upside-down emotions, aided and abetted by alcohol, had led her to think that revenge by infidelity was what he so richly deserved.

However, even with those mitigating circumstances, Josh wasn't sure he could ever forgive her if she had been unfaithful. She was his girl. He also wanted someone who could trust him, as he should rightly be trusted. It was difficult and frustrating, Rosa being so bloody jealous.

If only love was less complicated, then maybe it would be less powerful. But if it was less powerful, none of us would keep falling into it. Those warning red flags would be waving, and we would all say, 'Thanks for letting me know, red flags. I am not going to jump into this flawed and complicated relationship and waste years of my life.'

How far removed was he from the glorious setting of Cockleberry Bay, sitting here in his plush office in the City. Would he miss it when he left? Definitely not the stress and difficulties a frenetic trading environment brought, that was for sure. He took a small sip of hot coffee in anticipation of listening to his messages. It was so bittersweet hearing Rosa's desperate and sometimes very funny messages every day, but he had to see this through. Missing Rosa gave him a pain in his stomach, and he had given up his customary beer after work with the boys on a Wednesday and had started running instead. Anything to distract his mind and body from the perpetual nagging grief of her absence.

He could have cried as he listened to Rosa's message from the night before. She was trying to sound upbeat but he could tell she was hurting.

'Hello, husband. Guess who. Me, me, me, me.' Hot barked in the background. 'Oh, and him too.' Josh bit his lip. 'You'd better be listening to these messages, or they sure are a waste of my breath.'

'I'm listening, chick,' Josh said softly as his wife carried on her one-sided conversation.

'So, SURPRISE…I miss you. Hot misses you. Lots. I'm more than sorry for what I might have done. OK. I will say that every night until I see you again. And if you are listening, I'm sure that you do smile sometimes when I talk to you like this.'

Was he being mean, doing this to her? No, he had to do it, for both their sakes. Make sure the time was right. 'Yes,' he said aloud, then gulped some more coffee down. That was it. Her birthday would be perfect to get everything settled this end and in the Bay. He would work towards that. It was bad enough he was missing Valentine's Day and the anniversary of the shop opening. He vowed that he wouldn't miss her birthday, not ever – from now on. Rosa might hate Christmas, but she always loved her birthday.

He yawned and dialled a number. 'Alec, it's Josh. How's it all going?'

CHAPTER FORTY THREE

'A cigarette, you say?' Rosa stared at the detective who had taken a seat on the sofa next to her and was now devouring his fifth shortbread biscuit, baked at home by Mary, to one of Queenie's old-fashioned recipes. 'But no one here smokes. I don't understand.'

'There's not much *to* understand. It's quite straightforward. The fire was started by somebody putting a smouldering cigarette in your bin in the back kitchen of your shop.' He wiped crumbs from his neatly trimmed beard. 'Your employee is Patricia Whittaker, known as Titch – that's right, isn't it? You said she doesn't smoke. So, could it have been a customer out the back maybe?'

'No, I don't let anyone go through the back from the shop side uninvited, but delivery drivers come through that way sometimes.'

'Ah, OK. Did you have a delivery that day?'

'I can't remember, I will need to check my records. Do you want me to look now?'

'Yes, yes, please do.'

Rosa went to her desk in the spare bedroom, fetched her laptop and fired it up.

'Do you have any deliveries directly from abroad?'

'Not usually. Why?'

'We found a butt and an empty cigarette packet just inside your back gate, a foreign brand. Unfortunately, both ended up in a puddle so there was simply no way to retrieve any sort of DNA.' The detective showed Rosa an image of a red and white branded cigarette packet.

'Some of the guys who deliver are not English, but to be fair, that doesn't mean they smoke foreign cigarettes. Ah yes, we did have a delivery that morning,' Rosa said, peering at her laptop. 'It was from Hastings, my pet-food supplier. They are based in London. I guess that answers why the back gate wasn't locked after they'd left, which meant that someone could get in. Titch does have a habit of forgetting, especially if we're busy.'

'Do you trust your employee?'

'Detective Clarke, what sort of question is that? Of course, I trust her! And remember, her baby was sleeping upstairs when the fire started.'

The bearded man tapped a chewed pen on his phone case. 'Good, good. Anyone you've had a disagreement with recently?'

'Only my husband,' Rosa said with a sigh. 'Seb Watkins is back in the Bay now though.'

DC Clarke remained silent for a second, then looked up as if in thought. 'With a pretty strong alibi.'

'Was he with Sheila Hannafore, by chance?'

'I'm not at liberty to say, Mrs Smith, not whilst we are still mid-inquiry. But I will need to contact Hastings – have you got a number handy, please? It could be as simple as a delivery driver putting his stray fag in the bin on his way out without checking it was properly extinguished. Because you don't smoke, there wouldn't have been an ashtray in the kitchen – that's one thought. Yes, it could have been a simple accident.'

'Let's hope so, eh? I could do with getting it all sorted with the insurance people, although I know these things take time.'

'You're a very sensible young lady. Thank you for your time and for the biscuits, they went down a treat. I'll be in touch as soon as I can. It's always nice to get a case closed.'

Rosa showed him out via the balcony stairs and down to the back gate so he could retrace the steps of somebody coming through the back kitchen. She then went through into the shop.

'What did he have to say?' Titch was sat on the counter stool, looking at her phone.

'That Seb has a strong alibi.'

'Yeah, right. Of course, he does. Didn't Jacob tell you that he thought Old Ma Hannafore was guilty of setting his stockroom alight too, back in the day?'

'That's right. I was trying to think of motives, and there are a few. If Seb knew you were here alone, setting off a fire would have really shaken you up or worse! And Lucas going back to London really did piss his mother off, plus we did try and frame them for the hit-and-run.' Rosa let out a big sigh. 'Anyway, I can't hurt my brain thinking about it any more.' Josh had been on at her about upping security for ages, despite her claim that surely nobody would be interested in nicking dog biscuits or shell bracelets.

'The CCTV company are coming tomorrow to install one at the rear, so the back yard will be fully covered, and we just need to make sure to put the alarm on whenever we go out,' Rosa told Titch. 'Plus, please remember to lock the back gate straight after a delivery.'

'I will, I promise. I realise I've been bad at that. Right, I'd better get going.' Titch got her handbag from under the counter. 'What you up to tonight? Anything?'

Rosa blew out a loud breath. 'I dunno, the usual, leave a

message for Josh, drink some wine, cry about Josh, drink some more wine, watch a bit of TV then go to bed. I've made a decision. If he's not back here by my birthday, then I'm going to London to have it out with him.'

'But that's ages away.'

'Two months to be exact – April the thirteenth – but I've set that timescale as I'm sure he will back by then.' Rosa looked at her friend and told her, 'He'd bloody better be!'

CHAPTER FORTY FOUR

The Seven Lessons
Three: Identity

Vicki Cliss was one of those people who, as soon as you meet them, you know that you are in safe hands. In her early thirties, she was plain but pretty with no make-up and sported a neat dark bob. A tiny pregnancy bump was visible through her open coat. She smiled warmly as Rosa approached her at the edge of the glorious Polhampton Sands. Hot, already feeling the vet's good energy, gave his little bark of approval and began running around her, nuzzling her boots and, excited by the smells of other animals, started cocking his leg against one of them before Rosa noticed and hastily tugged him away.

'Hey, Vicki. Ooh, sorry about that.'

'No problem.' Vicki smiled. 'Well, there's not a lot wrong with him, is there? Shall we go down to the edge and see how he moves? I just want to check that he didn't crick his spine during the fire.'

'Yes, please.' Rosa looked around, marvelling. 'I've only seen this beach from afar before. It makes our bay look like a lake.'

'Did you get the bus?'

'No, I got Ralph Weeks to bring me over in the one and only Cockleberry taxi. The bus is just too slow, if you're busy. And I'm always that at the moment.' Rosa looked to Vicki's tummy. 'Your first?'

'No, my third. I must be mad. But Stuart always wanted a football team. We've got two boys already.'

'Let's hope he's content with a five-a-side then.'

They both laughed.

'I bet this is beautiful in the summer.' Rosa looked right and left at the beach, which seemed to stretch for miles.

'It really is. Best to come out early or late though, as it gets mobbed by holidaymakers.'

'So, do you have a house here as well as your veterinary practice?'

'Yes, the surgery adjoins the house, I took over an existing business, so it was really quite easy to get set up.'

'Our vision is to get a house eventually if we start a family. Well, that's if Josh comes back. He's left me, you see.'

'Oh dear, I won't ask.'

'It's a long-convoluted story and yes, it's not good but I'm ever hopeful things will work out.'

'Having a family is pretty cool if you do.'

'Is it? My observation is that it's bloody hard work and I'm not sure if I'm ready to give up my freedom yet. I look at Titch and it's just such a different way of life.'

'Does Josh want kids?'

'He'd have us competing against your little football team if he had his way.'

'Don't get me wrong, I love being a vet, the training was worth every minute, but my kids are my greatest achievement. They kind of make you look from the outside to the inside.

Make you realise what's important.'

'Ah. I didn't have that much fun as a kid, never really had a family as such. I was in care, you see. I don't want to lose my sense of identity, not now when it has taken me so long to find it.'

Vicki nodded. 'I can understand, but I reckon that's even more reason to have a family of your own, to feel that love, because there is a lot of it to feel. I can't even explain the emotion that will run through you when you are handed that little screaming new-born. You will fall in love and never fall out of it again.'

'Has Josh been paying you to say all this?'

Vicki looked suddenly awkward, then laughed, joking, 'I will invoice him.' The two women walked along in comfortable silence for a bit.

'About what you were saying about giving things up, Rosa.' Vicki broke the silence. 'I've got a good job and can afford a cleaner and a gardener and to pay for babysitters if I need them, but Stuart is a stay-at-home dad, so we've managed that way. We always wanted to be present parents. And he says it's not about what he's given up but what he's gained from seeing his children develop and grow.'

'Not everyone is as lucky as you.' Rosa knew she sounded ungracious, but she was hurting.

'I realise that, and I'm grateful every day. I suppose what I'm saying is that you *can* make it work and have it all – if that's what you want, Rosa.'

The wind started to whip up and they looked at Hot, who was scampering along the sea's edge barking at unsuspecting seagulls. 'Like I said earlier, I don't think we need to worry about him.' Vicki shivered. 'Let's go back up to the surgery if you don't mind. My car's just over there in the car park. We can give him a proper going-over then. I want to listen to his chest.'

Rosa hoisted a sandy Hot onto the vet's examination table.

'He seemed fine on the beach, but how's he been since he rescued little Theo?' Vicki caressed the dachshund behind one long ear. 'They have a sixth sense, dogs. And dachshunds are great bodyguards. Has he been sneezing a lot? Have you noticed a hoarse cough?'

'Thankfully, he does seem OK. He's sneezed a few times, but it's usually when I've been dusting or when he's put his nose too close to something pungent. And his bark is just as loud and irritating as usual. I have read up about intervertebral disc disease, of course, as I know a quarter of little dachshunds get spinal problems but we are careful not to leave Hot anywhere he can jump down and jar his spine. We have a set of stairs for him to get up onto and down from the sofa.'

'That's good to hear.' Vicki gently pushed and prodded his spine and manipulated his hips, much to Hot's wriggling annoyance. She then examined his paws, which made him jump, as he was very ticklish, especially on his back paws, before informing Rosa, 'All completely normal so far.' She then put her stethoscope to his chest while Rosa held him still. Dropping it back around her neck, the vet smiled. 'Well, his heart and lungs are fine. He's a healthy little chap with a big heart in many ways, this one. You can put him down now.'

They moved out into the reception area and Vicki said, 'Right, I'd better go. It's feeding time at the zoo and my turn to do dinner tonight.'

'What do I owe you?'

'A friend of Jacob's is a friend of mine, so nothing – but I will be angling for cuddles when you do decide to take the baby plunge.'

'We'll see.' Rosa smiled as she put ten pounds in the animal welfare charity box on the counter. 'And thanks so much, that's really kind. Good luck with your new one. When are you due?'

'Ages, yet. I'm only sixteen weeks. Now, are you OK to get back?'

'Yes, I'll text Ralph, he said to let him know when we're done.' Rosa produced a chunk of cucumber wrapped in foil from her pocket and brandished it to get her dog out of the surgery and away from its plethora of fascinating smells.

Later, as Rosa sat in the back seat of the taxi with a snoozing Hot on her lap, she found that Ralph was in a talkative mood.

'Like children, our animals, aren't they?' said the balding, middle-aged taxi driver, smiling at her in the rear-view mirror. 'And Vicki's the best. We always come here, as we've got two guinea pigs, a rabbit, a tank of stick insects, two rescue kittens, an aquarium of tropical fish and a cockatoo called Conker. It's a right menagerie in our house.'

'You could open a zoo,' Rosa giggled, then rested her head back and shut her eyes. She needed to think about things. Vicki had made the idea of having children seem magical, rather than a necessary chore of evolution. Visions of the miscarriage straight after her wedding flooded back. How could she have made so light of that to herself? How could she not have shared something so sad and distressing with Josh? She hadn't done a pregnancy test, but she was never late, so even a few days overdue and feeling not quite herself had been a big sign to her that she was well on the way.

Despite everything, Rosa was honest enough to admit that the prospect of having children still terrified her. Imagine if she was a bad mother… The thought of inflicting her chaotic background and insecurities on another human being was just too much to contemplate.

CHAPTER FORTY FIVE

Valentine's Day and not even a phone message from Josh.
Rosa was convinced now that he would never forgive her for
something she didn't even know she'd done!

It had been a horrible day. She had felt so down that she
couldn't even be bothered to go ahead with the raffle she had
organised to celebrate the first anniversary of the shop having
been open. There was nobody to talk to, to share her pain, for
Jacob and Raff were full to capacity at the Lobster Pot and Titch
was out on her date with Ritchie. Titch hadn't even needed Rosa
to babysit as her mum was happy to do it. Rosa's mum Mary was
working a late shift at the Co-op and really, what was the point
of calling Josh?

Finding a small bottle of wine in the downstairs fridge, Rosa
necked it, then opened a bottle of wine upstairs. Two large
glasses later and with her head reeling slightly she put on Hot's
lead and woolly coat and set off to clear her head.

It was chilly, and with the sky bright with stars above her, Rosa
couldn't resist the magic of the night. Much to Hot's delight, she
started running in and out of the waves with him. Puffing, and
realising how cold it was, she walked back to the usual bench, sat
down and took her phone from her jacket pocket. Hot trotted

after her, stopping to bark at seagulls swooping overhead.

Seb was rolling a cigarette outside the pub when he heard the distinctive London accent of Rosa as she slurred, 'Shut up, Hot, an' shut your beaks, seagulls. A bit of hush, if you don't mind. I'm phoning my ex-husband.'

'Ex-husband, eh?' Seb silently appeared by her side. 'We always thought he was a bit too much of a posh toff for you.'

Rosa stood up. 'At least he's not a criminal.'

'Not guilty on all counts.' The ginger ruffian took a long toke on his weed-loaded cigarette.

'Must try harder when you are attempting arson though.' Rosa shook her finger at him.

'Oh, I'd be far less obvious, girl, give me some credit. And whatever you think of me, attempting to kill a kid isn't in my repertoire.'

'The fire was started by a lit cigarette, and you smoke.'

Seb laughed out loud. 'So do half of the inhabitants of the Bay, girl, but not those cheap-shit Spanish cigarettes the plod was trying to pin on me.' And as Rosa teetered slightly and sat back down on the bench, Seb wandered off along the beach as noiselessly as he had appeared.

Ignoring the biting wind and crashing waves, Rosa scrolled through her phone contacts, struggling to hear the answerphone message when it eventually kicked in.

'Josheee, oh Josheee. Hello, ex-husband, and Happy Valentine's Day. I hope you got my card. I thought it was funny anyway. I love you. Hot loves you. We both love you. Please come home. I don't think I've done anything bad. It's so pointless without you. Drunk, that's me. Drunk! Just like my mother – isn't that what you said? You told me to call you when I liked myself. Well, you obviously don't like me, and I still don't like myself either. There – I said it.'

216

Rosa dropped the phone onto the sand and with the message still running let out an almighty sob.

'Rosa, Rosa.' On opening her eyes, she saw the familiar face of Alec. 'Come on, let's get you up, it's freezing. What are you doing down here, heh?' His voice was full of care.

Rosa squinted and shook herself. She made a little moaning noise. 'What time is it?' A shivering Hot had not left her side on the bench.

'Time we got you home, little lady.'

'Doctor Alec.' Her voice and body shook, and she began to cry. 'Nobody loves me.'

'Rosa. Of course they do. Now, let's get you home, shall we?'

He zoomed his torch around her, retrieved her phone and put it in his pocket. Then ensuring Hot's lead was fixed firmly around his wrist, the gentle giant lifted the troubled girl like a babe in arms and began to carry her up the hill.

CHAPTER FORTY SIX

The Seven Lessons
Four: Addiction

Rosa had been dreaming that her phone was ringing, then realised that it was.

'Rose, it's Titch.'

Rosa groaned and checked back to her phone. 'Shit, is that the time?'

'Are you not up?'

'I am now.'

'Well, get your arse into gear as a delivery man is at the back gate. I'm not in until two today, you know that; luckily they had my number too.'

Still fully clothed, Rosa scrabbled for her keys from the bedside table and noticed a hand-written note beside it, reading: *Meet me at West Cliffs path at 2.30 today. Alec.*

Hating herself for the night before, when she'd put Hot in danger yet again by passing out on the beach and then sleeping way past his breakfast-time, she had pulled her hat down as far as it would go and tied a scarf up to her nose.

Alec was met by two bloodshot eyes and a very timid Rosa. 'Didn't realise it was fancy dress,' he joked gently.

Rosa looked up to the tall man, the fifteen-inch difference in height feeling very significant today. Alec could see tears forming in her eyes. 'Shall we?' He guided her through the entrance to the coast path and then remained silent as they began their ascent.

'Josh always said it was easier to walk and talk if problems needed ironing out,' Rosa said eventually.

'Did he?'

'Yes, because sometimes if you are not looking directly at a person it's easier to speak openly.' They carried on walking, until she spoke again. 'What were you doing down the beach at that time, anyway? I mean, I'm so glad you were, and I will never be able to thank you enough.'

'Oh, I was just giving Brown his before-bed walk,' Alec lied, remembering how in his hurry to get to her after Josh's frantic call he'd gone out in odd shoes. 'Where's Hot?'

'At home. He needs rest and warmth after what I did to him. I needed to concentrate on what I have to say to you, Alec. I wanted to tell you I'm so sorry for you having to find me like that, and more worryingly, do you think I have a drink problem?'

'No, but I do think you have a problem with drink. That, combined with sadness, is a very different thing. You drink to mask the pain but, once unmasked, your inner demons come out and you become destructive.'

'I can't bear it that Josh is not with me at night. I get so lonely.'

'I think you'd be lonely in a room full of Josh's at the moment.'

'Oh, don't go all therapy-speak on me, Alec. What do you mean, exactly?'

'You just don't like being alone with yourself.'

Rosa put her gloved hand to her face. 'Shit! That is exactly what Josh said when we had our final row. He said that I didn't like myself, actually.' She brushed her hair out of her eyes. 'Talking of therapy, Alec, I'm so sorry I ran out of our session. It was really rude of me.'

'No apology required.' Alec thought for a moment then went on, 'It's hard being alone with ourselves, with no alcohol or distractions. Especially when, as you say, you don't like who you are very much. That is particularly challenging.'

With plumes of breath coming from their faces, they carried on walking until Rosa stopped and grabbed onto Alec's arm.

'What's wrong?' he asked immediately. 'What is it?'

'That's where we fell, Hot and I – just there.' Rosa shuddered. 'I can't even look over there now, although I've done it once.' Darren the lifeboat man's words suddenly hit her: 'The fears we don't face become our limits.'

'Show me.'

Hiding behind the big man's bulk, Rosa pointed with a shaky hand and let him lead the way. Holding onto his arm, she gestured down the cliff to the ledge where she and Hot had landed on that fateful snowy evening.

'See? You just did it. You were drunk then too, weren't you?'

'Yes. Yes, I was.' Her voice cracked. 'But even that didn't stop me from getting pissed last night and ending up lying on a bench, like some kind of tramp. Hot and I could have bloody frozen to death. I don't deserve to have him.' She wept.

'Yes, you could, but you didn't. I reckon your mum would say those angels have given you one more chance.' Alec took her hand and led her to a rock where they perched together uncomfortably in the cold. He blew out a long breath and watched it slowly dissipate in the cold air. He knew it was so important to reach her. Turning slowly to her, and looking Rosa in the eye, he made a decision.

'Rosa, I'm going to tell you something that I don't share with many people unless I know them very well.'

Why did everyone confide in her? Rosa thought back to Raff's admission that he was adopted. It made her feel proud, that he had trusted her with this intimate fact. She waited quietly to hear what Alec had to say.

'I'm an alcoholic, Rosa.'

'Woah! Not another one,' she said clumsily, not knowing how to react. 'Just having Mum to worry about is enough.'

Alec said firmly, 'You need to worry about yourself, not us, please – and I haven't touched a drop for nineteen years, five months and four days.'

'Blimey, you started young!' Rosa bit her lip. Another crass remark.

'I'm forty-eight, so not that young,' he said calmly.

'Wow, you look good. I had you at late thirties.'

The big man grinned. 'Not drinking and working out does help!' He became serious again. 'Let's just say I got far too used to drinking vodka at university. My dad died when I was just twenty years old – and that was it. I was lost. The shame I feel for not looking after my mum or being there for my younger sister at that time still haunts me. But that's what addicts are like, Rosa. We are selfish, we tell lies, we make excuses, we let people down. We look for our next fix – in my case a drink. But it could be drugs or gambling or sex in some cases.'

Alec looked at the sea for a long moment before resuming. 'My rock bottom was getting into a fight and waking up in the morning with not only my front teeth and wallet missing, but in a police cell charged with a public order offence. Somehow my dear mum managed to get me off, blaming it on the death of my father. It was at that precise moment that I realised I wanted to turn my life around. I got help, talked through my grief, started on an alcohol recovery programme, which led to me training to be a therapist, and I've not had a drink since that fateful night. I went on to meet my wife, Alesha, who I still adore even though things didn't work out, and she bore me our most beautiful son.' He squeezed Rosa's hand and told her, 'My life is still enhanced by abstaining.'

'But Josh and you went for a drink that night and he came home hammered.'

'Yes, he did, but I drink soft drinks – that's my life. I like to socialise. I do everything that a drinker does but without the alcohol, so it's the same life as everybody else. I just see things clearer. Always remember what I've said the night before and never end up in a police cell with broken front teeth,' Alec smiled. 'It's my choice, and for me, it's a good choice.' He let his words sink in.

Rosa said slowly, 'Most of the trouble I get myself into is when I am drunk. If I hadn't been drunk that night Luke and I…well, we wouldn't have been together. Alec, it's terrible – I don't even know if I had sex with the man!'

'And do you really think that by knowing what happened, it would make things any better? Would you feel any differently?'

'I suppose if I knew for sure that we didn't have sex, I wouldn't feel quite so bad. I would know that I hadn't cheated.'

'I think it's time to look at the bigger picture. That particular event is past, it's gone. What's important is what happens moving forward. Stop beating yourself up, Rosa. People don't just stop loving you because you make a mistake, you know. People who really care will stick by you. Will forgive you.'

'My mum left me,' Rosa whispered.

'No, your mum left herself to drink. She was an addict to

alcohol. It's almost as if just calling it alcoholism doesn't make it seem so bad. I think it should be labelled Alcohol Addiction.' His voice softened. 'But whatever it is, it's a very hard thing to control and give up. She loved you as well as she could under the circumstances. If she hadn't dropped you and cut your face, she would have kept you by her side and done the best by you, and she's told you that. Your being taken away from her – that was her rock bottom. After that, she cleaned up her act. And although it may not help right now, you need to understand that behind the scenes there was a great family love looking out for you. And when the time was right, your great-grandfather and great grand-mother, as well as your mother, they searched and found you. They never stopped loving you, Rosa, not for one minute. Your mother's heart was full of cracks from missing you. Her baby. Cracks which she is slowly filling by giving you the love now that she was unable to give you when you were her little girl.'

Rosa swallowed down her emotion. 'How do you know all this about me?' she asked in a faint voice.

'Josh told me. He is so proud at the way you have coped with everything since finding out about your long-lost family, and also by how adeptly you manage the shop.'

'He didn't say that when he was angry with me.'

'Anger is futile. All that happens is the person giving it gets themselves into an unnecessary state of upset, says ridiculous things they don't often mean and the person receiving it goes into defence mode, so doesn't listen anyway.' Alec gave a bark of laughter. 'It's a waste of good energy.'

'But what do you do with anger if you don't let it out? One of the lads at my second children's home told me it would go back down my throat and start burning my organs. I always believed it was true so made sure that every little bit of anger exploded out of me like a firework.'

Alec looked at the damaged but blossoming young woman by his side. 'Oh, Rosa. It's hard but I always say, try to turn that angry feeling into a positive energy.'

'Like what?'

'What did Josh say? "Come back when you like yourself", or something similar?'

'Yes, but I don't understand.'

'Put your energy into liking yourself, Rosa. Take positive steps to help yourself feel better. Your friends tell you how great you are, so does your mum and especially your husband. He didn't mean to hurt you with those words. He thought you had made the ultimate betrayal. And you know, most of what he said – well, it wasn't true anyway. And,' Alec paused, 'keep on what you are doing with the shop. You have created an amazing little business there and that was all down to your hard work. You should be continually patting yourself on the back for that.'

Alec beamed at her. 'You are a great girl, Rosa. Believe it.'

'Thank you. Does that mean that you think I should give up drinking, then?'

'You will do what you do, Rosa. I can't answer that or tell you what to do. I will say that maybe just having one or two would be better with your current state of mind, and if you could stop, for a little while at least, then you will be surprised at how much easier life becomes.'

'OK. That does make sense. I just need to put it into practice. What I know for sure though is that I've decided I am giving Josh until my birthday to come back. You see, Alec, I'm beginning to get cross with him. He knows I'm hurting. I leave a message for him every single night without fail – and nothing. No response. I need to talk to him. I need to tell him how much I love him.'

'Oh Rosa, he knows that. From the little I've seen of him he knows a lot more about you than you realise. All I am going to say is, listen to Josh's silence because it has so much to say. We human beings get confused about this love business. In fact, it was Rumi who said that "Love is not an emotion, it's our very existence".'

'Rumi? Don't tell me he was hanging out with Kahlil.' Rosa broke into a grin. 'My mother would be beside herself.'

Alex laughed. 'In a previous life maybe.'

They reached the top of the cliff path where it plateaued out into a wonderful flat area of grass. Wild flowers were attempting to push their heads up into spring. 'Oh, that's so pretty.' Rosa leant down to look closer at a cluster of purplish flowers.

'Don't touch!' Alec shouted causing her to flinch in shock.

'Sorry to shout,' he apologised to the shaken girl, 'but that's bittersweet. It's highly poisonous.'

'You know so much.'

'That's thanks to many holidays I spent down here with my son and wife – that plus an incessant yearning for more knowledge.'

'Do you still see your wife?'

'Not since the divorce, but like I said, we are on perfectly friendly terms.'

'Bittersweet, eh?'

'Very good! We just fell out of love, wanted different things. She's a beautiful person, an intensive-care nurse. We met on holiday, a true holiday romance. I used to say, I went to the Caribbean to seek solace and I came back with a trouble and strife; as in cockney rhyming slang for wife, you know.'

Rosa smiled. 'Yes, I do know. Mary tells me I was born within the sound of Bow Bells, which evidently makes me a right proper cock-er-ney.' She was ready to go home now. 'We'd better start walking down before it gets dark. Come on.' Rosa

225

linked arms with the big man, thinking that it was the first time she had ever felt some kind of fatherly guidance. Throughout her life, she had spent so much time grieving about not having a mother that it had never occurred to her to fret about a missing father figure.

'Alec, could you explain more about love not being an emotion?' she asked. 'I do so need to try and work out in my head what I am feeling.'

'Right, so how shall I put it… Here goes: love doesn't behave the way emotions do. When we love truly, we can experience all our free-flowing mood states as well as intense emotions including fear, rage, hatred, grief and funnily enough, shame. But love does not increase or decrease in response to its environment. Love is much deeper than any emotion. I guess what I am trying to say is that Josh will not be loving you any less at this moment; he is just going through his emotions to try and make sense of what has happened.'

'You think?'

'I know. He won't be having a good time of it in London. He'll be showing up at work as usual every day, but there will be sorrow behind his smile.'

'Really?'

'Yes, Rosa, really. Give him time. You hurt him.'

As they started walking back down to the beach, Rosa looked out to sea. 'I didn't even know what a horizon looked like until I arrived in Cockleberry Bay.'

'I don't think you really knew what *you* looked like until you arrived in Cockleberry Bay.' Alec put a comforting arm round her shoulder.

A tear rolled down Rosa's cheek. 'Yes. And now, I am learning.'

CHAPTER FORTY SEVEN

'Happy Easter! Here's a bottle of red for the table, but I'm on Diet Coke today.' Rosa and Hot bustled into Jacob and Raff's beautiful home – a converted church overlooking Polhampton Sands. She handed Jacob a second carrier bag, saying, 'In here are some eggs for us all to share.'

'Ooh, you are good.' Jacob kissed her on both cheeks and took her coat. Ugly, Pongo and the Duchess flew into the hall to greet her and Hot. The four hounds then proceeded to tear out of the door into the huge landscaped gardens.

'I forgot how gorgeous it is here,' Rosa said dreamily. 'You certainly give Greenway a run for its money with your beautiful garden.'

'It's only because the gardener is so damn hot,' Jacob drawled. 'We give him far too many hours just to see him riding, top off, on the electric mower during the summer.'

Rosa laughed. 'What are you like!'

Just then, Raff appeared from the garden and kissed her too. 'I've hidden the eggs out of reach of the dogs, as the chocolate is poisonous for them.' He looked slightly perturbed. 'We never do this Easter-egg hunting in Italy; you Brits have some strange habits, but finding them should keep the children quiet, for a minute anyway.'

'It will keep me quiet too,' Rosa beamed.

'So, Signora Rosa, we have roast beef on the menu today, not as good as your mother's, I am sure, but I will try.' The young Italian grinned and headed back to the kitchen.

'Does he ever get a day off?' Rosa asked Jacob.

'He loves cooking for the family, which includes you, of course, and Vicki and Stuart are joining us too, with their brood. Can't beat a Sunday lunch with friends.' Sensing Rosa's sadness, Jacob kissed her lightly on the cheek. 'So, Mrs Smith, how are you?'

'My arm is back to normal, thanks. As for me, I'm doing all right. I'm on countdown to contacting Josh now. I've figured that by setting a deadline of my birthday I can deal with that. Maybe he will see sense before then, who knows? I'm not even thinking the unthinkable – that he won't want to come home.'

'He just needs some time, Rosa.'

'That's what Alec said. He's such a nice bloke.'

'Yes,' Jacob replied and quickly moved on. 'Can I get you a drink? Just Diet Coke, yes?'

'Yes, please.' It felt alien to Rosa not going straight for the wine, but she couldn't do it any more. All the signs were saying to stay off it, at least for a while. If Alec and her mother could refrain from drinking and they were 'proper' alcoholics, she was certain it wouldn't be that much of a hardship for her.

'Who are you?' the inquisitive blue-eyed five-year-old boy greeted Rosa.

'I'm Rosa, and who are you?'

'My mum likes Rosas, don't you, Mum? Daddy brings her them sometimes when she shouts at us.'

Vicki Cliss walked into the large conservatory overlooking the bay and corrected her son. 'It's roses, Arthur.'

'That's what I said.' The cheeky, dark-haired lad turned and ran out towards the garden, nearly knocking over his two-year-old brother in the process, and shouting, 'Chocolaaate!'

'How many eggs has he had already?' Vicki turned to Jacob.

'Well, I think Raff only put fifteen small ones out there for them both to find, but poor little Stan doesn't seem to be getting many of them.'

Stan came toddling towards them. 'Arthur pig, Mummy.'

Vicki swept him up in her arms, above her now-visible bump. 'Come on, baby boy, let's go and find some eggs for you.'

At that moment, all four dogs came running in and started to charge around Rosa's legs, barking loudly.

'Oi, you lot!' she chided them and couldn't resist picking up the Duchess for a cuddle. A stocky, brown-haired man came in from the garden, grumbling good-naturedly,

'They say never work with children or animals, but why do they never warn you not to live with them either?'

'I thought you wanted a football team?' Rosa laughed. 'You must be Stuart. I'm Rosa Smith.' She put the Duchess into the big dog-bed and shook hands with Vicki's husband.

'Nice to meet you – and no, I wouldn't swap them for the world…when they are asleep.' Rosa smiled as Stuart Cliss continued his faux sarcasm. 'And great – in another few months we'll have baby number three!'

'All right, Stu? Can I get a drink for you?' Jacob appeared from the kitchen.

'What softies have you got? Looking at that storm brewing, I may not be here long.' Just as Rosa was going to ask why, she heard a shrill bleeping sound coming from his pocket. 'Damn! I bloody knew it! I'll have to go.'

Stuart bumped into his wife in the doorway. Her expression showed her disappointment. 'Have you really got to?'

'I'm so sorry, darling. The crew's a couple down this weekend. See you later.' He kissed her then blew a kiss to his sons, who were still running around looking for eggs despite the wind now whipping up quite strongly. 'Get back in the house, boys,' he shouted as he got into his car and screeched down the hill.

Vicki sighed. 'I shouldn't complain. When I'm working, he's with the boys so he can't go out on the boat, and he does love it.' She called Arthur and Stan in from the garden. 'Come and watch Daddy go off in the lifeboat.'

Rosa caught Vicki rubbing her pregnancy bump. 'Are you feeling all right?' she asked.

'Yes, just a bit of a pain, that's all. He or maybe she this time is having a growing spurt, I expect.'

From the large window of the conservatory it was plain to see that the wind and swelling waves were causing a few unsuspecting boats to make a hasty retreat into harbour.

Vicki went off to the toilet as her boys sat down quietly at the window waiting to see the lifeboat launch down below. Even the three older dogs were all squashed together with the tiny Duchess in the big cashmere-lined dog bed, enjoying each other's warmth.

'Stuart wasn't on the lifeboat when I disgraced myself, was he?' Rosa whispered.

Jacob shook his head. 'Don't worry. It's all fine. He is a lovely guy, as great as Vicki.'

Raff popped his head around the door. 'I'm just going to have a quick smoke, then dinner will be served.' The door flew open and a rush of wind caused an envelope to fly off the hall table as Raff headed outside.

'Dadddeee!' Arthur and Stan pushed their faces to the window. Vicki rushed in to see the lifeboat way down below shooting down the ramp into the now very turbulent sea. 'And, breathe,' she whispered to herself, but they all heard.

Jacob took her hand, murmuring, 'He'll be fine, he always is.'

'We are ready! Here is the roast beef with all his trimmings.' Raffaele carried a big platter into the conservatory and placed it on the long, beautifully decorated Easter table. Jacob looked at his husband and blew him a kiss, thinking him even more adorable when he got his words slightly wrong.

Vicki was just putting Stan into his high chair when she suddenly turned very white. Handing the toddler to Jacob, she headed swiftly back to the toilet. Sensing something was wrong, Rosa followed close behind. On reaching the bathroom door, the pregnant woman turned around and with a complete look of panic in her eyes, told her, 'Rosa, call an ambulance, please. My waters have just broken.'

With an ambulance on its way and Jacob amusing the unsuspecting children at the dinner table, Rosa's experience with Titch and the birth of Theo came into their own. With the help of Raff, she had assisted Vicki up the stairs, to lie down in a spare bedroom on top of three thick bath-towels hastily fetched by Raff, then she'd eased down the shaking woman's jeans and pants, covered her and placed two pillows under her feet, hoping she was doing the right thing. Blood was seeping out of Vicki non-stop. Raff had dashed off to fetch more towels. The panic when delivering Titch's baby was the same, but sadly, with all this blood, and the birth being so early, Rosa knew the outcome would most probably be very different.

Even in this situation, the ever-stoical vet was remaining as calm as she could. 'I know I've lost it. I just know. Ow, it hurts so much.' She put her hands on her abdomen and let out a stifled scream. 'You have to reach Stuart.'

'Jacob has called him.' Rosa knelt and held her hand, not

daring to say that of course Stuart wouldn't be picking up his mobile in the middle of rough seas and a rescue mission.

Vicki couldn't help herself; she started to cry. Concerned at how much blood she could see, Rosa comforted the distressed woman and kept checking her phone. Where the hell was the ambulance? This was an emergency!

Just then, her phone rang with an unidentified number. She answered immediately, thinking it might be the paramedics trying to find the house, but instead…

'Rosa, it's Lucas. I think we need to talk.'

CHAPTER FORTY EIGHT

Ritchie smiled down at Theo as he pushed his pram along the beach path. 'Cute just like his mother, this one.'

Titch held onto the side of the pram. 'Yes, isn't he? He's getting big now. It's hard to believe how quickly the past six months have gone.' She pulled the baby's blanket up to his chin. 'I can't wait for some sunshine. We can take him down to the beach and play with him in the sand then.'

'We? As in you and me?'

Titch went uncharacteristically shy for a minute. 'Maybe.'

'I really enjoy it when we go out together, don't you?'

'Yes, I told you I do. It's so nice to get out and feel free for a while.'

'Look at us being all grown up, as if we are proper courting or something,' Ritchie said.

'Courting?'

'Yes, it was what our great-grandparents did evidently, back in the day. It means dating, I think. Hardly anyone used to shag before marriage then either.'

'Well, we are courting then.' Titch then added, 'And there's not much hope of the other, at least, not at the moment.'

'Not helped by the fact that we are both still living at

home. And somehow, lying down in the back of the fish and chip van like we did of old doesn't hold the same appeal any more.' Although they'd always been friends, the two had tried experimenting in their early teens.

'Do you remember when we were caught coming out of the back of your mum and dad's old van and you told your mum we had seen a bird hop in there and were trying to save it.'

Ritchie laughed so much he nearly choked. 'And you had half a haddock stuck to the back of your head. Bloody hilarious.'

With tears streaming down their cheeks, they doubled over with laughter. Every time one of them tried to say something they couldn't get the words out. Eventually Theo stirred, causing them to stop and Titch to pull his blanket up again and settle him. They carried on walking.

'Joking aside, you do realise that your mother's hated me ever since er…Fishgate?' Titch tried hard not to start laughing.

Ritchie snorted. 'Don't set me off again, you. I think hate is a bit strong, but I won't deny she's a funny old stick about having a baby out of wedlock, and can't even comprehend that you dared sleep with someone from outside of the Bay.'

'You'll have to keep me a secret then.'

'No, I bloody won't. I'll be proud to have you on my arm, Titch Whittaker.' He leaned down and kissed her gently on the lips.

'I'm hopefully going to rent the flat above the shop when Rosa and Josh sort themselves out, so that will be easier for us all. We can just relax then, rather than have to go out all of the time to be alone.'

'Still no word from the big lad then, I take it?'

'No, they still haven't spoken. I can't believe it. It's been like this since Christmas. Saying that, what would you do if you thought your wife had slept with someone else, but she couldn't

234

confirm or deny for sure as she was so drunk?'

'If you were the wife in question, I would forgive you instantly,' Ritchie replied quietly.

It was the nicest thing a man had ever said to her in her whole life. Titch's eyes filled with tears. Putting her hand over his on the pram handle, she looked up to her gangly companion. 'This is all right, isn't it?'

Ritchie nodded. 'It's more than all right. And now that we are officially courting…' Titch laughed at the word as her new beau continued, 'I wondered if you'd like to spend a night at a hotel of your choosing with me. If it's easier we can bring Theo, but if you can get a babysitter then obviously that would be better.'

'Aw, that would be amazing! Let me talk to Rosa. She gets lonely and needs to be kept busy, to keep her mind off Josh, so hopefully she will say yes. We'll have to work it around the shop hours though.'

Ritchie's grin said it all. 'Just let me know. Right, we'd better get back up that hill. I'm on chip duty tonight.'

CHAPTER FORTY NINE

The Seven Lessons
Five: Motherhood

As a sobbing Rosa came up for air, Mary took a deep puff on her inhaler, held her breath to allow the drug to do its work, then exhaled slowly.

Rosa's outpouring of sorrow continued as her mother gently rocked her on her lap.

'It's just not fair, poor Vicki. She loves children so much and then that happened to her. I tried to help her, but I couldn't save the little mite.'

'It wasn't your fault, duck. If babies want to stay in, then nothing will budge them. If they need to come out, then that's nature's way too. That little soul obviously wasn't ready for this world.'

Rosa sobbed again. 'Is that what happened to me then? Mine and Josh's little soul wasn't ready. Seeing Vicki's face, I remembered the terrible pain that I felt too. I just sat on the toilet with blood coming out of me. Josh was watching the rugby in the lounge and I didn't tell him – I didn't even tell you.'

'Oh, darling girl.' Mary pulled her in tighter.

'It was just so scary and so horrible, and I knew it was a miscarriage, but I didn't want anyone else to know because I thought it was my fault. I thought I'd willed that baby to fall out of me because…because…'

'Ssh, now take your time, duckie.'

'I wasn't ready, Mum; I just wasn't ready. I think I will make a terrible mother.'

'Well, I think you'd make a great mother, Rosa. And that's coming from a pretty rubbish one.'

Mary strained to reach a book on the kitchen table with one hand. It was a copy of *The Prophet* by her favourite author, Kahlil Gibran. 'Listen now, I'm going to read this to you,' she said and cleared her throat.

'"Your children are not your children. They come through you but not from you, and though they are with you, yet they belong not to you. You are the bows from which your children as living arrows are sent forth".'

She put the book down. 'OK, so I sent you forth from a very wonky bow and for that I will be forever sorry, but reading this takes the worry away slightly, doesn't it, Rosa? You can create and guide the little person who comes from you, but fundamentally they are their own person.'

Rosa stood up, took her mother's head in both her hands and kissed her hard on the forehead.

'You know what, Mary Teresa Cobb? I'm so glad I came from your bow. You may have been a bit late to the match, but I couldn't have asked for a better archer, and even though I flew away from you, this living arrow will never leave you again.'

CHAPTER FIFTY

'You look like the cat that's got the cream, Titch Whittaker,' Rosa said sternly. 'What have you been up to?'

'I officially have a boyfriend.'

'Ooh, how exciting. You mean Ritchie, I take it?'

'No, Ed Sheeran has moved to Cockleberry Bay. Duh…of course it's Ritchie. I need to ask you a favour actually.'

'Go on.'

'I know it's a big ask, but would you mind having Theo overnight one night soon? I will work around our shop shifts, of course, so it could be a week night. It's just, Ritchie wants to take me to a hotel for the night – and well, I haven't ever stayed in a hotel with a boyfriend and…'

'Yes.'

'And I know you haven't done it before and…' Titch looked up and smiled. 'Yes?'

'Of course, I will. It would be a pleasure and I'm honoured that you trust me enough to do that.'

'Aw, thanks, Rose. It's just I don't want to put on Mum all night.'

'It's fine, just have your phone handy and I'll be happy to look after him. I hardly sleep now due to stressing over Josh until the early hours, so it will be company for me if the little darling wants to play, not settle. A win-win all round.'

Titch went to put her coat in the back kitchen and make some tea, and Rosa came out to join her. Leaning against the worktop, she said, 'Guess what? Lucas phoned me.'

Titch gasped. 'Really? What did he say?'

'Well, this is the thing. Just as poor Vicki was losing the baby, he rang. Typical Luke! Wrong place, wrong time. I obviously wasn't thinking straight and said I would have to call him back. The thing is, he rang from a withheld number, so I can't.'

'He'll call back, I'm sure.'

'He might not. Because of what was happening, I was really abrupt with him. And he doesn't know I'm not with Josh, so maybe he just won't bother, thinking I'm not interested.'

'You could get his number from Sheila maybe?' Titch said doubtfully.

'Are you mad? I want nothing to do with that woman. Last time I saw her she accused me of running her darling son out of Cockleberry Bay. I wouldn't give her the satisfaction of refusing to give me his number. Because that is obviously what she would do.'

'Talking of the Hannafores, any more news on the fire?'

'No. DC Clarke said he'd update me as soon as he had anything else.'

'Ah, OK. It's all a bit loose on evidence, isn't it?' Titch put teabags in two china dachshund mugs.

Rosa got the milk out of the fridge as Titch poured boiling water in. 'How are you feeling, anyway?' Titch wanted to know.

'About what? The fire, Lucas, Josh or everything?'

'Hmm. It is all going on, isn't it? So yeah, everything.'

'OK, so let's go in order. About the fire, I really don't want to believe that someone would deliberately do something so wicked. About Lucas, I've also got over the fact that I might

239

have slept with him, but I know that Josh won't have, so that of course bothers me the most. Jacob, Raff and Alec said from a man's point of view to just give him time. He needs to stay in his man-cave for a bit. But he's been in there for bloody months now. And why the bastard won't return any of my calls I don't know. I'm leaving a message every day like you said.'

'Well, there's nothing more you can do.'

'Aside go and see him, but Jacob urged me not to, saying that if I could wait until my birthday that would be a very good idea. In fact, even Mary said that.'

'That's not so long now.'

Rosa stirred her tea and lifted out the teabag with her spoon before dropping it into the bin. 'Titch, there is something else that is really worrying me.'

'Go on.'

'What if Josh has found someone else? What if he thinks that I am a complete slut and that he must sleep with someone else too, to even it up. I mean, we all have carnal desires.'

'OK, I know I am younger than you, Rose, but what I do understand about love is what my mum told me one day after my dad died. She told me that when someone else's happiness is your happiness, that is true love.' Titch sniffed. 'Josh was buying you the café, for goodness sake. To make you happy!'

'I know, I know. And that is such a sweet quote. Your poor mum, she must miss him still.'

Titch took a deep breath. 'I know. I was so happy when Mary told me that it wasn't my fault about him taking his life.'

Rosa smiled inwardly. Gift or no gift, her mother was a very wise woman.

'I'm so chuffed for you, Titch. That must be such a relief.' Rosa hugged her.

They drank their tea. After a while, Rosa confessed, 'What

I've realised recently is that my feelings for Luke, and I won't deny there were feelings, were far more sexual than loving.'

'Well, it wouldn't have taken Mary's crystal ball to work that one out,' Titch helped herself to more sugar.

'The other night I imagined myself sitting in an empty room in front of a door and thought about who in the whole world I would most like to come through it.' Rosa paused. 'And it had to be Josh. Without a doubt, he is the love of my life.'

'Well, trust in that and him then, please.'

'I shall try.'

'How's the no-drinking going too?'

'I'm not saying I'm not not drinking, just cutting down. Mind, it was a blessing that I didn't have a drink at Jacob's the other Sunday as I was able to be present and sober while Vicki was in her hour of need.'

Ding! Rosa poked her head around from the kitchen as the shop door opened. 'Hello, DC Clarke, your ears must have just been burning.'

'I'm not sure that's the sort of wording you should be using after the turn of events here, is it now, Mrs Smith?'

'Ha! You're right.'

'Do you have a minute?'

'Yes, of course. Fancy a cuppa?'

'Ooh yes, please, and do you have any of those lovely shortbread biscuits?'

Rosa tried not to laugh as Titch puffed out her cheeks in a pig-like gesture behind his back while Titch put a fresh cup of tea, plus the biscuit tin and Rosa's half-finished mug on a tray for her to carry up.

Once settled in the lounge, Rosa with Hot asleep on her lap, the policeman informed her, 'I haven't got any concrete news, I'm afraid, Rosa. The Managing Director of Hastings insisted

241

'none of his delivery guys smoke the same brand of cigarette we found out the back of here.' He looked at her sympathetically as he held a biscuit in the air. 'I think you said that you have insurance?'

'Yes, but it's become too much of a hassle so I've decided to let it go. They'll only go and put the premium up if I claim, so what's the point.'

'Oh, I see.' The policeman frowned.

'I have a business to run. And Seb Watkins, and Sheila Hannafore – what about them? I know they both dislike me intensely.'

'We actually have CCTV footage of Seb at an MOT garage where he said he was at the time of the incident.' So, he had been telling the truth, Rosa thought.

'We didn't need to question Sheila directly,' the police officer went on, 'just made some discreet inquiries and found out that she had been working the lunchtime bar as usual that day, with a number of witnesses. With no other suspects in the frame, we will be putting this case on the back burner for now. Oops.' The usually stern-faced detective laughed. 'I'm at it now.'

Rosa felt suddenly relieved that Old Ma Hannafore didn't have to hate her for another accusation. 'We'll just have to assume that it was a delivery driver who dropped a stray cigarette by mistake, then?'

'We must never assume, as that makes an ass out of you and me.' The detective shook again with mirth. 'Oh, what fun we are having today.'

Rosa, wanting to laugh at him, not with him, carried on: 'I know I wouldn't fess up if I had dropped the ciggie in the bin, especially as nobody got hurt.'

The detective greedily shoved a third biscuit into his mouth and got up from the sofa. At that moment, Hot moved around a bit in his sleep, and a very pungent smell seeped into the room.

Rosa waved a hand in front of her face. 'Ooh, sorry about that, DC Clarke.'

'It's fine, I find these biscuits give me wind too.'

Rosa put Hot down, and somehow managing to stop herself from guffawing, she opened the French doors to let in some fresh air and to allow the policeman to leave by the spiral stairs.

'Right, must get on,' he said self-importantly. 'More Cockleberry crimes to solve.'

Considering last year's hit-and-run was the biggest thing that had happened in the Bay since the tragic death of six fishermen in the 1960s, Rosa wasn't quite sure exactly what he did all day. The detective stood in the doorway. Seagulls were mewing their pleasure at the crisp but sunny late March day. 'Well, thank you, Mrs Smith, and please do let me know if anything else comes to light, and we will do likewise.'

'Of course, and careful on those stairs!' Rosa shouted after him. She then shut the French doors and bent down to stroke her flatulent hound, who was whiffling up the biscuit crumbs on the carpet near where DC Clarke had been sitting.

'Greedy and lazy,' Rosa tutted aloud. Two of the traits she least admired in a person. It made her realise how lucky she was that her life was becoming full of people with values and traits that she *did* admire.

CHAPTER FIFTY ONE

'Let's see how long we can keep this shiny new high-chair clean shall we, baby boy?' Rosa chatted away to Theo. 'Right, Auntie Rosa is going to feed you some nice warm organic chicken and carrots; yum.' Dipping her finger in and tasting the food in the Peppa Pig bowl, she then turned away to make a gagging sound. 'Ew, rather you than me.'

Rosa widened her smile until the little curly-haired and dark-eyed beauty smiled and gurgled back at her. She had never understood the baby voices that everyone put on around children but now, faced with little Theo, she was doing the exactly the same thing. She felt such an affinity with him, probably due to the fact that she had not only helped deliver him, so was the first person ever to see him, but had spent a lot of his first six months close to him.

Titch had gone off with Ritchie to the hotel, obviously slightly concerned about leaving her son for the first time all night but also looking so radiant. It was lovely to see her like that and despite the slight downside of being the offspring of that bigoted old bag Edie Rogers, Ritchie had many good qualities ,and showed them by being extremely kind and protective of his new love.

Rosa was delighted that Theo ate not only his chicken and carrots but also some of the banana that Titch had said he would take or leave. She laughed at his cheekiness as he threw his water cup onto the floor a couple of times; however, on realising it was a game she had to put a stop to it before he flattened an already damp and disgruntled Hot.

Later, after managing to rock the baby gently to sleep in her arms and laying him in his carry-cot, Rosa felt proud of herself; maybe this baby lark wasn't quite as frightening or hard as she had imagined.

Shutting the bedroom door quietly behind her, she tiptoed back to the lounge and turned on the TV and the baby monitor. She wanted to be on full alert in case Theo woke up. Going back to the kitchen, she opened the fridge, and on seeing a half-full bottle of white wine, took it out and emptied it down the sink. Alec was right, she could conduct her life with everything the same, just not with a drink in her hand. Pouring herself a lemonade, she thought back: yes, she had had some fun drinking – or had she? Had she really, if she was honest with herself? Stealing traffic cones and taking them back to Josh's front garden, or having to escape politely the morning after from men she'd slept with the night before wasn't really that much fun, was it? Not in the cold light of sober day.

She even felt calmer about Josh tonight for some reason, probably because she had something to take her mind off him. So calm was she, in fact, that she chose not to leave him a message. Just as a new ITV drama that she fancied watching was about to start, Theo began to stir; she was getting up to go and see what he wanted when her phone rang. The sight of a withheld number caused her heart to beat faster. It was such bad bloody timing again that it had to be Luke.

Waah! Waah! Waah! Theo's lungs started to show off.

Rosa picked up the phone. Just at the sound of Lucas's voice, Rosa's hands began to shake. 'Yes, yes,' she said into the phone. 'It's me, Rosa. I just need to pick up the baby, hang on.'

Waah! Waah! Waah!

'Ssh now, my lovely, hush now.' Rosa put the phone on the bedside table, lifted the baby onto her shoulder and started rubbing his back. She put her mobile on to the speaker setting.

'Sorry.' Theo started to settle and make blubbing noises against her neck. 'I'm babysitting.'

'I just wanted to phone to see how you are.'

'I'm fine, Luke.'

'I…it's just that you were really drunk, and I didn't want you to think that—'

'Think what, Luke?'

Waah! Theo started again.

Luke spoke more loudly. 'Look, I didn't sleep with you in case you were worried about that – that's what I am trying to say. I fancy you, but necrophilia ain't really my style. Blimey, can't you stick a dummy in his boat race?'

Theo suddenly stopped crying, for which Rosa was so grateful. 'Luke,' she said, glad for the chance to talk without interruption, 'it's really nice of you to tell me that, but it's not as if I would let myself forget such a thing – nor as if I'd give you the bloody pleasure again, either.'

The baby now sucked noisily as the dummy did its job.

Lucas smiled to himself, knowing he had done the right thing in calling her back. He could hear the relief in her voice. She had obviously assumed he had been as drunk as her and wouldn't remember anything either! Two swigs of a beer didn't exactly count, did it? He had wanted to be sober, to remember every moment with her. Rosa was so streetwise in some ways, but so naïve in others.

'Hmm,' he teased. 'I'm not sure what I'm going to do to get you to break those marriage vows now, young lady.'

Rosa wondered whether to ask how she had got back to the flat on the night in question, and also why his mother was so angry that he had left the Bay.

Luke broke the silence. 'Anyway, I just wanted you to know that.'

'It surprises me that you seem to care so much about what I think, Luke.'

Lucas bit his lip at the end of the phone and made a pained expression. This was his chance to say exactly how he felt about her.

Instead, all he managed was a cocky, 'Got to keep all options open for when I come back down to the Bay, haven't I?'

Rosa sighed. 'Luke?'

'What's up, sexy?'

'I just want to say thank you.'

'For what?'

'Calling me.'

'You can't kid a kidder, kidder.'

'Oi, that's my line you've nicked there! I just need to convince Josh of my innocence now that he's moved back to London too.'

'Shit, that serious, eh? Well, if he ain't listening, you know where I am.'

Rosa went silent. Then Hot started barking, which made Theo spit out his dummy and start crying again. Lucas cringed at his ill-judged quip and, realising just how futile his attempts at making a play for her were now, felt even more deflated.

'Aw, is that Mr Sausage I can hear?' Lucas felt a wave of nostalgia. 'And was I right in thinking that your old man wasn't having an affair himself then?'

'Yes, smartarse, you were.' Rosa sighed again. 'So, *are* you coming back down at all?'

'Not for a while, no, Rosa. My life's in London again now.' The cockney lad felt his throat burning with misery. 'Need to start being a grown-up, stop messing around with other people's feelings.' He paused. 'And my own.'

As he hung up, Rosa began to sob in unison with the disgruntled baby. Lucas hadn't needed to do that, hadn't needed to do that at all. He wasn't such a bad lad, after all. Now all she had to do was convince Josh. But now she was in a Catch 22 situation, as firstly how would he react knowing that she had had further contact with Lucas? And secondly, why should he believe her anyway?

Lucas brushed his tears away as if swatting flies from his face. These emotions were just so alien to him. He'd never cried over a woman in his life. He'd obviously never loved a woman in his life either. Until now, that was. If this was what unrequited love felt like, you could keep it.

He got himself a beer from the fridge and flopped down onto the sofa. With memories of *that* kiss running through his mind, he sighed loudly. He thought back to hearing someone in the pub one night – it may even have been Titch – saying that when someone else's happiness is your happiness, that is true love. He took a slurp from his beer bottle and with that thought in mind, realised that he had just one more thing left to do.

CHAPTER FIFTY TWO

With Theo not letting up on his screaming, Mary had suggested on the phone that a change of temperature might settle him. Rosa didn't want to call Titch and worry her just yet, so she wrapped the baby up and put him in his pram. With Mary on standby to see if she could help, Rosa marched down towards the bay, sending out soothing noises as she did so, then started singing the first nursery rhymes that came into her head. Looking down, she became concerned as Theo was now kicking off his covers and pulling his little legs up like he had done on the night when he had been taken so ill. His face was also beetroot red and his distress obvious.

She was hurriedly turning the pram around, thinking that her mum would have to step in and give her opinion when she heard the calming voice of Alec behind her. Brown, his old Labrador, was shambling along at his heels.

'Hey, everything OK as it can be with a screaming baby on board?' Alec asked pleasantly.

'Oh Alec, I'm a bit worried to be honest. I've done everything on the list Titch gave me to do if he started playing up, but he just won't stop crying – and this is how he looked when he was really poorly.'

Theo's howls didn't let up.

'OK, come to mine. I can settle Brown and then we can have a proper look at him.'

They walked back between the two lions and into the warmth of Alec's house.

'Now, young man, what's all the noise about?' The big man lifted the baby up to his chest, causing Theo to stop crying momentarily. 'He looks so like my son did when he was a baby. I forgot just how cute he was. So much black curly hair too.' Theo whimpered and Alec turned to Rosa. 'You'll get to meet him soon – my lad is coming down in the morning, in fact. Spending the last few days of the Easter holidays with his old dad before he goes back to medical school.'

'That's nice. You'll both enjoy that.' And when Theo remained calm: 'See? Look at you, you're so natural with him. It's got to be my fault. I can't even look after a baby for a night properly.' Then, as if pandering to her insecurities, Theo began to scream again and dramatically draw his knees up to his chest. 'He's fed, I've changed his nappy, I tried to get him off to sleep. What's worrying me is this is how he was when he had his bowel problem before, and I'm sure the doctor said there was a chance that it could come back.' Rosa jiggled up and down nervously. 'Should I phone Titch, do you think?'

'Let's phone the emergency doctor first to rule that out.'

'I thought you were a doctor?'

'Not of medicine. It could just be it's the first time he's been left with anyone else and it would be a shame to worry your friend for nothing. Although his little face is burning up... Actually Rosa, let's be on the safe side and dial 999.'

Titch and Ritchie ran into A&E, their faces as white as a sheet. Ritchie was wearing just one sock and Titch was totally mismatched in joggers and a sparkly going-out top.

'Where is he? Where's my boy?' she wept.

'It's OK, it's OK,' Rosa soothed. 'He's had to go straight into emergency surgery. They said that your verbal consent on the phone was enough to go ahead with the operation as they couldn't wait for you to get here.'

'I drove as quickly as that bloody van would allow me,' Ritchie said wretchedly.

'It's not your fault.' Titch squeezed his hand. 'OK, did they say how long they'd be this time?'

'It all depends on how bad it is.'

'Oh, my poor little Theo. Was he doing what he did before then?'

'Yes, everything I told you on the phone earlier was exactly how it was.' Rosa took a deep panicky breath.

Alec butted in. 'I was with Rosa when he started getting distressed. We couldn't have acted any faster.'

'Thank you.' Titch let out a little groaning noise. 'I knew I shouldn't have gone away.'

Ever the calming influence, Alec put his hand on her arm. 'It could have happened anywhere and at any time, but he's in the best place now and he'll be seeing his mum very soon.'

They all sat in the waiting area, each one praying for the little boy to pull through.

At that moment a nurse bustled into the room. 'Mrs Whittaker?'

'It's Miss Whittaker, but how is he?'

'We've got him through this latest crisis, but we urgently need to get more blood supplies in. We don't hold a massive amount of the Ro subtype that we need, as you know. The surgeon said that you were hoping to get in touch with Theo's father to see if he was a match.'

Titch put her hand to her mouth and began to cry. 'I haven't found him yet.'

'All right, don't panic, dear, we will be able to source some,' the nurse replied and hurried back out of the room.

'I need to get home,' Alec declared suddenly. 'Rosa, do you want to come with me?' Rosa looked to Titch who nodded.

'It's fine. Ritchie, can you stay all night?'

The young man tried hard not to show disbelief at his new lover's question. Instead, he reached for her hand and promised, his love and commitment evident in every word: 'I can stay all night, all day – every day of my life if you need me, Titch.'

CHAPTER FIFTY THREE

Rosa had forgotten to set her alarm in all the drama, and was awoken by somebody banging on the shop door. It was already eight-thirty, but as she never opened until nine, at least it wouldn't be a disgruntled customer. Hot, too, had been deeply asleep after the disturbed night, but now he jumped up and hurtled towards the French doors, which Rosa quickly opened so he could have a pee. After shaking out a bowl of his dried food for his breakfast, she then pulled on her dressing-gown and headed downstairs.

'Oh, hi Jacob, everything OK?' The Duchess's head was sweetly poking out of his jacket. On realising she was in her furry mate's place, the young doggie started to whimper with excitement.

'Sorry, darling, I thought you'd have been up for hours.' Jacob inwardly hoped that his friend hadn't been drinking again.

Rosa yawned and stroked the little dachshund's ears. 'We had a bit of a late bedtime here. I was at the hospital with Titch again last night, as Theo was taken ill while I was looking after him. Oh Jacob, he's had to have another op.'

'Shit, that's terrible.'

'I know, and they are also worried about having enough

blood supplies for the little mite. I *told* Titch she should have made more of an effort finding his dad.'

'Don't be harsh on her.'

Rosa tutted. 'Of course, I won't, it's just my anxiety speaking – and there is no guarantee he'd be a match anyway.' She pulled herself together. 'So, what brings you here at this early hour?'

'A big favour actually, but if you haven't got Titch today, I don't want to put on you.'

'Go on, what is it?' Rosa asked. 'I am a fantastic plate-juggler, you know that.'

'Twinkle toes here hasn't been quite herself these past couple of days; she's off her food slightly and a bit whingy. I've got to go to the dentist and Raff is on his own in the kitchen today, so could you just mind her for a couple of hours from eleven o'clock? Ugly and Pongo can amuse themselves.'

'Of course, I can. Hot will love it and I will keep a close eye on the little munchkin. In fact, Vicki said that she's going to pop by with her boys at lunchtime. They want to go crabbing. The bay is a crustacean paradise, evidently. So how about I ask her to give the Duchess a once-over whilst she's here?'

'Bloody perfect.' Jacob was relieved. 'I was going to try and see Vicki later, so that's another worry less.'

'Good, aren't I? Why not just leave her with me now – you get on.'

'Hey, that'd be great, thanks so much. Keep me posted about Theo, won't you?'

'I will. See you later.'

As Jacob shut the door behind him, Rosa scooped the Duchess up in her arms and checked her phone messages. There was one from Titch. *Same as before! He's out of any danger, in special unit, will keep him in for the moment. I'm staying here. Told Ritchie to go to work. Could you pop over later maybe?*

Rosa quickly texted back to say OK and to send her love. It was great that Ritchie was by Titch's side now. He could share the load. Rosa had always felt slightly responsible for Titch in a big sister kind of way. Something else she would sadly never experience. Sibling love.

Rosa checked her watch. April Fool's Day. There was nothing funny about anything that was happening now, but at least that did mean in less than two weeks she would be on her way to London to see Josh. She would know her fate. So much had been going on that she had completely forgotten to leave a message for him again. She had had to deal with many dramas without him this week. He would understand. Let him miss her for a change. Realise that it wasn't all about him. Maybe she should start thinking of herself a lot more.

Yes, she'd make a mistake, but she was prepared to change. Rosa nodded to herself at her positive thinking. Everything would be OK, because she would make it OK. She had a sudden flashback to her dear darling Josh walking on the beach after she had confessed that she had been with Luke. Titch was right, if Rosa had just found out the same about him, she would have been distraught. Her jealousy was so off the scale that she wasn't sure what action she would have taken, but whatever it was, it wouldn't have been walking away from him or keeping silent. Josh was so wise sometimes.

Just as she was settling the Duchess and Hot in with their toys and some treats in two rubber kongs to keep them busy, Rosa's mobile rang on the shop counter downstairs. Not getting to it in time or recognising the number, she waited in case a voice message came through. It did. 'Oh, hi Rosa, it's Sara Jenkins here. I… er…look, can you meet me at the ice-cream kiosk on the front at eleven o'clock tomorrow morning? If I don't hear from you, I will take it that you *can* make it.'

It was 9.15 – quarter of an hour overdue for opening time. Fortunately, there were no customers as yet, as she wasn't even dressed. Putting the *Back in 20 minutes* notice on the door, Rosa dashed back upstairs to gather some clothes. However, before she disappeared into the bathroom for the world's fastest shower, she went to check that all was well with the puppy. She couldn't resist playing with the tiny Duchess for a few moments. Not wanting to be left out, Hot came bounding over, sniffed around the pretty bitch then barked loudly. Sweeping him up onto her lap, Rosa murmured fondly, 'My Hotty boy...' Then squashing his pointed jaw and tickly black whiskers against her cheek, she mumbled, 'Sara Jenkins, eh? What an earth does *she* want?'

CHAPTER FIFTY FOUR

Titch could barely speak for tiredness. In fact, at this precise moment she thought she might also be hallucinating.

'Your *son*, you say?' She looked at Alec and then at the handsome young man to the side of him. 'Ben? Oh, my goodness. Cardiff Ben from the stag party in the Ship – is that you?'

'Er…Oh hi. Do I know you?' Ben Burton looked confused. Then, putting his hand to his forehead, 'Oh lord. Yes, it's all coming back now.' He gazed at the little dark-haired bundle in the incubator and it was his turn to be open-mouthed.

At that point Ritchie, having just been to get coffees for everyone, returned to the unit.

'You already know each other?' Alec looked puzzled.

'Who are you?' Ritchie asked the newcomer warily.

'Well, this is awkward.' Titch paused and braced herself. 'And not quite how I had imagined this moment to be.' She sighed. 'Ritchie, this is Ben, Alec's son.' She put her hand gently on her baby's forehead. 'And Ben, this is Theo. Your son.'

CHAPTER FIFTY FIVE

'Imagine Jacob's face when I tell him he's going to be a grandfather,' Rosa laughed as she walked along the edge of the beach with Vicki Cliss. The Duchess had seemed to brighten up, and she and Hot were gleefully chasing each other. Arthur and Stan were crabbing. Buckets of water at the ready, the two young lads were eager to capture the ten-legged pinchers when they greedily grabbed the bacon bait that Stuart had just carefully put on the hooks for them.

Easter holidaymakers, making the most of the joyous spring sunshine, were starting to arrive and set up mini-camps. Seagulls, ecstatic that a free lunch would most definitely be on the cards, cawed their appreciation.

'I just knew when you said she was off her food that there could be a chance she was pregnant, but those sore nipples are the giveaway.' Vicki reached down to tickle the Duchess, who had her paws tangled in some seaweed. 'She's very young, but we will get her through it. I wonder if they know who the father is?'

'No, they don't – but I do!' Rosa was every inch the proud grandmother.

Vicki laughed out loud. 'Of course, I saw you hadn't had him done when I examined him.'

'Randy little bugger,' Rosa said fondly. 'I remember now having to pull him off her the other day. I naively didn't think he would be having his wicked way with her. And I've left them together a few times. How exciting – though it's odd that I'm going to be a grannie before I'm a mum. Oh dear, I'm really sorry, Vicki. So tactless.' Rosa put her hand on the vet's shoulder. 'How are you doing?'

'Remarkably well, thank you. I had a small op to clear out my womb. Left hospital the next morning, then spent a day in bed. I'm lucky I'm fit. It's the mind more than the body that needs to be looked after when something like this happens.' Vicki blinked to stop her tears falling and blew her nose. 'It was another little boy.'

Rosa now felt tears welling too. 'Vicki…how sad.'

'My boys have already moved on. Bump has gone to heaven and maybe one day another Bump will come to Mummy. If only Stuart and I could move on that quickly.'

'It's so hard, isn't it, bless you. If you ever need to chat, I'm here.'

'Thanks – I may take you up on that. I'm so lucky in having Stuart. He's an empathetic man. He gets it, you know. That's why he's so good on the lifeboats. That's why he's over there and has left us to chat over here. So thoughtful.'

'Like my Josh,' Rosa said softly. Realising that whatever she had thrown at him, he had been there for her. Her rock. But even rocks have a breaking point and she cringed at the enormity of distress he must have felt to finally reach his.

'It won't be long before you see him. You said your birthday, didn't you? You must be excited.'

'Excited, scared, feel a bit sick. But I love him, Vicki. Every day I am away from him makes me realise that he is the man

I do want to spend the rest of my life with. I bloody miss him.'

They sat down on a rock and lifted their heads to the warm spring sunshine.

'What if he's not ready or doesn't want to see me?' Rosa lamented.

'Hold your hand out and splay your fingers,' Vicki instructed. Rosa quizzically did as she was told as the vet continued, 'It may not be long now until you see him, but whenever you feel alone look at the spaces between your fingers and just remember that's where his fit yours perfectly.'

'That's so lovely.'

'Words cost nothing but mean more than the world sometimes. Saying that, this is for you.' Vicki reached into her pocket and handed over a pink gift box. Her eyes filled with tears again. 'Thank you, Rosa. For being there.' She started to cry. 'You got me through the toughest day in my life and I will never forget that. You held more than my hand. You helped to hold my heart together when it was pretty much breaking in two.'

Rosa was crying now. 'You made me face up to my own miscarriage. You helped *me* so much, too.'

'Oh Rosa, I didn't know. I'm sorry for your pain.'

'It's all good.' Rosa smiled between the tears. 'I'm facing my fears and life as a grown-up now.' She opened the box in front of her to find a beautiful light-pink stone bracelet with a heart attached.

'It's rose quartz, they don't do a Rosa quartz, or I would have obviously got you that.' Vicki sniffed and smiled too. 'Jacob told me you liked things like this. I hope you don't think me out of turn, but rose quartz is recognised as a stone of fertility. It's thought to nurture life and vibrancy below the skin, as well as to relieve stress. So I'm told by the lovely lady in the crystal shop in

Polhampton anyway. She also said that a woman should place a quartz stone on her stomach during pregnancy, and then give the stone to her baby after birth, as the rose quartz mineral is believed to welcome new life.'

'It's exquisite and not at all out of turn. Thank you, Vicki, it's beautiful. I will treasure it.'

'I even got one for myself…ready for the next time.'

At that moment, Vicki's oldest boy rushed over to show off his bounty of very unhappy crabs, who were scrabbling frantically to the top of the bucket trying to make their escape. Stuart had lifted a now-screaming Stan to his shoulders and was making his way up the beach.

'Mummy, Daddy says we have to set them free,' Arthur complained. 'It's not fair! Why can't we take them home?'

'Because life isn't fair sometimes, Arthur, that's why.'

CHAPTER FIFTY SIX

Rosa sat opposite a yawning Titch in the hospital café. The young mum groaned and reached for two sachets of sugar to stir into her insipid-looking tea.

'Here, let me.' Rosa took them from her to rip open and finish the job in hand. 'You poor thing. You look exhausted.'

'Theo can come home tomorrow, thank goodness. Oh Rose, it's been so stressful.'

'I know, mate. So, have they sorted the problem for good now, do they think?'

'They are very hopeful. I need to keep him on a special diet for a while and bring him for regular check-ups from now on, but the prognosis is good.' She perked up. 'He's so strong, my little lad, and he's been such a brave boy considering everything he's had to go through.'

'Like his mother.' Rosa reached over the table to touch her hand.

Titch's expression was pained. 'I'm glad to be here on my own now though.'

'Is Ritchie not being so helpful then?' Rosa was surprised.

'He is being a dream, but I had to see you face-to-face because something major has happened.'

'Go on.' Rosa started to unwrap her chocolate bar.

'You know Ben, as in Big Ben, as in father of my child?'

'Er…yes.'

'He's only Alec Burton's son!'

'Shut up! No way! That's mental.'

'Tell me about it. They both waltzed in here yesterday. Alec was beside himself with delight as Ben proved a match to Theo's blood group. He hadn't wanted to mention it to anyone the other night in case it didn't work out. He is such a nice guy, Rose.'

'That's right,' Rosa remembered. 'Alec told me that he'd met his wife in the Caribbean as a holiday romance. I didn't realise that she was from that part of the world. Oh, it all makes sense now.'

'Yes, it does. Ben is studying medicine in Cardiff; he recommended the South-west for the stag weekend as he had holidayed down here loads when he was younger. Little did he know at that time that his dad would decide to move down this way. The group spent most of their time in Newquay down in Cornwall, but Ben also loved Cockleberry Bay and wanted them to see it, hence their night at the Ship.'

'So what happened? How did you feel about seeing him?'

'I could tell that Ritchie was devastated, but he was really mature about it and went off outside so that I could speak to Ben in private. Ben was obviously gobsmacked, but when Theo opened his eyes it was such a special moment. You should have seen his face. He couldn't lift him as there were too many tubes connected to him, but he was so gentle in his touch and words. He's so handsome too, Rose, I can't tell you.'

'So, what did Ben say?' Rosa was wide-eyed.

'He is so sensible.' Titch stuffed a piece of carrot cake in.

'With a dad like Alec, that's not surprising,' Rosa butted in.

'He said he needed to sleep on everything as he wanted to do right by Theo and me, so he came back this morning, minus Alec, and we just pulled the curtains round and with Theo in between us we chatted.'

'So, what did you both decide?'

'Ben is studying hard and was honest and said that it had been a one-night stand and he wasn't a believer in making something work for the sake of it. He was just so happy that he is the right blood match for our Theo. He can't give me a monthly allowance yet, but when he is getting a decent salary he will. However, listen to this. He just got an inheritance from his grandmother on his mother's side and would like to give me two thousand pounds of it to help me towards a deposit on a flat or house when the time is right.'

'That Titchy Titch fund is going to be doing really well soon.' Rosa added.

'You just need to move out of your flat now so Ritchie and I can move in.' Titch grinned. 'Ben did also say for me to give him my bank account details and as and when he has some spare cash, he will pop it in. He would also like a say in Theo's future too. I can't believe how fair he has been, considering he's young like me too.'

'Titch, that is amazing. What a nice man.'

'I'm so lucky. I could tell we were worlds apart though. He speaks so eloquently, and he is so, so clever. We never would have matched in the real world.'

'Love has no boundaries and all that. I mean, look at me and Josh.'

'That's different, you have a foundation, we had a drunken bunk-up. Also, yes, he said that obviously because of his doctor training, if ever I need to call him to ask him to advise on some health issue, however trivial it may seem, that I must do so.'

'Excellent. And no doubt Ben will have to tell his mother she's a grandmother too. I don't envy him that, although Alec is such a cool guy, he just takes everything in his stride.' Rosa then asked carefully, 'How is Ritchie?'

'I've texted him to say that everything is still the same between us. But I know he feels threatened. He can't fathom why I'd rather be with a fish and chip server than a doctor. He's picking us up in the morning in his mum's car with a proper car seat in it, so we are not just holding Theo like before. That was so irresponsible of us, Rose.'

'It was an emergency when we took him the first time, so don't even think about that. We did the same in Alec's car the other night too.'

Titch looked haggard. 'I'm so tired, Rose.'

'I know, darling. And don't worry about Ritchie. He adores you, mate.'

'I really like him too. The plan tomorrow is to get Theo settled, then Mum said she'd sit with him for an hour so we can talk properly. I thought we could go to Coffee, Tea or Sea. It's so calming in there with the sea view.'

'Talking of that, I'm meeting Sara Jenkins tomorrow.'

'No! Why?'

'I dunno. She left a message saying she wanted to meet me. Maybe she will tell me more about the café or maybe she has spoken to Josh, who knows, but I want to hear what she has to say.'

'It's all going on.' Titch finished her tea.

'It certainly is.' Rosa laughed suddenly, remembering that she hadn't yet told Titch her own news. 'And by the way, you'll never guess who else is having children out of wedlock.'

'Who?' Titch sat up, her mouth full of carrot cake.

'The Duchess! And Hot is the father.'

Titch's shoulders began to shake with laughter. 'The Duchess? But she's so tiny, and so young too! What a slut. But your Hot must have taken advantage of her.'

'Oi, watch out. Hot had a troubled childhood, don't you know.'

'Don't you be sticking up for him. That's so sweet though.' Titch wriggled with excitement. 'I of course want one of the puppies. Ritchie and Theo will be over the moon. How long is the pregnancy?'

'Around sixty-five days, so they will be summer babies.' Rosa beamed with joy. 'Titch, I'm going to be a grandmother!'

'And dare I mention Grandpa Josh?'

'You can mention him, but I've not heard a thing. My plan is to get the train to London on the morning of my birthday. It's a Sunday so I'm just gonna shut up shop for two days.'

'I could . . .'

'No, you couldn't.' Rosa stopped Titch in her tracks. 'One hundred per cent take some time out. I also want to pay you for two shifts for two weeks as a holiday payment, how's that?'

'That's so kind, thank you, Rose.'

'Right, I'm getting off. Ralph Weeks is taking me back to the Bay.'

'Thanks for coming. I know it's a ball-ache to get here without a car.'

'Ooh, you'll have to watch your language as Theo grows bigger, and so will I.' Rosa hugged her friend. 'I love you, mate, and your little man.' She stood up. 'Good luck with Ritchie tomorrow. I'm sure it will be fine.'

'Likewise, with Sara. We will need a drink after all that.'

'Tea, maybe, now I'm teetotal and all that.' Rosa did a funny little dance.

'You're crazy.' Titch pushed her chair in, stood up and kissed her friend on the cheek.

'Takes one to know one.' Rosa kissed Titch back. 'Now go and give that little man of yours a tiny squeeze from me – and then, Titch, try to get some sleep.'

CHAPTER FIFTY SEVEN

The Seven Lessons
Six: Jealousy

Rosa didn't like shutting the shop during peak hours, but with Titch at home nursing a thankfully recovering Theo, and Mary working at the Co-op, she had no alternative. Meeting Sara Jenkins was important to her and she felt ready to face whatever it was the woman was going to say to her.

Leaving Hot dozing under a blanket in his crate upstairs, Rosa made her way down the hill to the beach. It was a glorious April day and she loved the fact that for the first time in ages she didn't need to wear a jacket. When the weather was good in Cockleberry Bay it confirmed her decision that she didn't ever want to leave. The local shops now had racks outside displaying their wares, and savoury smells floated in the air as doors were opened to let in the warm breeze and also to welcome visitors in. The season had begun and everyone was busy.

'Well, this is slightly embarrassing.' Rosa held her hand out to Sara who was standing right by the ice-cream kiosk, looking much younger than her fifty years in long shorts and a trendy surf-style T-shirt.

'That's why I've got us an ice-cream breaker.' Sara smiled and pointed to the two cornets resting in a little rack on the counter. 'If you fancy one, that is?'

'Mr Whippy and a flake – are you joking?' Rosa smiled back. 'That is possibly my favourite treat, along with fish and chips, that is.'

'Well you're certainly living in the right place for both of those. Shall we walk?'

Rosa nodded as Sara handed her the overflowing ice-cream cone. Instead of just listening, she did her usual nervous trait of blurting out a long stream of words. 'I actually don't know how much you know, Sara, about what happened, but it's all pretty mortifying and I'm not proud of the way I behaved. Especially right in front of your café. I've no idea what is happening with the café either, so if that is why you want to talk to me . . .'

'It's not, actually.'

'I've made a conscious note of not even looking to see if the green tarpaulin is still there hiding half of my name as the memories still make me cringe.' Rosa then realised what Sara had said. 'It's not? I just – I haven't even spoken to Josh and I'm so sorry if it's put you in a terrible financial position. Mary, that's my mum, she said you were moving to St Ives. Have I ruined your plans?'

'No. In fact, Rosa, you've done me a massive favour.'

'I have?'

'Yes. You see, I always rush into decisions. And as it turns out, I'm not ready to leave. Thinking that running a guest-house in St Ives would make my life easier was plain foolish. After taking time to really think it through, I realised that it would be even harder work than running the café. What's more, I don't like the thought of having strangers in my home every day. My friends are here in the Bay too – and look at it.' She pointed over to the beach where kids were running in and out of the sea's edge, screaming in delight.

'St Ives is a magical place too,' she went on, 'but this is my home and it is so beautiful here in Cockleberry Bay, come rain or come shine.' The sun was now causing the very blue sea to twinkle, and everyone within metres of it to breathe a little bit deeper. 'So, I have to thank you, Rosa. You stopped me in my tracks. Made me think about what I really wanted.'

'That is such a relief. I felt so guilty that I must confess I've been avoiding you.'

Sara tutted. 'Oh Rosa. Half the time people aren't thinking what you imagine they are thinking. When you realise that, life becomes a whole lot easier and I do have to say that if I had seen that mail exchange between me and your husband, I would have acted the same way as you. In fact, if I had been you, in a previous life I probably would have been storming down to this café and throwing a hot cup of coffee over me!'

'Oh my God, really?'

'Yes. I had a massive jealousy problem when I was younger.'

'You seem so together.'

'Ah, but that's a bit like realising that people aren't thinking what you imagine they are thinking.' Sara took a long lick of her ice-cream, which was running down the cone. 'Just because people have a calm exterior doesn't mean their mind isn't ugly and ravaged with pain.'

'I guess so. I didn't realise myself until recently that I have been masking my own pain with various coping mechanisms.'

'Well, I am sad to say that my own jealousy caused the most shattering event in my whole life.'

'Oh no! That sounds terrible. Come on, let's head up South

Cliffs. Have you got some free time?'

'Yes.' The café-owner took a deep breath. 'Jealousy is a natural emotion, but it must be tamed. Untamed, the words "green-eyed monster" are so damn relevant.'

'Do you mind me asking what happened?'

Sara opened the gate leading up to South Cliffs. 'I am an only child, and my dad left when I was at primary school. We didn't live round here at the time. He cleared off with his secretary – oh so clichéd. Left my mum in pieces and me never trusting anyone again.'

'I completely understand that. I was brought up in foster care and learned to trust nobody. I'm doing my best now to change that, I hope. I interrupted you, go on, sorry.'

'It's fine.' Sara made an exasperated noise. 'Even thinking about what happened makes me feel slightly ill but I have to tell you about it, Rosa. I'd always played at relationships, could never settle. Never believed anyone would truly want me.'

'But you are so beautiful.'

'Externally maybe, but I was really quite dark on the inside.' Sara threw the end of her cone in a bin. 'But then I met Steve.' Her voice cracked. 'He filled me with love, he completed me; we had the same goals, the same sense of humour. I bloody loved that man.'

'What happened?' Rosa asked gently.

'I saw him talking to another woman.' Sara blew out a huge breath. 'I'd arranged to meet him in a pub for lunch as we sometimes did if he was working and got a break or, you know, just general life stuff. He knew what I was like and managed our relationship as best he could around my jealousy. The poor bastard was literally just making small talk at the bar, I expect. Chatting about the weather or something. But I went completely crazy, lunged at him, reached for a drink of someone's else's off

271

the bar and threw it over her. Steve was so embarrassed. I know I humiliated him and myself too by making such a silly scene. He managed to get me outside and tried to talk me down like he usually did, but I wasn't having any of it.'

'I hear you loud and clear. It's so hard to control it sometimes, isn't it? I mean, look at me kicking off outside your café that day. That wasn't jealousy though; that was pure frustration.'

Sara stopped walking for a second. 'It gets worse.'

'Oh Sara.'

'He did what he usually did, said that he loved me and that he'd see me later when I had calmed down, then he got into his car and drove off. They were the last words he ever said to me.'

'No! What happened?'

'A deer ran out in front of him on the coast road. He swerved and hit an oncoming car, which brought on a heart attack. He died instantly.' The woman shuddered, and it was a moment before she could speak again. This time, Rosa wisely held her tongue.

'I'm telling you all this as I don't want you to make the same mistake. If you think your husband is The One, then trust him. Realise that not everybody will leave you. Not everyone is a bad person and out to hurt you, Rosa. By the sound of it, the likes of you and me are quite capable of doing that to ourselves.'

'I'm so, so sorry, Sara.'

'I just wish our last moments together hadn't been so awful. That *his* last moments hadn't been so awful.'

'He knew how much you loved him.'

'I made his life so hellish though. It must be so difficult for the other partner if they are not trusted. I didn't even think of that before…you know…before what happened.'

'You are so brave.'

'I'm not, Rosa, but what's the alternative of not picking

myself up and getting on with it? Life goes on. But that's why I find myself single and childless at fifty. Nobody has matched up to Steve yet, and I'm not sure if I will ever be able to let anyone else in.'

'I'm sure you will one day.'

'Yes, hopefully. The past couple of years I've been having the most intensive relationship I've ever had with anyone in my whole life. A therapist. I'm not embarrassed to admit it either. It's the best money I've spent on me in a long time. And if I can help someone else through something that in reality is quite easy to fix, then I will. So, stop your jealousy, Rosa.'

'I am going to try so hard now – that is, if Josh comes back.'

'He'll be back.'

'You don't know that.'

'Steve loved me. He always came back…' Her voice tailed off for a second. 'Work on yourself and that green-eyed monster. Even though it's such a hard topic to discuss, acknowledging its presence can help people strengthen their relationships. Exploring the emotions that underpin it, notably the fear of losing someone who is loved, can avert angry arguments. I just wish I hadn't been too late to find that out.'

'I hear you.'

'So, *when* Josh comes back, pave the way for a productive conversation about what the relationship might be missing and how you can repair the bond. Please don't get to my age and realise you have wasted time and energy on such an unnecessary emotion.'

'Blimey, you have been to therapy, haven't you?' Rosa teased kindly. 'Thank you, Sara.'

'Whatever age we are, we are always learning.' Sara closed her eyes for a moment then opened them and smiled, saying, 'Right – I'd better get back. Poor old Kitty will be starting to panic if

I'm not there for the lunchtime rush.'

Sara stopped just before they reached the café. She looked directly at Rosa. 'The R and O are still painted behind the tarpaulin in case you were wondering.'

'I don't even want to think about what that might mean.'

'It's not for me to say any more on the matter, but I felt I had to have that conversation with you.'

'I appreciate that, and it has definitely helped me to look at jealousy in a different way. I've also had a thought. I think I know someone who might make you smile again.'

'Oh?'

'Yes. I should imagine he's as stubborn as you, but he's a good bloke, so how does a blind date grab you?'

'You're talking to someone who hasn't been grabbed for years.' They both laughed. Sara reached for the purse in her pocket and handed Rosa a Coffee, Tea or Sea business card. 'Here's my number.'

CHAPTER FIFTY EIGHT

'Not even bribery with my favourite German sausage will dampen my disappointment at this news, Rosa Smith.' Jacob waved his arm in the air and went back to spooning fresh coffee grounds into his cafetière. Raff was busy outside tending their vegetable patch.

Rosa had gifted her friend five different types of mini-sausage and a secondhand pair of slippers and a pipe she had just picked up from the charity shop in Polhampton.

'Grandad quite suits you, I think.' Raff breezed in and kissed his husband on the cheek. 'You know I love an older man.' He and Rosa laughed, whilst Jacob tried hard not to smile.

The Duchess came into the kitchen yapping for food, followed swiftly by Hot with the pugs panting at his heels.

'Little madam! Under-age sex, she had. You do realise that, don't you?'

Rosa laughed out loud. 'Oh, don't be cross. It's going to be so lovely when the pups arrive.'

'For you, maybe, in the Corner Shop with just Hot to look after, whilst I have to run around here, pick up the shit and try to keep our beautiful home from being chewed.'

'I think Ugly and Pongo make a good enough job of that.

Anyway, the pups will be pedigree, so you can sell them, you old misery. Provided you keep one for me and one for Titch.' Rosa picked her handbag up off the kitchen worktop. 'Right, I'm not stopping, I just wanted to say hi and bring you gifts. I've got a meeting with a card supplier in town. Evidently pet birthday cards are quite a big market nowadays.'

'OK darling, see you soon.' Jacob blew her air kisses. 'Talking of birthdays, are you still intending to go and hunt down that errant husband of yours?'

'Yep. There's still been no word at all from him. I'm obviously desperate to see him, but I'm angry with him as well. I have everything planned that I want to say when I do see him, but let's face it – I will probably just end up a crying wreck.'

'Maybe it's not such a good idea then, Rosa.'

She harrumphed. 'I can't wait any longer. And if Josh can't get over what happened, then I need to know.'

'OK, but which day are you leaving, on your birthday or before?'

'Why the sudden interest?'

'Because maybe your friends want to treat you to a lovely birthday meal,' Raffaele piped up.

'Oh, that's nice. I need to look at train times. I promise I will let you know. Right, I must go.'

'Do you want a lift down the hill, Princess?' Raff slurped on his coffee and started flicking through a newspaper.

'No thanks, it's fine. Hot needs the walk.' Rosa leaned down and gently pulled Hot away from the Duchess. 'Come on, Muttley. You can see your girlfriend another day.'

Rosa took in the stunning views as she walked down the hill from her friends' house. Polhampton Sands was indeed a beautiful seaside town and it would be the perfect place to live and bring up a young family, as there was so much to do.

With half an hour to spare until her meeting, it was too good a chance not to spend time in the sunshine; she even fancied venturing down for a paddle.

Hot charged off on his usual fruitless task of chasing seagulls and Rosa was just bending down to unlace her trainers and go for a paddle when a familiar voice spoke to her.

'You wouldn't happen to have a light, would you?'

Rosa straightened up. 'I didn't know you smoked.' The shock of realising who it was caused Becca Fox to drop her red and white cigarette packet on to the sand.

'Spanish cigarettes?' Rosa noted, recognising the brand. 'Interesting.'

'Yes, I...er...my mum lives in Spain. And I – well, they are cheap and...er...I've only just started smoking again.'

Rosa felt anger rising through her body. She shut her eyes and saw a vision, firstly of Queenie saying, 'Sometimes, Rosa, it's better to just wait and say nothing at all', and then of her mother: 'Ask yourself, Rosa, is it necessary, is it kind?' A white feather then dropped out of the air and onto her hand, causing her whole body to tingle slightly.

'Smoking is bad for your health, so they tell me,' she managed.

'Not quite as bad as men though, hey, Rosa?' Becca rummaged through her handbag and found some matches. 'Thank God.' She lit her cigarette and took a huge drag, went to walk away, then stopped in her tracks.

'I know you had an affair with my husband, Rosa.'

'I...' Rosa was stuck for words.

'There's no point in lying about it now. Especially as he's moved on to his next conquest.'

Rosa thought for a minute, then confessed, 'I'm so sorry, Becca. Please believe me that I honestly knew nothing about you. He was so clever in the way he manipulated me. When

I found out about you and the children, it was a devastating shock. He nearly broke my heart, as a matter of fact.'

'So you didn't come to the house to check me and my kids out that day then?'

'No, far from it. My mother and great-grandmother set me up to show me exactly who and what Joe Fox was. And as soon as I found out, I ended it. I dropped him in it on local radio first, of course.'

'Ah, yes, the imaginary stomach bug to get away from you that day. He thinks he's so bloody clever, but he's not.' Becca shook her head and sighed. 'I found out eventually, about you and him, I mean. I managed to work out his phone code and found messages to you. I don't even like the name Rosie, but to see him squirm every time I use it actually quite amuses me.'

'I'm so very sorry. If I had known – girl code and all that. I would never have had anything to do with him.'

Becca put her hand up to stop Rosa talking and took another deep drag on her cigarette. 'There was a fire in my shop.' Rosa looked directly at the woman, whose usually glossy blonde locks were greasy and hanging around her face. Her T-shirt was clearly un-ironed. She looked so dejected and downtrodden – but who wouldn't, Rosa thought, married to a creep like Joe Fox.

'Yes, I heard about the fire.' She mumbled, 'Right, I must go. I need to fetch Rosie from nursery. Bye.'

'Did you start the fire in my shop, Becca?' Rosa carried on calmly.

Becca started to cry and turned to walk off again.

'Did you!' Rosa shouted after her.

Becca whirled around ferociously. 'I thought he was seeing you again; he was showing all the usual signs, dog-walking for hours, late nights at work. And when he came out with the story that you had fallen from the cliff and how he had to see you at the shop, well, I just assumed that it had started up again.' She threw her cigarette butt in the sand and covered it with her foot. 'You can go to the police if you like and I'll admit it. I might as well go to prison. My life is like hell, with four children to look after on my own now, and he is just such a tosser. Who else will take me on, eh?'

Rosa couldn't even imagine what the other woman was going through. At least when Joe had broken her heart, she had only herself to think about. Yes, the woman standing in front of her had done a terrible thing, but Rosa couldn't be sure that the old Rosa wouldn't have done the same in the circumstances. I mean, look at what she'd done when there wasn't any proof that Josh had had an affair? She set out to sleep with somebody else.

'I understand now why you wanted to use my back toilet and suss out the back entrance. It all makes sense now. And taking my mobile number so you could sneakily check his bill again, I guess?'

'You should be a detective not a shop-owner.' Becca sniffed tiredly. 'I'm not running because I know you will find me, so do you want me to call the police or will you do it?' She went to hand Rosa her phone.

Rosa pushed the phone back and ran her hand through her wind-blown brown curls and thought. If somebody had been hurt, this would be a very different scenario. As it was, the damage had cost more time than money. 'So, are you getting divorced now? How will you manage?'

'As if you care,' the woman said dully. Hot ran back up the beach and looked curiously up at Becca, sensing some discord in the air. She sighed deeply. 'I've actually put everything into place to move to Spain and live with Mum. My eldest is at university now, so it's just the twins and Rosie. There's a good international school for them in Barcelona, but I guess that will all change now.' She made a funny laugh-type noise. 'When I'm locked up.'

Hot knocked Becca's bag with his jumping and her packet of cigarettes fell to the sand. Rosa picked them up and crushed them in her hand.

'Becca, go home. Get rid of all the cigarettes you have like these and book your flights to Spain.'

'But...' Becca looked at her in disbelief.

'You've been through enough, living with that philandering bastard. And I'm afraid your eldest son might not turn out much better, if someone doesn't take him in hand. He's got a nasty temper. You getting locked away from your three little ones who need you won't make *me* feel better. That would be awful. I'm just happy knowing who did it.' Rosa gave a smile. It was another lesson in the perils of jealousy.

Becca was open-mouthed. All she could manage was, 'But...' Rosa checked her watch and tightened her laces.

'I need to go. Goodbye, Becca. Enjoy your new life in Spain.'

CHAPTER FIFTY NINE

Ritchie gazed nervously across the table in Coffee, Tea or Sea at a very tired-looking Titch.

'Sorry I look such a fright,' she apologised.

'Titch Whittaker, you always look beautiful to me. How's our little chap doing, anyway?'

'He's so much better, thank heavens. He had baby rice for breakfast and Mum just got him to take a whole bottle and get him off to sleep, so we should have a decent bit of time until he wakes, I hope. The doctors said we should hold back on giving him too many solids. I think we may have started him too early anyway – everyone says a baby should be six months old, these days.'

'I wouldn't have a clue,' Richie said honestly, 'but it's fantastic news, to hear that he is settling so well. Talking of feeding, I already ordered a hot chocolate and a croissant for you as I know they are your favourites, just in case we didn't have much time.'

'You're so sweet, Ritchie Rogers.' Titch reached over to hold both of his hands. 'And thank you so much.'

'For what?'

'Just being there. I couldn't have got through this without

you.'

Ritchie tried to sound casual when he said, 'That Ben seems like a decent bloke.'

'Yes, he is, and he is going to do right by me and Theo, which is just so comforting.'

The colour drained from Ritchie's face. 'As in, he's going to marry you?' He could barely get the words out.

Titch laughed. 'No, silly. Just help with finances, and obviously he can advise re Theo's health issues, plus readily give blood if required.'

Ritchie gave a sigh of relief. 'That's all right then.' He leaped up from his seat and went around to her side of the table.

'Where are you going?' Titch took a slurp from her hot chocolate.

When Ritchie got down on one knee and held out a little green jewellery box, the few people in the café went silent.

'I know this may seem like a short courtship,' Ritchie began, and Titch put her hand to her mouth. 'But it's one we started at school, many years ago, so it's not really. I adore you. I adore that little boy of yours. And I would be the happiest man in the world if you would agree to be my wife. Patricia Irene Whittaker, will you marry me?'

Tears started to flow down Titch's pale, tired face. She looked into Ritchie's eyes. On paper, they had been dating for just weeks, but the kindness he had shown to both her and Theo over the past few days proved that where love is concerned, time doesn't really matter. Just as love isn't an emotion, it isn't ruled by a stopwatch either.

So, when Ritchie placed a simple but exquisite white-gold diamond ring on her finger, Titch meant it with every part of her little bruised heart when she said, 'Yes, yes, I'll marry you.'

Sara found a couple of party poppers that had been left in the drawer at Christmas and set them off over the pair. Everybody cheered.

As they walked back up the hill, stopping to kiss momentarily, Ritchie held both Titch's hands.

'Do you know what made my mind up?'

'My incredible beauty? My hour-glass figure?' Titch giggled.

'No. It was when you corrected the nurse to say you were a miss in the hospital and I just thought, "That miss ain't gonna be a miss for much longer".'

'You're crazy.'

'I know, but I plan to be the best husband in the world, and with your permission I plan to be the best father figure I can be for Theo. Of course, his real dad will be in his life, but I will be in his heart from the start. He will be such a loved little boy.'

'I'm so happy!' Titch did a little dance in the street. 'I can't wait to tell Rosa. When shall we do it and where shall we live and…'

'Let's get Theo completely better first. Then we can start making plans.'

'That's so sensible.'

'Well, it's a good job one of us is, eh?' Ritchie hugged his fiancée tightly. 'Come on, let's go and shout our news from the rooftops of Cockleberry Bay.'

CHAPTER SIXTY

Josh was just getting ready to leave his office for the evening when his secretary poked her head around his office door.

'You off, Katie?' he asked.

'Yes, but I've just had a call from Reception. There is somebody here to see you.'

'Oh, that's odd. There's nothing in my diary. Who is it – do you know?'

'It's a Lucas Hannafore, and he said you will know what it's about.'

Josh grimaced.

'Everything all right?' Katie had noticed his frown.

'Yeah, yeah. Can you say I'll meet him downstairs in ten minutes, please?'

CHAPTER SIXTY ONE

'Married! Oh my God, we need to open some champagne with immediate effect – well, lemonade for me.' Rosa hugged Titch tightly and gave Ritchie a friendly poke in the ribs. 'This is just so wonderful. So tell me when and where. I obviously want to be chief bridesmaid.'

Titch laughed. 'Ritchie's literally only just asked me, so we have no idea yet but yes, of course, you can be my matron of honour.'

'No, that makes me sound far too old.' Rosa went to the back kitchen and checked the fridge. 'Dry as a bone, this place, I'm afraid. But we will celebrate soon.'

'I was going up to tell Mum first but as you were outside the shop, I couldn't contain myself.'

'I should think not. How's our little Theo doing?'

'Fingers crossed he's still asleep now, but yes, he's definitely turned a corner.' Emotion suddenly hit her and Titch felt a bit faint. She had to sit down behind the counter.

With Ritchie in the toilet, Rosa whispered, 'I'm so happy for you, mate. He seems such a good man. He has really shown his true colours this week too.'

'He is and he has.' Titch's eyes were moist. 'Now we just

need to get you back on track,' she said to Rosa. 'Are you still intending to go to London?'

'Yes. Tonight, in fact.'

'Tonight? But you can't!'

Ritchie appeared from the toilet. 'Can't what?'

'Rosa can't go up to London tonight.'

Rosa made a face. 'Why not?'

'Erm, because it's your birthday tomorrow and I want to see you on your birthday.'

'Don't be weird, Titch. I'll probably be on the next train back when Josh shows me the divorce papers anyway.'

'What time are you going tonight then?'

'In a couple of hours. Ralph Weeks is picking me up. I only need a small bag so I'm all packed and ready.'

'Don't you think it might be better to call Josh and let him know?'

'And give him the chance to say no? No way.'

'OK, come on, Ritchie. We need to get home, right now!'

'Ooh, I love it when you are so demanding.'

'See you soon, Rose, and Happy Birthday for tomorrow.' Titch kissed her friend on the cheek and hot-footed it out onto the street.

Rosa's cry of 'Congratulations!' was lost in the wind as the happy couple power-walked their way up the hill to the Lobster Pot.

CHAPTER SIXTY TWO

Josh was greeted by a more subdued version of the cockney plumber than he had encountered on previous occasions. It felt weird to see Lucas Hannafore in a city setting.

'What do you want?' Josh was abrupt.

'Can we talk, mate? It will only take a few minutes.'

'Very well. There's a bench in the square over there.'

Josh, terrified of what he was about to hear, walked along in silence. Rosa hadn't messaged him for the past few nights, and it was an ominous sign. Maybe she had never truly loved him at all; maybe all his attempts to help her had been totally in vain. That her reckless attitude to life and love made it easy for her to throw everything away. Maybe she had fallen for the plumber and Lucas was giving Josh the bad news as Rosa was too chicken to do it herself.

Luke broke the silence. 'I'm working on a site near here so thought it better I see you face to face, man to man like, and all that.'

'Who told you where I worked?'

'I may be a tradesman, but I know what LinkedIn is, mate.'

'Is Rosa OK?'

'She's more than OK.' Lucas stopped. 'We don't need to chat

287

on a bench, I can say it all here.' A police car tearing by with sirens blaring interrupted his speech. 'That night, you know – well, I *was* with your wife. But we were chatting, that's all. I found her on the beach, in a shocking state. Her phone had smashed and she had no coat on and was falling down drunk She thought it was you who was playing around. I helped her, whilst you were off gallivanting.'

'But I so wasn't, and Rosa knows that now.'

Lucas ignored him and carried on. 'Don't get me wrong, I fancy your old woman – who wouldn't? Your Rosa is hot.' Josh closed his eyes, dreading what else was going to come out of the plumber's mouth. 'But as I said, she was drunk – and call me old-fashioned, but it's not my thing to try it on with drunk women.'

'Did you kiss her?'

Luke thought long and hard before he answered. Imagining the sweet lips of Rosa pushed against his, he lied for her sake. 'Nah. She was too busy putting a can of Pina Colada to that pretty boat-race of hers to have time for that either.'

Josh tried to hide his relief. 'So why come and find me, why not just try and call me or text me?'

'Like I said, I was in the area and…' Wishing he'd stopped there, his voice tailed off.

'And what?'

With his heart burning with sadness, Lucas said reluctantly, 'Falling in love, now that's easy. Having sex, even easier. But meeting someone who can spark your soul, now that's rare. She deserves to be happy, mate; that's what.'

With that, Lucas headed off into the busy London street, leaving Josh slightly shocked at the lucidity of the man's delivery and with the words *thank you* teetering momentarily on his lips.

CHAPTER SIXTY THREE

Jacob was flapping his arms around behind the bar.

'I knew it. It is so Rosa to decide to do something she said she wouldn't. I should have just given it to her earlier. And her bloody battery has died now. Bugger! Raff, where's my phone? I need to call Josh.'

'Here, he's sent a text, look.'

'Oh Lordy.' Jacob began to flap even more. 'He's left early too. He's going to be coming one way on the M4, and she'll be passing him on the train tracks going the other way.'

Raff, looking particularly handsome in his chef's whites, started to laugh.

'It's not funny, husband.'

'I said, didn't I, that we should have just told her that Josh was coming.'

'And where would the romance have been in that, eh?' Jacob stopped frowning. 'Ah, no worries. It's going to be fine. I have a cunning plan...'

Rosa was thankful that Hot had finally got used to the train and the other passengers and, worn out, was fast asleep on her lap. She liked the warm weight of him and hoped the peace would last. Five hours of him being restless on a train was just too much to contemplate. She had brought his evening biscuits and a bottle of water to go in his metal dish, and just hoped he wouldn't disgrace her during the five-hour journey. Knowing Hot, it was something of a vain hope.

Rosa couldn't understand why Jacob had got all uptight when she'd informed him that she had changed her plans and was leaving early. He'd wanted to make a fuss of her for her birthday and dish out some gifts, but surely it was far more important for her to sort out her marriage once and for all. Nor could she work out why he was so keen to find out which side of the train she was sitting on. In fact, thinking about it now, he had been acting very strangely.

Just as he was about to say something else, her phone battery had died. A train guard said there were charging points in first class that she could use if she was desperate, but for now she was happy just to relax. Escape from the real world for a bit. Because the real world as she knew it could well be changing for ever when she reached London. A gamut of emotions began to run through her. She was half-excited, half-scared of seeing Josh. She had found her key to the London house, so if for some reason he wasn't in, at least she could wait in comfort for him. And she had done her hair and nails and was wearing a new outfit form Polhampton and a pair of sexy knickers. Just in case. She *had* to do this. If Josh was going to be a coward about it, then she was going to take the situation by the balls. Thanks to Lucas her guilt had been absolved and Josh would just have to believe that she had remembered everything and that nothing had happened between them.

As the train started to pull out of Combe Marian station, she rested her head against the window to try and have a little snooze. Just as her eyes were getting heavy, she saw what looked like the gangly figure of Ritchie running along the platform at full speed. She strained back down the track to see if she had been imagining things, but she had no direct view.

She checked her watch. They'd only been travelling for twenty minutes, but it seemed a lot longer. Hot was still sprawled on her lap, so taking the time to have more of a snooze herself, she leaned her head back against the window. Just as they were pulling out of the next station, it happened again: there was a figure looking exactly like Ritchie running along the platform at top speed, with what looked like a piece of white paper in his hand. She craned to see and spotted the gangly figure in the distance with hands on hips and head down completely exhausted. She'd better get her phone charged, Rosa thought. What if it was Ritchie and something was wrong with Titch or the baby?

She put Hot in his travelling crate and asked the lady across the aisle to keep an eye on him for a couple of minutes. Then, with the train pulling into its final Devon stop before it headed directly to London, she started to make her way towards first class to charge her phone. As she stood up, she saw the tall, gangly figure again and realised that yes, it was indeed Ritchie. When the train stopped and he caught her eye, the look of relief on his face was huge. Panting like a dog, he held the crumpled piece of white paper up to the window. It said simply:

Meet me where the sky touches the sea, tomorrow at 10 am.

CHAPTER SIXTY FOUR

The Seven Lessons
Seven: Love

As Rosa made her way up to the top of West Cliffs, her heart began beating like that of a frightened bird. Spring had most definitely sprung in Cockleberry Bay, and the morning sunshine had lightened the sea to a topaz blue; the wave tops were sparkling like diamonds. Seagulls and other coastal birds whipped around in the light breeze shouting their appreciation at such a glorious day.

There was only one person who would know to meet her where the sky touched the sea, and the thought of seeing him again filled her with incredible joy – and undulating fear. She wondered if Queenie and Ned, her great-grandparents, had felt this way when they used to meet here all those decades ago. Just thinking about them made her put her hand to her heart. How life had changed since she'd inherited the Corner Shop, found her birth mother and married Josh; it was as if all the sorrows of her past had been lifted and she could now soar like a seagull into the brightness of her future. Except for her folly, which had brought sorrow back into that happy life.

As she walked the cliff path, the past few months began to speed through her mind. She was now able to stride with confidence past the ledge where she and Hot had fallen. She had also gone nearly a month without alcohol and was beginning to feel so much better in herself both physically and mentally. There were also a lot more hours in the day to achieve what she wanted to do. Rather than sit and wallow with a glass of wine in the evenings, she had even had time to paint flowers onto some of her pots on the roof terrace, and Raff was taking the time to teach her how to speak Italian.

It had been a tragic way to start a friendship, but the strong bond between herself and Vicki Cliss had very much influenced Rosa's attitude to family life. Looking at jealousy and anger in a different way had made her think deeply about how she reacted in certain situations; she had learned that if anger was turned into a positive, it could be a very life-affirming force. And as for jealousy, if ever she felt that green-eyed monster rising, she would think back to the heart-breaking tale of Sara and her late partner, Steve. Rosa was also beginning to feel that she *did* deserve all that was happening to her and that somebody could perhaps love and cherish her without wanting to leave her.

She puffed slightly as she reached the top of the path and the clearing where she and Josh had so often sat and looked out to sea, putting the world to rights.

She heard the music before she saw him. She didn't know the song but recognised the velvety tones of Etta James. Queenie and Mary would quite often have her music on in the background when Rosa went to Seaspray Cottage for Sunday lunch. 'Trust in Me'. That was it! On realising, Rosa smiled. Maybe that had been their subliminal message to her too.

Just in case what Josh was going to say would blow her world apart forever, the girl stood still and listened. Both the music and lyrics were haunting, but as soon as the chorus floated out over the cliffs, the sky and the rolling sea, with its message about trust and the magical words 'love will see us through', she somehow knew everything was going to be all right.

Starting to move her body to the music, she rounded the corner and looked at the place where they always used to sit. He was there. Rosa put her hand to her heart and tears started to fall. With his back to her, looking out to sea, sitting on a white rug with his blue wireless speaker and surrounded by rose petals, was her one true love. The voice of Etta James drifted away, to be replaced by the Altered Images tune of 'Happy Birthday' which was now blaring out through the tranquil air.

She knew he could sense her presence, but that didn't stop her from creeping up behind him – and just as she was about to put her hands over his eyes, he turned around and grabbed her.

She squealed in both delight and then annoyance, and started to beat his back with her little fists, crying, 'Let me go.'

She stood up and stared down at her husband with wild eyes. 'Do you realise how many messages I have left you? How many nights I've waited in the hope that you might call me back? Yes, I did wrong by seeing Lucas, but I now know I didn't sleep with him and I don't feel I deserve that silent treatment. There's been a fire at the shop. I fell down a cliff. Theo was ill. So many things! You didn't even care!'

'Slow down, my gorgeous wife. I cared more than you'll ever know.'

Josh gazed at her, glorying in the sight before him. 'Oh Rosa, do you really think I would go away for nearly four months and not be caring about you every single second? I have missed you so much. I want you, only you, and all of you.

Unconditionally.'

'It's a bit late to care now,' Rosa replied bitterly. 'And I don't understand. If you say all you want is me, then why did you stay away, make me feel so terrible? That was cruel – and love is supposed to be kind.'

Josh stood up and took her in his arms. 'I had to do it.'

She pushed him away, and continued her soliloquy of heart. 'Had to do it? You know I have my issues, but saying that, I think I've turned a corner since you've been gone, Josh.'

'In what way, Birthday Girl?'

'It doesn't matter now.'

'I'm sure it does.' Josh held her close.

She looked up at him. 'You are so bloody handsome, and I've missed you so much.'

Josh kissed her softly. 'I so want you to realise how amazing you are. I choose you. And I'll choose you over and over and over. Without pause, without a doubt, in a heartbeat. I'll keep choosing you. I sat on my own in the London house, it was so quiet without you and Hot, and whilst I was sitting there, I realised that you're all my heart ever talks about.'

He let go of her and said, 'Come on, sit down. In this rucksack, not only do I have cold lemonade, I have your favourite warm bacon and egg in crusty white rolls, plus two cream cakes, as it is your birthday after all.' Josh laid out the little feast on the rug. 'Happy Birthday, darling wife.'

'Lemonade? No champagne then?'

'A little bird told me you'd stopped drinking.'

'Sounds like there's been some pretty big-mouthed birds around here.' Rosa took a hungry bite of her roll.

'So, tell me how else you think you may have turned a corner then. I'm intrigued.'

'Hmm. Well, I never usually see Raff on his own but he helped me a lot, and so did Sara Jenkins. They made me think about stuff in a different way. Made me value myself. And Alec Burton is just such a lovely man.' She rested back and put her face in the morning sunshine. 'You didn't mention that he doesn't drink.'

'I hadn't even noticed, to be honest.'

Rosa sipped some lemonade, then put the plastic glass down and holding Josh's gaze, she let her striking green eyes bore into his soul.

'It was you, wasn't it?'

'What do you mean?'

Rosa's voice was cracking. 'Whilst it was happening, I didn't have the time to stop and think about it, but now all those notes with "Meet Me" on them begin to make sense. Raff, Vicki, Alec, even Sara – you set them up, didn't you?' She shook her head in disbelief. 'All those lessons so relevant to me and you… Oh Josh.'

Josh felt very emotional. 'I met you,' he said, 'thought you were perfect, and so I loved you. Then I saw that you weren't perfect, as I am not perfect, and I loved you even more. But because of what has happened in your past, without some kind of intervention you would always have had that fear of abandonment, that fear of never being good enough, that lack of trust. I had to do something, or we never would have made it.'

'Your "come back when you like yourself" comment was said in anger but you were so right.'

'I'm so sorry, Rosa, that I said all those hurtful things that day, but you broke me. To think of you sleeping with another man, well, it was too much to bear. But I too needed that time, to come to understand that you weren't really directing anything at me, it was all at yourself.'

'So you set up the therapy session too?'

'Yes, but in true Rosa fashion, you kicked back, which I fully respect.' Josh laughed. 'I then thought that maybe other people who'd been through different experiences could open your mind up, without you feeling pressured.'

'And you spoke to Darren, the lifeboat man?'

'Yep.'

'I thought that was a bit odd, him being in the right place at the right time!'

'The thought of you never being able to walk up here again broke my heart. I couldn't let that happen. Your family is all around us...where the sky touches the sea.'

'You are so bloody thoughtful.'

'I do my best.' Josh leaned down and kissed her on the nose.

'Such a sad story about Sara losing her partner. And I guess Jacob told you about Vicki losing her baby?'

'I also heard how amazing you were, getting her through that day.'

'It was nothing.'

'It was a lot for you to cope with.'

'I had a miscarriage, Josh.'

'No!' He paled. He hadn't expected this. 'Baby girl, when?'

'Just after we married.'

'Why on earth didn't you tell me? I can't believe I didn't realise!'

'It was just a heavy period really; it was so early and...'

'Never ever not tell me something like that again. OK?' He hugged her tightly.

Rosa's voice was quiet. 'OK – and Josh?'

'Yes, my love?'

'I'm not good at all this emotion stuff, but I love you. In fact, I love you more than I have ever found a way to say to you. And for all the pretty bad things I've done in my life, the one thing

I did do right was give my heart to you. I'm sorry about not trusting you, about being crazy, about not liking your planning or being dismissive about having children.'

Josh put his fingers to her lips. 'It's all OK now. You can't rush something you want to last for ever. I had to go away, to put us back together, as it's where we belong.' He put on the Etta James track again, took his wife's hand and started to smooch with her. She squirmed as he whispered in her ear, his hot breath tickling her like Hot's whiskers.

'I love you to where the sun touches the sky, Rosa Smith, and don't you ever forget that.'

EPILOGUE

'I don't want to go in the café,' Rosa sulked. 'I want to get you home where you can give me a proper birthday present.'

Josh could think of nothing he'd like more, either. But: 'You're such a little minx, Rosa Smith, but come on – a quick coffee by the beach will make this morning complete.'

'SURPRISE!' Rosa jumped a foot in the air as party poppers exploded all over her. A life-size dachshund cake with twenty-seven candles was the centrepiece of the café counter. Hot, wearing a pointed pink party hat set at a jaunty angle, came rushing forward and jumped up at Josh's lower legs, howling and whining in the excitement of seeing his daddy again.

'Happy Birthday, Rosa duck, and may we have many more together now.' Mary came forward, kissed her daughter's cheek and handed her a gift. Rosa hugged her back and thanked her mum.

Rosa then looked around at the packed café. Jacob, Raff and their three hounds were all present, as were Vicki, Stuart and their boys. Titch and Ritchie had brought Titch's mum to the party, with a helium balloon attached to her wheelchair. Theo was sparko in his pram tucked around the back. Rosa smiled and waved as she saw Darren with an attractive lady, probably his wife, in the corner. Alec, she saw, was helping Sara pour coffees for everyone and was chatting animatedly to her. A blind date didn't need arranging now, Rosa thought to herself with a smile.

The room was full of love.

'Speech!' Jacob shouted.

'I want to say something first; in fact, you all need to follow me outside.' Josh headed for the door with his arm in the air like a tour guide.

'I don't want to be any trouble – I'll stay here,' Titch's mum said anxiously.

'Oh no, you won't,' Ritchie told her. 'I'm steering.'

The seagulls were mewing their content at the wonderful sunny day and, of course, the pending excitement of food being left by the weekend tourists.

'Pull this.' Josh handed Rosa a rope with a heart on the end. Keeping a safe distance, she tugged, and the green tarpaulin fell to the ground to reveal the word ROSA'S, sign-written in red paint. The painting of Hot wearing his tartan doggie coat with a string of sausages in his mouth finished the sign off beautifully.

Everybody cheered. Rosa looked quizzically at Josh, and then at Sara. 'But Sara wants to stay,' she said.

'I know she does,' Josh interjected. 'The RO is for Rosa's half and the SA for Sara's half.'

Sara stepped to the front. 'I shall be staying in the Bay that I love, and running the business that I love full-time for a while. Josh has bought into the business so then, Rosa, this is where you come in. If you fancy it, of course, you can come and join me at a later stage when we can run this little outfit together. By sharing it, this will allow us to have our own time, in your case for the Corner Shop, and in my case to have a bit of much-needed rest and relaxation.'

Everyone filed back into the café ready for cake. Rosa stayed outside with Josh. She nuzzled into her husband's side. 'This is the best birthday present I've ever had in my life.'

'Not just me coming home, then?'

Hot came running outside with the Duchess, who was much fatter than usual. 'Oh, and I forgot to tell you that this little lady is pregnant with our boy's babies.'

Josh started laughing. 'That's brilliant, just hilarious. What fun we'll all have, when they come. I bet Jacob is mortified though.'

'He's pretending to be.' The pair of wieners trotted off down to the sea's edge. 'I've been thinking a lot about babies, actually.' Rosa smiled. 'And I think you'd make a bloody great dad.'

Josh had tears in his eyes. 'And I didn't choose just any old mongrel for a mate, you know.'

'Oi.' Rosa poked him in the ribs. 'But I want to wait until you finish in London, so I'm not left holding the baby, especially as I've got a café to run now, too.'

'Er…that's something else I was going to surprise you with later, actually.'

'What?' Rosa's mouth was open in shock. 'Don't tell me you don't have to go back to work – is that it?'

Josh nodded.

Rosa screeched and started twirling around on the spot. 'That is the most amazing news. I am so happy.'

'Well, aside from a couple of days' consulting a month, but yes, I'll be here. We will get a basic income from the café, whether we work it or not. My life with you is too important for me not to be here. And financially, that's why I took some time to come back. I wanted to make sure everything was in place before I did. The London house is rented to a couple I know who work in the City, so that should keep Ethel Beanacre on her nosey toes. In fact, everything is pretty damn amazing.'

Josh kissed his wife on the lips before forcing himself away and slapping her gently on the behind. 'Right,' he said a little breathlessly, 'I think you'd better go in and cut that cake, madam.'

'Josh?'

'What's up?'

'Thank you for helping me to like myself.'

He ruffled her wild curls and smiled widely.

'You, my gorgeous wife, did that all by yourself.'

END

Word-of-mouth is crucial for any author to succeed. If you enjoyed your time down in Cockleberry Bay, please could you leave a review on Amazon. Even if it's just a sentence or two, it would make all the difference and would be very much appreciated.

Love, Nicola xx

ABOUT THE AUTHOR

Meet Me in Cockleberry Bay is prize-winning author Nicola May's tenth novel and the sequel to the No. 1 bestselling *The Corner Shop in Cockleberry Bay*. Nicola likes to write about love, life and friendship in a realistic way, describing her novels as 'chicklit with a kick'.

Nicola lives near the famous Windsor Castle with her black-and-white rescue cat, Stan. Her hobbies include watching films that involve a lot of swooning, crabbing in South Devon, eating flapjacks and enjoying a flutter on the horses at Ascot racecourse.

Find out more at www.nicolamay.com.
Twitter: @nicolamay1
Instagram: author_nicola
Nicola has her own Facebook page.

BY THE SAME AUTHOR